C000186287

Hybrid

Also by Shaun Hutson

Assassin
Breeding Ground
Captives
Compulsion
Deadhead
Death Day
Erebus
Exit Wounds
Heathen
Knife Edge
Lucy's Child
Nemesis
Purity
Relics
Renegades
Shadows
Slugs
Spawn
Stolen Angels
Victims
Warhol's Prophecy
White Ghost

Hybrid

Shaun Hutson

timewarner
books

A *Time Warner* Book
First published in Great Britain in 2002
by Time Warner Books

Copyright © Shaun Hutson 2002

The moral right of the author has been asserted.

*All characters in this publication are fictitious
and any resemblance to real persons, living or dead,
is purely coincidental.*

All rights reserved.
No part of this publication may be reproduced,
stored in a retrieval system, or transmitted, in any
form or by any means, without the prior
permission in writing of the publisher, nor be
otherwise circulated in any form of binding or
cover other than that in which it is published and
without a similar condition including this
condition being imposed on the subsequent purchaser.

A CIP catalogue record for this book
is available from the British Library.

ISBN HB: 0 316 86075 1
ISBN CF: 0 316 86154 5

Typeset by Palimpsest Book Production Limited,
Polmont, Stirlingshire
Printed and bound in Great Britain by
Clays, St Ives plc

Time Warner Books UK
Brettenham House
Lancaster Place
London WC2E 7EN

www.TimeWarnerBooks.co.uk

Fifty per cent of this book is dedicated to Mr Peter Nichols, for his expertise, skill and very moderate fees.

The other fifty per cent is dedicated to my wife. For everything.

ACKNOWLEDGEMENTS

Well, here we are again. The bit of the book that I know many of you look out for more eagerly than chapter one. I don't know if this list of people, places and things that inspired, helped, encouraged or supported me during the writing of this one is shorter or longer (I'm sure someone will tell me). All I know is that the writing of this particular novel was, to use a technical phrase, 'a bit of a bastard' . . .

But enough of the literary stuff. Here's the list and, as usual, those on it should know why, those *not* on it probably won't give a toss and those who think they *should* be on it will probably get the hump. Ah, well, as a very great man once wrote, 'It ain't like it used to be but it'll do.'

Many thanks to my agent, Sara Fisher, for her patience amongst other things.

Very special thanks to Barbara Boote, Andy Edwards, Sarah Shrubb, Andy Hine and everyone else at my publisher. It's nice to be home. Special thanks to the sales team.

Thanks to everyone at Chancery. To Jack Taylor, Tom Sharp, Barbara Grant, Karen and Jim at the Clydesdale Bank in Piccadilly.

To Zena, Dee, Julie and Andy, Nicky, Terri, Becky and Rachel.

Special thanks to Sanctuary Music, particularly Rod Smallwood and Steve McTaggart. Also to Wally Grove and his ever-expanding world of cheese. And, of course, to Steve, Dave, Adrian, Bruce, Janick and Nicko.

As ever, many thanks to James Whale. Also to Melinda and to Frisbee . . . And, of course, to Ash.

Many, many thanks to Martin 'gooner' Phillips. A true friend, worthy adversary (when Arsenal are at Anfield) and owner of ITV digital . . . Thanks, mate.

Thanks also to Ian 'I saw that a month ago' Austin. The scourge of the car salesman.

To Hailey Owen, wherever you are and whatever you're doing, I know you're enjoying it. Thanks also to Claire at Centurion.

As ever, I must thank Ted and Molly who, whenever they're out in their garden, run the risk of being floored by a stray football . . . On which note, thank you to Nike football boots.

Indirect thanks, as always, to Sam Peckinpah and Bill Hicks. Always missed.

A very big thank you to all the staff and management at Cineworld in Milton Keynes. Look, some blokes blow their money down the pub, I blow it at the pictures. Anyway, to all of you, many thanks from 'Cappuccino Man'.

Massive thanks to Graeme Sayer and Callum Hughes and all the incredible work they have done and continue to do at www.shaunhutson.com. Thanks also to everyone who's contacted or visited the site.

Thank you seems somewhat inappropriate a word to say to Liverpool Football Club, especially for *those* afternoons in Cardiff and *that* night in Dortmund. Not forgetting the continuing moments of extreme delight you bring me. I would say on a Saturday at three o'clock but Sky seem determined to screw that time slot up once and for all. So, to the mighty Reds I salute you. Sky, I continue to curse you for not giving a toss about *real* fans.

The last few thanks are for those closest to me. My Mum and Dad. I say it every time but it's still true. Thank you is too small a word to sum up what they do.

Even more so for my wife, Belinda. Many think I *should* be locked up, without her I *would* be. This book was particularly hard on her so my gratitude is even more boundless than usual.

It was probably pretty rough on the other girl in my life too. But she never complains (well, not unless you count saying that, in the mornings, I'm like one of the monsters out of

Scooby Doo . . . You'll find us at the pictures on the Saturdays when the mighty Reds don't have a game. Sometimes you'll find her with me when they're playing. This book, like everything I do, is for my beautiful, wonderful daughter, with love.

Last thank you. For you, my readers. For the new and the more well seasoned I humbly offer this latest journey.

Let's go.

Shaun Hutson

Cos I'm losing my sight, losing my mind, wish somebody would tell me I'm fine . . .

Papa Roach

Psychoanalyse the chapters,
on the path to my darkest day.
Searching for the answers,
all I see is damage through the haze.
Queensryche

LIVING DEATH

The fly was caught in the web.

He watched it writhe helplessly, tangling itself even more surely in the sticky strands that ensnared it.

The web had been spun across one of the windows of his office and it was the frantic buzzing and struggling of the fly that had first alerted him to its plight.

Now he sat back in his chair and watched.

And waited.

The spider emerged slowly from its hiding place. A bloated, corpulent specimen that barely seemed able to haul itself along the gossamer snare towards its victim.

But it came with lethal intent.

He watched as it stretched out one leg and placed it on the struggling fly. Then, with surprising speed, it hugged its swollen body to the insect, drew it close and injected venom from its fangs. Clung on tightly as its victim was immobilised.

As living death took over.

Finally it began to weave a silken cocoon around the fly before hauling itself back to its hiding place.

It would feed later. On the still-living fly.

Christopher Ward watched for a moment longer then looked back at his desk.

The screen of his computer was blank. It had been for the last two hours. He hadn't managed one single, solitary word since he'd wandered out of the house at ten that morning.

The cup of coffee he'd drunk at eleven hadn't sparked any thoughts. Neither had wandering backwards and forwards in the office.

It was like that some days. Most days.

He stared at the screen. He placed his fingers on the keys and he waited.

And nothing happened. No outpouring of creativity. No flood of story-telling genius.

Just a blank screen. And a blank mind.

It wasn't writer's block. He knew how that felt. This was something new. More painful.

This was living death.

He glanced at the fly still suspended in the web. It twitched helplessly every now and then. He wondered if it was aware of its impending doom. He doubted it. Man was alone in being able to contemplate his own end. The only species able to appreciate the finality and inevitability of death.

Christopher Ward was caught in a web of his own.

LIVING IN THE PAST

Ward was in his early forties. Some people told him he looked younger. That on a good day he could pass for thirty-eight or thirty-nine.

But good days had been in short supply for the last two or three months.

Most mornings when he looked in the bathroom mirror the face that looked back at him was tired and pale. There were dark rings beneath his blue-grey eyes. Hair that had once reached his shoulders had recently been cut to just above his collar. And now there was a little too much grey in those once-lustrous locks.

Twelve years ago it had all been so different. He'd greeted each day with optimism. Life was worth living then. So much happening. So much to look forward to.

And now what? Every day was a battle. It was a struggle to get out of bed. A battle to work. To force himself into his office for each day of a life that had changed so drastically.

Twelve years ago he had known only success. There had been more money than he knew what to do with. Exotic holidays. Parties. Expensive lunches. Exorbitantly priced dinners.

And women. Lots of them. All eager. Wanting him.

He had seen no end to it. Why should there be an end?

But that end was looming. Waiting over the horizon.

Waiting like a bloated, hungry spider ready to devour him. To suck the life from him. The life he had loved so much. The life he had never really stopped to appreciate.

He'd read that life is like a train journey and the trouble

with most people is that they rarely get off the train to enjoy the sights.

Ward had been one of those people. And he regretted that now.

Regretted it because he knew that those days were gone for ever.

And he knew why. From deep inside he felt a twinge of a welcome and long absent emotion.

Anger. Anger at what he was about to lose. From anger grew hatred. From hatred rose fury.

He would use these feelings.

He glanced at the blank screen of the computer once more.

Ward pressed his finger down on one of the keys and held it there.

fffffffffffffffffffffffffffffffffffffffffffffffffffffffffffffffffffffffffffffffffffffffff

At least, he mused, there was something on the screen at last.

He got to his feet and wandered over to the top of the stairs. His office was a converted garage about ten yards from his house. A white door led into the side of the building, and fourteen steps led up to the place where he had worked for the last twelve years. The room was about twenty-feet long, half that across.

Within these confines Ward had positioned two black ash desks, one supporting an old manual typewriter and the larger one a computer, several bookcases, a small stereo system and a sofa bed. A second door led to a toilet and shower.

He had a sink in one corner. A kettle stood beside it with tea bags, coffee and a jug of milk. He was self-sufficient inside his little kingdom.

He walked out of the house at ten in the morning and he walked back in at four in the afternoon. Same routine every day.

It was all he knew. All he had ever known. No matter where he had lived. The one-bedroom flat over a billiard hall at the beginning. The two-bedroom terraced-house he'd bought after the success of his first half-a-dozen novels. The four-bedroom house with the tiny paved area at the back, sandwiched between a bakery and an old woman who he had known only as Mrs B.

And what he had now. What he'd had for the last twelve years. Financed with his success that seemed a hundred years in the past.

All that mattered now was the present and the future.

If he had one.

MARKET FORCES

Ward opened the back door and walked in. The house was silent.

He crossed to the sink, filled the kettle then plugged it in and waited for it to boil.

Ward wandered into the hall and saw that there was mail lying on the mat. Bills. Junk mail. The usual.

Instead of returning to the kitchen he took a detour into the study. A huge bookcase lined one wall and in the centre section were his own books. Twenty titles under his name and the same number again under the various pseudonyms he had used over the years.

He looked at them blankly. They all counted for nothing now.

It was these books that had made him his money. Given him the lifestyle so many others could only envy. And it was these books that he still *wanted* to write but which no one wanted.

No publisher. No agent. They had told him that sales had not been good. Markets had changed. Same old shit.

Well, fuck them. Fuck them all.

Something different was needed, apparently. Something original but easily pigeon-holed.

Books by celebrities were very popular. Models, second-rate comedians, has-been soap stars (those that weren't trying to make it in the music business), even footballers were writing books. Any talentless cunt with enough money to pay a ghost-writer and a good editor was capable of churning out a book and earning shitloads of cash for it.

And then there were the household names who milked their own brand of repetitious bullshit while fawning publishers knelt at their feet to push ever-larger cheques into their grasping hands.

Add to these the comfortable middle-class writers who lectured on real life from the security of knowing it was a world they would never have to inhabit. People with millions in the bank who crowed that money wasn't everything, who complained about invasion of privacy during their six-page interviews, who were proud of how they'd been single mothers or record-shop employees or advertising men before they'd made it big. And who whined about how hard they'd had to work to get published when all it took was a generous publisher and an even more generous publicity department.

Ward despised them all. Even when he'd been successful he'd despised them. The whole fucking business stank. It stank of cowardice. Of duplicity. Of betrayal.

He heard the kettle boiling. Fuck it. He needed something stronger than coffee.

GASPING FOR AIR

Ward poured himself a large measure of Glenfiddich and swallowed it. He felt the amber liquid burn its way to his stomach, waited a moment then poured himself another.

It was cool in the sitting room despite the heat outside. The sun was shining and he could hear the sound of a lawnmower in the distance. One of his neighbours cutting the grass. Or perhaps one of their gardeners.

He smiled to himself.

He'd have one more drink then he'd go back out to the office. See if the break had released some trickle of creative juice.

It took two more drinks before he could bring himself to move.

Ward stood at the back door and peered towards his office. On one side of the building was a huge oak tree whose branches brushed against the windows and stonework like skeletal fingers. The sun glinted on the roof windows and he shielded his eyes. It really was a beautiful day.

He thought about the fly trapped and paralysed in the spider's web.

A beautiful day.

Ward ran a hand through his hair and set off across the garden towards the office.

As he reached the door he heard the fax machine ringing, and hurried inside and up the stairs in time to see paper oozing from it.

Anything important?

No. It never was. Not any more.

He looked at the blank screen of the computer for a moment then sat down almost reluctantly in his chair.

'Come on, come on,' he murmured to himself. He could smell the whisky on his breath when he spoke.

Again he rested his fingers on the keys. Again he pressed one key a little too hard.

jjjjjjjjjjjjjjjjjjjjjjjjjjjjjjjjjjjjjjjjjjjjjjjjjjjjjjjjjjjjjjjjjjjjjjjjjjjj

It wasn't funny this time.

He got to his feet and crossed to the bookshelf on the far side of the room.

Look at a book. There might be inspiration in there some-where.

He stared at the titles.

Who Killed Hanratty?

Helter Skelter

Beyond Belief

Cannibalism: The Last Taboo

The Shrine Of Jeffrey Dahmer

The Encyclopaedia Of Serial Killers

Something clicked. Ward frowned. He read a few pages of *Hunting Humans* then put it down and returned to his desk.

There was a small plastic carriage clock on his desk. It showed 1.36.

He was still staring at it two hours later.

ROUTINE

One of the things that Christopher Ward had discovered during twenty-three years of professional writing was that routine was vital. Treat the whole thing as a job. Nothing more.

Despite what the pretentious bastards on *The South Bank Show* said, it was a job. End of story.

Every day he set himself a target of three thousand words. Ten pages.

At the beginning, he'd written fifteen, sometimes twenty in a day. That time of fresh enthusiasm and burning ambition, when the desire for success was paramount.

Once that success had been attained, the urgency faltered. He went from writing five novels in a year to just one. Earning that kind of money didn't require him to burn the candle at both ends.

He had had it all. Big house. Big bank account. Big reputation. He was at the top of the tree.

But from the top there's only one way to go. And it was the most uncomfortable ride Christopher Ward had ever experienced.

Now he was lucky if he completed five pages a day. But the routine still had to be adhered to. He could not leave the office without having written something. At least one page before he would allow himself to move from his desk and return to the house. Or to wherever else he went to forget about what he'd just been through in the office.

It was important to keep the job and normal life separate, and never to think about the job when you weren't behind the desk. Never.

He stared at the blank screen. Then at his notes. Then at his synopsis.

Christopher Ward began to type.

Fresh Skins
by
Christopher Ward

PREFACE

JANUARY 23rd, 1991:

The grave was no more than three feet deep but it had taken over an hour to dig using the small shovel they'd given him.

They'd watched him toiling in the frost-hardened earth, and when he'd paused every now and then to catch his breath, they'd urged him on, forcing him to finish the task quickly. They were anxious to be out of the freezing night and back in the warmth. Away from this place.

Despite the cold he was sweating. Not all of it was due to his exertions.

A wreath of condensation clouded around him like a shroud.

Perhaps he would have been able to dig more quickly had one of the bones of his right forearm and several of his fingers not been broken. The cuts and bruises on his face and the cigarette burns on his arms weren't helping either.

He hurled another shovelful of earth on to the pile before pausing for a second.

He could see them moving about agitatedly in the gloom. One of them visible only by the glowing tip of his cigarette. The other was pacing back and forth in an attempt to keep warm, stopping every so often to stamp his feet, trying to revive his circulation.

Christ, it was cold.

The sky was cloudless. There'd been snow showers during the last twenty-four hours and a thin powdery layer was still covering the ground, hardened by the frost that dug icy barbs into everything.

The man standing in the grave had not seen the snow fall. The blindfold that had been over his eyes had ensured he saw nothing. It had only been removed an hour or so earlier. Then they had pushed the shovel at him and told him to dig.

One of the men wandered to the edge of the hole and peered down into the depths. His companion glanced in too. They murmured something about it being deep enough. Three or four feet would do.

One snatched the spade from him. The other told him to stand still.

The man in the grave looked up but couldn't make out their features in the blackness.

Not that it mattered any more.

He heard the slide on the automatic being worked. A metallic click in the freezing silence. He knew a round had been chambered.

The shot came seconds later. It caught him in the back of the head.

So did the second. And the third. The fourth was hardly necessary. Or the fifth.

The muzzle flashes erupted vividly in the blackness. The boom of the discharges were deafening in the stillness.

They waited until the sound had died on the wind then one reached for the shovel and the other began kicking clods into the freshly dug grave.

It would take a lot less time to fill it in, and for that they were thankful.

It was so cold.

One of them hawked and spat on the body then they continued covering it with earth. The other flicked a spent cigarette butt into the crude resting place.

Three or four feet was enough to hide the smell from carrion creatures. Foxes wouldn't dig down that deep. And even if one did, who cared?

At least the job of filling in the grave warmed them up a little.

One of them looked at his watch.
Soon be done.

It was a start.

He glanced at the plastic carriage clock, then at his watch. He switched off the power and sat gazing at his own reflection in the blank monitor for a second.

Three pages. Better than nothing.

He got to his feet and headed for the stairs.

ESCAPE

Christopher Ward had found that one of the prerequisites for being a writer was a liking for solitude. He'd never been a very sociable person anyway, preferring his own company to that of others from an early age. Even so, when he wanted he could be as gregarious as the next person and actually appear to be enjoying it. But, deep down, Ward needed time on his own.

Even when he wasn't working days would pass without him speaking more than ten words. These days a few muttered syllables on the phone was the full extent of his social interaction. And, of course, his visits to the cinema.

He had loved the cinema for as long as he could remember. Ever since his mother first took him to their local fleapit, somewhat inappropriately named The Palace, to see *Planet of the Apes*.

Like everything else, his cinema-going had changed over the years too. Now his local was one of the sixteen-screen multiplexes that had sprung up in most large towns.

Ward spent a large amount of time in the one that was just ten minutes' drive from his house. So much time in fact that many of the staff spoke to him as if he were a friend.

He watched everything. He had endured films like *Pearl Harbor*, he had tolerated pictures like *Shakespeare in Love*, and he had marvelled at masterpieces such as *Gladiator*. They offered an escape for him. A chance to sit in darkness for two or three hours and concentrate on the images before him.

Anything to forget his present predicament.

This particular day was cheap day. It was also pension day

and most of the auditoria were populated by pensioners, usually complaining about how loud the sound was or muttering damning comments about the films shown in the trailers.

Ward parked his car in the large car park outside the building and walked in, glad to feel the air-conditioning after the heat of the sunshine. He took the escalator to the first floor where the cinemas were housed.

There were a number of restaurants and coffee bars on the same floor and he glanced over at them as he strode towards the box office.

He saw couples sitting talking. Laughing. Everyone, it seemed, had *someone.*

Except him.

He ambled into the short queue behind two pensioners and a couple of students and waited, scanning the electronic board behind the cashiers that displayed show times.

The pensioners were having trouble choosing between *Captain Corelli's Mandolin* or *Hannibal.* Both based on bestselling books, Ward noted with annoyance.

They were still deciding when the students slipped past them and bought tickets for *The Mummy Returns.*

He felt like giving the old sods a prod in the back, telling them that they wouldn't enjoy *Hannibal* and that *Captain Corelli's Mandolin* was bullshit. Instead, he too slipped past them and shoved a five-pound note through the small slot beneath the glass of the cashier's position. He collected his change and headed off to the theatre showing *X-Men 2.*

The girl who tore his ticket smiled at him. She was pretty. Early twenties. He glanced at her gold name badge. Sheree.

He hurried to find a seat. The lights were dimming as he sat down. He was free for another two hours.

COME THE NIGHT

W ard hated the night. It gave him time to think. Thoughts crowded in like unwanted spectres.

He sat in front of the television, the images before him barely registering. But after half a bottle of Jack Daniel's, very little of *anything* was registering.

Alcoholic anaesthetic.

Apparently every drink killed a thousand brain cells. The first to go were memory cells.

Ward poured himself another drink and murdered a few more recollections.

By the time he'd finished the bottle, the clock on top of his TV showed 1.03 a.m. He struggled to his feet and switched off the late-night film, some Jean-Claude Van Damme shite. It could have been anything.

He slammed the living-room door behind him, set the burglar alarm and wandered upstairs.

It was a humid night and Ward wasn't surprised to hear the first rumblings of thunder in the distance. He undressed in the darkness and stood gazing out over his considerable back garden and up at the cloud-filled sky.

Far away there was a silent fork of lightning. It cut through the clouds like a silver spear and was followed, seconds later, by a loud clap of thunder.

He watched the sky, watched the darkness. Felt his head spinning.

He glanced in the direction of his office, clearly visible from his bedroom window. There was a dull grey glow coming from inside.

Ward blinked hard and sighed. Had he forgotten to turn the monitor off again?

There was another flash of lightning, the silver gleam glinting on the velux windows of the office.

Ward sat on the edge of the bed for a moment then lay down.

The storm grew louder.

It was a long time before he slept.

RESUMING HOSTILITIES

Blank screen.
Headache.

Christopher Ward massaged the back of his neck with one hand and exhaled deeply.

It wasn't a hangover. He'd had enough of those over the years to know the difference.

The storm that had raged for most of the night had brought with it only a little rain and the grass had been virtually dry when he'd made his way out to the office that morning.

An hour ago to be precise. A painful, thought-free, tormented hour.

Finally he re-read what he'd written the day before.

Then he rested his fingers on the keys and began to type.

I

BELFAST, NORTHERN IRELAND, PRESENT DAY:

There were two pounds of explosive beneath the bus seat, wrapped carefully in a black plastic bin liner and secured by gaffer tape. No one but the bombers knew it was there.

Certainly none of the eighteen passengers who were crowded on to the vehicle as it moved through Belfast city centre.

Not the driver who brought the bus to a halt in North Street. He smiled courteously at every new passenger as they dropped their fare into the small metal dish. Some took the change. Others waved away the few pence he offered as if it were some kind of tip.

The driver smiled, waited until the last of the new batch was safely aboard then hit the button that shut the automatic doors. They closed with a loud hydraulic hiss and the bus pulled out into traffic once more.

As the driver swung into Royal Avenue he peered to one side to catch sight of the spire of St Anne's Cathedral jabbing skyward at the banks of cloud that were scudding over the city.

Most of the seats were already taken. In his rear-view mirror, the driver could see a young woman struggling to pull a baby's bottle from a bag. She offered it to her child and the boy (he assumed it was a boy as it was dressed in blue) sucked hungrily at the teat. Two middle-aged women were chatting animatedly, sometimes glancing back at the feeding child and murmuring happily to it while its mother ran a hand through her tousled hair and tried to stop her shopping bags from tumbling over as the bus rounded a corner.

There was another stop further ahead and two passengers rose, preparing to alight there. The driver could see more than a dozen people waiting to take their places.

He swung the bus in close behind a Datsun that was waiting in the bus lane, hazard lights blinking. He hit his hooter twice and the Datsun moved off.

The bus doors opened to expel the two passengers and welcome the newcomers. As they filed on, the driver looked at his watch. Shift nearly over, thank God.

The beginnings of a headache were gnawing at the base of his skull. He was sure his wife was right and he needed glasses. A combination of that and the concentration needed to guide a bus through Belfast's busy centre usually left him needing to swallow a couple of Nurofen by the end of the day. Perhaps once he got his glasses he wouldn't have that trouble. His appointment with the optician was at nine the following morning. Or was it nine-thirty? He'd check when he got home.

He was about to close the doors when three young children came hurtling towards the bus shouting and gesturing. They were all wearing grey uniforms with ties askew and buttons undone. Pulled off in one case, he noticed. No more than eleven or twelve years old.

They hurried aboard and dumped their money in the tray. The last of them broke wind as he passed and looked apologetically at the driver who merely waved him away. A chorus of chuckles greeted the boy.

They made their way noisily towards the back, past the young woman feeding her baby. Past the middle-aged women still chatting loudly. Past an old man counting coins in the palm of his hand.

The boys sat down and one reached into his satchel for a bag of pick 'n' mix.

They started chattering, their voices mingling with those of the other passengers.

The driver swung the vehicle into Castle Street, narrowly

avoiding a cyclist. Who in their right mind rode a bloody bike in a city centre? The driver shook his head.

Four seconds later the bomb exploded.

2

In places blood had sprayed several feet across the road and pavement. It radiated from the gutted remains of the bus, its coppery odour mingling with the stink of petrol, burnt rubber, incinerated metal and, worst of all, the sickly sweet stench of seared flesh.

As well as the remains of the bus chassis, shattered glass from the vehicle and also from nearby shops was spread all over the thoroughfare like crystal confetti. Twisted metal hurled in all directions by the murderous blast was also strewn over a wide area.

Cars caught in the explosion stood abandoned. Those closest were almost as pulverised as the bus itself. Windscreens, smashed by the massive concussion blast, looked as if they'd been staved in by an invisible hammer. A wheel lay in the road. Close by was a scorched air freshener in the shape of a pine tree, and the head of a 'Kenny from *South Park*' figure, ripped from the foam-filled body by the force of the detonation.

Each one of these pieces of debris had blue-and-white or yellow tape around them. A larger piece of tape had been tied around the entire twenty-yard radius of the bomb-blasted bus. It bore the legend: POLICE LINE DO NOT CROSS.

Uniformed RUC men moved back and forth, some charged merely with keeping ever-curious passers-by from stopping too long to gaze at the scene of carnage.

For every man dressed in the familiar blue serge uniform of the local constabulary, there were plain clothes officers, bomb-squad members and forensics men. The full complement of experts needed in the aftermath of such an event and God alone knew their expertise had been needed often enough in the city during the past thirty years.

Several police cars, their blue lights turning silently, were parked at both ends of the street. Further barriers to those who could bear to peer at the devastation.

All of the dead and injured had been ferried away by a fleet of ambulances more than two hours ago. Those that remained within the cordoned-off area had a purpose.

All those *outside* looked on with a mixture of revulsion and relief.

There but for the grace of God . . .

Sean Doyle brought the Orion to a halt close to one of the RUC cars and swung himself out. He dug a hand into the pocket of his leather jacket and retrieved a packet of Rothmans, glancing around as he lit a cigarette, shielding the flame of the Zippo with his hand. He sucked on the cigarette then walked purposefully towards the blue-and-white tape, his long, brown hair blowing in the breeze that had sprung up in the last half hour.

Doyle ducked under the tape and looked impassively at the remains of the bus. There was a huge hole in one side of the chassis and most of the roof was missing. What remained was blackened and twisted. He stepped over the remnants of a double seat as he advanced through the maelstrom of activity.

'Hey.'

He heard the voice but didn't stop walking. Heavy footsteps behind him.

'You're not allowed in here,' said the same voice close to his ear.

He turned and saw a tall RUC constable looming before him.

Doyle sucked on his cigarette and slipped one hand into the pocket of his jeans. He pulled out a slim leather wallet and flipped it open allowing the policeman to see the ID.

'All right?' said Doyle flatly. He held the man's gaze.

The tall man nodded and watched as the leather-jacketed

newcomer made his way among the dozens of personnel, occasionally stopping to speak with one of them or examining a piece of wreckage.

Doyle stopped beside a particular piece of twisted metal and ran an index finger over it. He sniffed at the digit. The oily residue smelled of marzipan.

'Semtex,' he said to a suited man with round glasses who had joined him.

'About three pounds of it,' the man told him, removing his glasses and cleaning the lenses on his tie.

'Remote control or timer?'

The man looked vague.

'How did they detonate the fucking thing?' Doyle snapped.

'Remote control as far as we can tell. There wasn't much to go on as you can see.'

Doyle took a drag on his Rothmans.

'Who are you anyway?' the man wanted to know.

'Sean Doyle. Counter Terrorist Unit.'

The man looked him up and down.

'Where's the boss?' Doyle wanted to know.

The man hooked a thumb over his shoulder. 'He's busy.'

'So am I *now*,' Doyle said, and walked off in search of the man he sought.

3

Chief Inspector Peter Robinson was a powerfully built man with heavy jowls and sad eyes. He looked older than fifty. An illusion further fostered when he removed his cap to reveal a perfectly bald head.

Doyle wasn't really surprised that the years had taken their toll on the policeman's features. What had been happening in Northern Ireland over the past three decades was enough to give any bastard extra wrinkles. Especially those with the kind of responsibilities that Robinson held.

Doyle saw him standing with two plain clothes men close to the obliterated remains of the bus. The CI was gesturing this way and that, occasionally pausing to take a call on his mobile phone.

Doyle took a final drag on his cigarette, lit another and ambled towards the little gathering. One of the plain clothes men stepped towards him but Doyle flashed his ID and the man backed off again.

Robinson finished his call and pushed the Nokia back into his overcoat pocket. 'Doyle,' he said. 'When did you get here?'

'About four hours too late looking at this lot,' said the counter terrorist nodding towards the bus. 'What's the SP?'

'Five dead, twenty-six injured. Two on the critical list,' Robinson told him.

'Any ideas?'

'It was a bomb,' said one of the plain clothes men. 'I'd have thought that was fairly obvious.'

'No shit, Sherlock,' Doyle said sardonically. He blew a

stream of smoke in the man's direction. 'I meant about who planted it, dickhead.'

The man took a step towards Doyle who remained where he was, his grey eyes holding the man's gaze.

'The bomb squad aren't one hundred per cent sure yet,' Robinson interjected, waving his subordinate back. 'But it looks like the same kind of device that was used in Victoria Street a month ago.'

'But that was defused,' Doyle reminded him, digging his hands into the pockets of his leather jacket.

Robinson nodded almost imperceptibly.

'Any prints?' the counter terrorist continued.

'Not yet,' Robinson told him. 'Even if there are I doubt they're in the files.'

'Fresh skins?' Doyle mused.

Again Robinson nodded.

'The Provisionals have nothing to gain by this kind of action,' said the CI. 'It *has* to be some kind of splinter group. Continuity IRA. The Real IRA.'

'INLA?' Doyle murmured. 'UVF? You're spoilt for choice, aren't you?'

'There'd be no reason for a Protestant organisation to start planting bombs in the middle of the city,' offered one of the plain clothes men.

'There's been no reason behind most of what's happened here for the last thirty fucking years,' Doyle said dismissively.

'It looks like Continuity IRA,' Robinson said. 'That would make the most sense.'

Doyle wandered towards the wreckage of the bus and Robinson joined him.

'How close are you, Doyle?' the policeman asked.

'To finding who did this? Ask me in a couple of days.'

'I'm asking you *now*.' Robinson stepped in front of Doyle and stood motionless.

The counter terrorist regarded the policeman evenly for a second then shrugged. 'Two names keep cropping up,' he said. 'Matthew Finan and Declan Leary. They're not in your files. I checked with the Guarda *and* with my lot. No trace of them there either. If they're active, they're new to this game. Never been arrested. Never done time.'

'Fresh skins, like you said.'

Doyle nodded. 'It's difficult getting descriptions,' he continued. 'People aren't exactly falling over themselves to talk about the Continuity IRA. You know that. But I'll get them. Finan's got family in Turf Lodge. Word gets around. It's just a matter of time.'

'That's something we're a little short of, Doyle.'

The counter terrorist looked around at the remains of the bomb-blasted bus and drew hard on his cigarette.

'Tell me about it,' he murmured.

A BLESSING

Sometimes it just happened.

He didn't know why but sometimes Ward regained his concentration and his drive and he wrote.

The words and ideas flowed with ease. The way they used to.

He glanced at the plastic carriage clock. 12.16 p.m.

He could go inside the house now and make a sandwich. Lose his train of thought. Lose what he had. What it had taken him so long to find.

He re-read the last two pages he'd written, gazing at them on the screen.

The words began to flow once more.

4

COUNTY DONEGAL, THE REPUBLIC OF IRELAND:

Gravel crunched beneath the Renault's tyres as it turned into the small car park.

The driver glanced around as he brought the vehicle to a halt. His companion also scanned the area behind the Tinker's Dog, squinting into the gloom in an effort to pick out shapes.

There were only half a dozen cars so the pub was obviously quiet.

Declan Leary switched off the engine and sat back in his seat. 'It looks like we're early,' he said, running a hand through his short, brown hair.

'Maybe they're inside,' Matthew Finan speculated.

Both men were in their mid-twenties. Both dressed in jeans. Finan had a thick, black fleece on. Leary sported a denim jacket and sweatshirt.

Leary looked in the direction of the pub. 'Maybe,' he murmured.

Finan checked the dashboard clock then pushed open the passenger door and clambered out. He paused for a moment and looked around him.

The pub was surrounded on three sides by trees that grew thickly from gently sloping ground. The darkness made them appear impenetrable.

Finan moved quickly to the boot of the Renault and opened it. There was a long, slender, black leather bag inside. He took it out, tucked it under his arm and wandered past Leary, nodding as he did.

'Only if you have to, Matty,' said Leary quietly.

Finan nodded again and disappeared towards the trees.

Leary remained behind the wheel, closing his eyes for a moment. The drive had taken longer than he'd thought. He dug in the pocket of his jacket and pulled out a packet of aspirin. He swallowed one dry, wincing at the bitter taste it left in his mouth. He pulled open the glove compartment and found a half-empty bottle of Lucozade. He gulped it down gratefully then stuffed the empty bottle back where he'd found it.

Again he scrutinised the pub. He could go in. See if they were there.

Fuck it. Let them come to him.

He peered at the wooded area surrounding the car park but Finan had been swallowed by the darkness.

Leary stepped out of the car and lit a cigarette. As he moved his arm he felt the Glock 9mm automatic in the shoulder holster beneath his left arm.

He could hear the sound of running water nearby and realised that it was the river. The pub in Lifford was built very close to where the dark water of the Foyle divided in two, the fork of the Finn turning away into the Republic while the Mourne cut a path into the valleys below the Sperrin Mountains. The river divided just like the country, thought Leary, smiling at his philosophical musings. Perhaps that was why they had chosen to call the meeting here.

He sucked on his cigarette and waited.

Matthew Finan found a suitable spot about halfway up the slope. He turned and looked back into the dimly lit car park and found that he was able to pick out the shape of the Renault easily.

Moving quickly, he unzipped the black bag and removed the contents.

The Heckler and Koch HK81 rifle felt reassuringly heavy in his hands. He swung it up to his shoulder and peered through the nightscope, easily picking out Leary in its green hue.

Finan slammed in a twenty-round magazine and chambered one of the 7.62mm rounds, then he moved the weapon slowly and evenly until the cross-threads settled on Leary's head.

Finan lowered it again and released the bipod on the front of the barrel. He propped the twin metal legs against a tree stump and settled himself into position on the damp grass.

He unwrapped a piece of chewing gum and pushed it into his mouth.

He waited.

Leary took a final drag on the cigarette then dropped it and ground it out beneath his foot. He rubbed his hands together and decided that due to the chill in the air he might be better off in the car. After all, he didn't know how much longer he'd have to wait.

Leary closed the door and turned the key in the ignition. He allowed the heater to blow hot air for a few minutes, warming his hands at the vents, then he switched it off again.

'Come on,' he muttered, gazing first at his watch then at the dashboard clock. He leant forward to switch on the radio.

There was a light tapping on the passenger-side window.

Leary turned quickly. He saw a figure outside the car. Almost unconsciously he allowed one hand to touch the butt of the Glock as he reached to unlock the door.

'It's open,' he called.

The figure outside didn't move.

'I said, it's open,' Leary repeated. 'Get in the front.'

The door opened and a thin-faced man with thick, black hair slid into the seat.

For long seconds he and Leary regarded each other indifferently.

It was the older man who spoke first.

'You're late,' said James Mulvey.

'It was a long drive,' Leary told him. 'Perhaps if you'd picked somewhere nearer, I'd have got here sooner.'

Mulvey wasn't slow to pick up the edge in Leary's words. His eyes narrowed slightly.

'Where's Finan?' he wanted to know.

'He's around.'

'Why isn't he with you? He needs to hear what we've got to say too.'

'So, where's Donnelly?' Leary wanted to know.

Mulvey hooked a thumb over his shoulder. 'Inside.'

'Go and tell him to come out here.'

'It's warmer inside. Come on, I'll buy you a drink. The both of yous.' Mulvey prepared to open the Renault's door.

'I'm fine here,' Leary told him. 'Whatever you've got to say, say it.'

Mulvey drew in a deep breath. 'There's no need for this, you know,' he said gently. 'We're not the enemy.'

'Are you sure about that, Jimmy?' Leary chided.

Mulvey's face registered anger.

'You got me here to talk,' the younger man said. 'So talk.'

Matthew Finan readjusted the sight on the HK81 and pressed his eye more firmly to it. He carefully arranged the cross-threads so that Mulvey's head was at their centre.

Then he gently rested his finger on the trigger and waited.

5

James Mulvey shifted in his seat and allowed his gaze to travel from the windscreen to the interior of the car. There were several tapes scattered round the back seat. An old newspaper open at page three. Some sweet wrappers. The car smelt of cigarette smoke.

'It's like a bloody tip in here,' Mulvey observed.

'You didn't drag me halfway across Ireland to talk about the state of my fucking car, Jimmy,' Leary snapped. 'Now what do you want?'

Mulvey pulled at the lobe of one ear and regarded his younger companion.

'What you've been doing has got to stop,' he said finally.

Leary met his gaze and held it. 'Says who?' he wanted to know.

'Northern Command. What I'm telling you comes from the top. From the men in charge.'

'From the men in charge of *you*,' barked Leary, pointing an accusatory finger at the older man.

'What you're doing isn't helping the Cause,' Mulvey hissed. 'Fucking bombs here, there and Christ knows where. Those days are over, Declan.'

'For you, maybe.'

'We've won. The Brits are prepared to give us what we want. Prisoners are being released every week. Jesus, your own brother comes out in two weeks. They haven't insisted on decommissioning. There's no need to keep fighting.'

'It's still not our country though, is it? Why did you join the organisation in the first place, Jimmy? Can you remember?'

Mulvey exhaled deeply. 'I wanted my country back,' he said. 'I wanted the Brits out. I wanted guys like me to have the same kind of chance as any Proddie. I wanted an Ireland ruled by Irishmen. I wanted those six fucking counties over the border to be part of that Ireland.'

'So why have you given up?' Leary asked. 'Too old? Too tired? Did you lose your guts in the same jail cell you lost your ideals?'

Mulvey turned angrily in his seat. 'I was fighting for this country while your mother was still wiping your fucking arse,' he rasped.

'That was your choice. Just like it's my choice now. Ten years ago you'd have been patting me on the back, not telling me to stop.'

'Ten years is a long time. A lot's changed.'

'How long were you in Long Kesh?'

'Seven years.'

'And for what?'

'For what we've got now. We've got peace on *our* terms. We're as close to a united Ireland as we've ever been.'

'The six counties are still ruled from London, Jimmy. It doesn't matter what fancy names you give to those bastards who sit at Stormont. They're doing what the Brits tell them. In my book that doesn't make a united Ireland.'

'There are Sinn Fein delegates in London this week having talks with the British government. It's a politicians' game now, Declan, not a soldiers'.'

'So what are you telling me, Jimmy?'

'I'm telling you to lay off. You, Finan and the rest. You'll destroy everything we've fought for if you don't.'

'Bullshit. The Brits are never going to give us everything we want.'

'They will in time. But not while you and your boys are running around planting bombs on fucking buses.'

'You "sixty-niners" are all the same, Jimmy. You think because you started this that it'll end when *you* want it to.'

'I'm giving you an order, Declan.'

'I'm not even in your fucking army, Jimmy. So stick your

orders up your arse and tell Donnelly the same.'

'It could jeopardise your brother's release.'

'Fuck off.'

'Vincent could spend the rest of his life in jail because of you. They'll use you against him.'

'That's bollocks and you know it.'

'Is it? Do you really want to take that chance, Declan?'

'Don't threaten me, Jimmy, and you can tell Donnelly *and* Tracey what I've told you. We're not stopping. And there's nothing you can do about it.'

Mulvey regarded the younger man silently for a moment. 'You seem very sure of that, Declan.'

'What are you going to do?' asked Leary, his right hand sliding into his jacket pocket. 'Shoot me?'

'Just remember what I've told you,' Mulvey said.

Leary pulled his hand free of his pocket and the older man heard a familiar sound.

The swish-click of a flick knife.

Mulvey looked down quickly at the weapon now resting against his thigh.

The two men locked stares for interminable seconds.

'I don't care who I have to kill, Jimmy,' Leary told him. 'Understand?'

Mulvey finally pushed open the passenger door and swung one leg out.

'Let's hope it doesn't come to that, Declan,' he smiled crookedly.

He slammed the door behind him and stalked back across the car park towards the welcoming warmth of the pub.

Leary watched him in the rear-view mirror, seeing him pause for a moment before stepping inside. Only then did he push the flick knife shut and slip it back into his pocket.

JUST LIKE OLD TIMES

For two mornings on the trot Ward was in the office by ten. On both days he had sat straight down at his desk, re-read what he'd written the day before and began.

It felt wonderful.

6

Doyle heard footsteps outside the car.

He was already awake. He had been for the past half hour. But now, as he slowly turned over, he allowed his eyes to open a fraction.

There were four of them. Not one any older than ten. They peered in at him with the same puzzled amusement they would view a goldfish in its tank.

One of them tapped on the glass. The others giggled.

Doyle sat bolt upright and gestured angrily at the kids. 'Fuck off, you little bastards,' he shouted in a perfectly replicated Irish accent.

The kids scattered.

Doyle grinned to himself and stretched his arms before him. He heard the joints pop and crack.

'Shit,' he murmured.

His neck ached too. Everything fucking ached these days. Sleeping in the back of the Orion didn't help.

He pushed open the rear door and swung himself out into the street.

The counter terrorist reached for his cigarettes and lit one. He pulled on his leather jacket to ward off the early morning chill.

As he stood there, curious passers-by glanced in his direction, wondering who was this long-haired, unshaven man who had been sleeping on the back seat of his car for the past two days.

Strangers, he had found over the years, were not exactly welcome in the Turf Lodge area of Belfast but this most recent

foray had been greeted more with bemusement than suspicion by the locals.

Mothers walking their children to school regarded him
indifferently. Some muttered hushed words to each other.

An elderly man leading a collie on a long lead even nodded
a greeting in his direction.

Doyle returned the gesture and pulled up the collar of his
jacket. He rubbed his stomach as it rumbled and set off down
the street towards a newsagent's, hands buried deep in his
pockets.

There were several people inside the shop and Doyle
looked at each face, consigning it to his memory.

He bought a Mars bar, some crisps and a can of Red Bull
and got in the short queue behind a young woman dressed
in a pair of navy-blue leggings and a puffa jacket. Doyle ran
approving eyes over her buttocks while he waited.

As if aware of his prying gaze, the young woman turned
and looked at him. She was barely twenty *(half your age, you
dirty bastard)* and pretty even without make-up.

'Rough night?' she said smiling.

He nodded. 'Thanks to my missus,' he lied. 'I've been sleeping
on the back seat of the car.'

'Did she throw you out?' the young woman wanted to
know, moving closer to the till.

'I walked out,' Doyle continued. 'When I found out what
she'd been doing. I've been looking for her ever since. Now
I know where she is. *And* the bastard who's been fucking her
behind my back.' He smiled. 'If you'll excuse my French.'

The young woman chuckled and put her purchases on the
counter. 'So who is he?' she wanted to know.

'His name's Finan,' said Doyle. 'Matthew fucking Finan.
Bastard. I don't know how long it's been going on but I'll
catch them at it. I've been parked outside his house for the
last two nights. When he comes back I'll . . .' He allowed the
sentence to trail off.

The smile had faded from the young woman's face. 'Where's
your car?' she wanted to know.

'Round the corner in Glen Road. Outside number fifteen.'

'You'll have a long wait if it's Matthew Finan you're after,' said the shopkeeper, pushing the young woman's goods into a carrier bag. 'It's his sister who lives in Glen Road.'

'Shite,' hissed Doyle. 'Do you know where I could be after finding *him*?'

The shopkeeper shook his head.

The young woman picked up her carrier bag and left without looking back at Doyle.

So, you do *know him.*

Doyle paid for his breakfast then opened the can and took a long swig.

'What's his sister's name?' he asked, wiping his mouth with the back of his hand.

'I don't know,' the shopkeeper said briskly, suddenly more interested in tidying the newspapers laid out on his counter.

Doyle bought a *Daily Star*, jammed it into the back pocket of his jeans and headed for the door. He stopped outside the shop and took a bite of the Mars.

Finan's sister, eh?

It was another step closer.

7

NOVEMBER 16th, 1993:

M alcolm Porter knew he'd had too much to drink.
He'd been fairly sure of it when he'd left the joyously
rowdy atmosphere of the Bull. He'd stumbled twice as he
negotiated the steps that led from the public bar of the pub
to the pavement.

Now he was positive he'd drunk too much. He sucked in
a deep breath and stood still, propping himself against the
wall of a house wishing the world would stop spinning quite
so violently.

But what the hell, if a man couldn't celebrate after a victory
such as he'd just tasted then it was a pretty bad show. How
many times did anyone experience the exultation of being in
a darts team that had just won its regional league?

He glanced down at the trophy he still gripped in his right
hand. It was a silver-plated figure holding a dart. Poised, as *he*
had been, to make the winning shot. His name was inscribed
on the bottom of the plaque, just above the name of the pub.

He brandished the small trophy above his head with all the
pride of an FA cup-winning captain.

Porter giggled at his own actions (further proof that he
was pissed) and continued the walk home.

Normally it would have taken him less than ten minutes
to reach his house in Hopewell Avenue but the weight of
victory and the burden of booze were adding extra time to
the trek.

He chuckled again as he continued on his way.

Past a wall that bore the six-feet-high letters: NO SURRENDER TO THE IRA.

He glanced at them but they didn't register. He'd seen the same kind of graffiti for as long as he could remember. After a while it all blended into one, and became as much a part of the landscape as the terraced houses that wound through the city like files of troops.

He stood in front of the wall for a moment and saluted the words. This caused another ripple of giggling.

Sheila would be angry when he got home, he knew that. She'd go on at him for waking the kids and complain about his being drunk, but it would pass quickly enough. She could never stay mad at him for long and, besides, if a man couldn't enjoy a few drinks when he'd just won such a magnificent trophy then where was the justice in the world?

He already knew where he was going to place the trophy. There was a spot on the mantelpiece between his wedding photo and those of his two children. It would look suitably imposing there.

He brandished it before him once more and walked on.

Nearly home now.

As the car pulled up beside him he gave it only a cursory glance. He thought for a moment about stopping the vehicle and showing the occupants what he'd just won.

He giggled once more.

The car stopped and he was aware of the rear door opening.

Porter turned in the direction of the vehicle. Saw a man coming towards him. A man he didn't recognise.

He felt strong arms enveloping him, pulling him towards the waiting car.

He dropped his trophy and saw it land in the gutter.

For fleeting seconds he did nothing. By the time he attempted to fight back he was sprawled on the back seat next to another man.

Porter couldn't see faces. It was too dark inside the vehicle. He was about to say something when he saw the gun.

He almost giggled again. Almost asked if he could have his trophy back.

Two shots sounded, the muzzle flash and retort muffled, to a degree, by the silencer protruding from the barrel of the .22.

Both powered into his head.

The car drove off. As it did, one of the rear wheels crushed the trophy flat.

8

Doyle sat in the Orion and finished the rest of his breakfast. He balled up the empty crisp packet and Mars
wrapper and dropped them out of the window into the street.
Then he sipped at the Red Bull and watched the front door
of number 15 Glen Road.

The cassette was on, turned down low.

'. . . *You had time to waste, time to wonder . . .*'

Doyle looked down at the back of the paper spread out
on the passenger seat.

'. . . *Time, to become someone else . . .*'

He picked it up and re-read the previous night's match
report on the Liverpool versus Newcastle game. There was
a photo of Liverpool's winning goal and Doyle smiled to
himself as he scanned it. Then he dropped the paper and
returned his attention to the house.

He'd already been sitting there for a couple of hours. His
right leg was stiff so he massaged the thigh with one hand.

'Where the fuck are you?' he murmured to himself, eyes
never straying from the house.

As he leant forward he caught sight of his own reflection
in the rear-view mirror.

You look like shit.

His hair needed combing. He needed a shave. Needed a
fucking shower.

Doyle wondered how much of his life had been spent
sitting around in cars waiting for people. Watching.

All part of the job, old son.

Surveillance. Tailing. Stake-out.

He preferred the term hunting.

Doyle ran a hand through his long hair then scratched at one of the scars that were so much a feature of his visage. He couldn't remember where half of them had come from. Those *or* the ones that couldn't be seen until he took off his clothes.

Each one was a reminder of pain.

So much pain.

All crammed into forty-four years.

Some of them wasted?

He sat back in his seat.

'*. . . Might be a good thing, might be a bad thing . . .*'

He yawned.

'*. . . But you can't put your arms around a memory.*'

Doyle jabbed the cassette off as he saw the young woman approaching the door of number 15. Five-three. Early twenties. Dark hair tied back in a pony tail. Carrying three bags of shopping.

He watched as she fumbled for her key then let herself in.

Doyle looked at his watch. He'd give her ten minutes.

9

Shonagh Finan heard the knocking on the front door and put down her mug of tea.

She wandered through from the kitchen into the small living room, then out into the hall as another knock echoed through the house.

'All right, all right, don't knock the door down,' she called, unfastening the lock.

Doyle nodded a greeting as she opened the door, aware of her appraising gaze.

'Hi, there,' he said, his accent impeccable. 'Shonagh, right?'

She nodded. 'I don't know *you*,' she told him.

'Matt sent me,' Doyle lied. 'Can I come in?'

She hesitated a moment, hand still on the door knob.

'It's important,' Doyle continued.

She stepped back and ushered him inside.

Step one.

He kept his hands in his pockets and waited in the hall. 'Matt told me to meet him here,' the counter terrorist informed her. 'He said he'd ring you. Tell you I was coming.'

'I haven't spoken to him,' she said. 'And I still don't know who *you* are.'

'Frank McKean,' Doyle lied, pulling his right hand from his pocket and pushing it towards her by way of greeting.

Shonagh looked at the proffered appendage but declined to grasp it.

Doyle, with all the accomplishment of a seasoned actor, waved the hand in the air, embarrassed, then jammed it back into his pocket again. He attempted a smile and shuffled nervously from one foot to the other.

'I'm a friend of Matt's,' he persisted.

'I know most of his friends. I've never heard him talk about you before. Frank . . .'

'McKean.'

'That's not a Belfast accent.'

'Neither is yours.'

She smiled wryly.

Keep going.

'I'm from the South,' he lied.

'Where?'

'A little place called Ennis.'

She nodded.

'Do you know it?' he said, almost hopefully.

Shonagh shook her head.

'Look, I'm sorry to just turn up on your doorstep like this but Matt said that I'd to meet him here,' Doyle continued. 'Him and Declan are interested in something I've got.'

Her expression changed slightly. 'You know Declan Leary?' she asked.

Bingo.

'Through Matt, yeah,' he told her.

'Perhaps I ought to ring Matt, tell him you're here.'

Doyle nodded. 'That'd be grand,' he said smiling. 'And if Declan answers the phone you can tell him he still owes me some money.'

The card was played now.

That's it. Call the bastard. Bring him straight to me.

She hesitated.

'Listen, if I'm intruding, I'm sorry,' said Doyle. 'I was supposed to meet him at my place but he said to come here. I don't want to put you out.'

'It's no trouble, Mr McKean, I . . .'

'Frank,' he said softly. 'Please, call me Frank.'

Shonagh smiled. 'You might as well have a drink while you're waiting,' she said. 'Come through.'

She ushered him into the kitchen and switched the kettle on.

Doyle looked around the small room then smiled at

Shonagh once again. She pointed towards a chair and he sat.

'How long have you known Matt?' she asked, standing close to the kettle as it boiled.

Doyle shrugged. 'A few months,' he said.

'Where did you meet him?'

The lie was ready. 'In a pub in Clonard,' he told her.

The water inside the kettle was bubbling now.

'He didn't tell me his sister was so good looking,' Doyle added with a grin.

'Nob off,' she chided, waving a hand at him dismissively, her cheeks colouring slightly.

The kettle boiled. She turned to pour the water into the mugs.

Doyle was on his feet in a second.

He caught Shonagh's hair in one strong hand and grabbed the kettle with the other.

She tried to scream but Doyle jerked harder on her hair.

'Keep your fucking mouth shut or I'll break your neck,' he hissed into her ear, all traces of his Irish accent now gone. 'Where's your brother? I want an address.'

'Fuck you,' she panted, struggling against him.

Doyle pushed her against the cupboards.

'An address,' he rasped.

She didn't speak.

He lifted the kettle and held it over her head, tilting it down slightly. She could see steam billowing from the spout.

'Tell me where I can find him or you'll need skin grafts for the rest of your fucking life,' snapped the counter terrorist.

She whimpered.

'I'll count to three,' he warned, upending the kettle full of scalding water a little more.

10

One single drop formed on the spout and fell on to her cheek. Shonagh yelped in pain and struggled more violently against Doyle but he held her firmly.

'An address,' he reminded her. 'That's all I need.'

'Fuck off,' she snapped.

'You're very brave for a girl about to lose her looks permanently.'

'Who *are* you?' she wanted to know.

'Just a guy doing his job. Now give me that address before I melt your fucking face.'

Another drop of red-hot liquid fell on to her cheek.

The counter terrorist could see a small red welt rising where the scalding water touched flesh.

'You can either tell me or the RUC,' Doyle said. 'Your choice.'

'I don't know what you're talking about.'

'Your brother's a member of the Continuity IRA. Maybe you knew that, maybe you didn't. Either way I couldn't give a fuck. All I want to know is where I can find him.'

She stopped struggling so frenziedly for a second but Doyle still held her firmly before him.

'That bomb that went off in the city centre a couple of days ago,' he continued. 'Your brother was involved with that. So was Declan Leary.'

'You can't prove that.'

'I can if I speak to him. He might not even be guilty. Give me an address where I can find him, let me speak to him. He might not be in any trouble.'

Yeah, right.

'I don't trust you,' she protested. 'How do I know you're not from some fucking Proddie organisation?'

'You don't. But seeing as I've got a kettle full of boiling water held over your face you're not really in a position to argue, are you?'

She was shaking.

'As it happens I'm with the Counter Terrorist Unit,' Doyle continued. 'Not that that really matters at the moment.'

'Are you going to hurt him?'

'It's a possibility,' Doyle said flatly. 'But right now I'll hurt *you* if you don't tell me where I can fucking find him.'

Another moment of silence.

'All right,' Shonagh gasped.

Doyle released his grip on her hair and stepped back a pace.

'Now, your brother *or* Declan Leary,' he snapped. 'Where are they?'

She put one hand to the cheek where the boiling water had dripped.

'You would have done it, wouldn't you?' she murmured. 'You would have scalded me.'

He nodded. 'If I had to. Give me an address.'

She regarded him venomously. 'You're a real fucking hard man, aren't you? Threatening a woman. Do you get off on that, you bastard?'

'The address.'

'Fuck you,' she hissed.

Doyle quickly slid one hand inside his leather jacket. It closed over the butt of the Beretta 92F 9mm automatic nestled in the shoulder holster and he pulled the pistol free.

'This'll do you more damage than boiling water,' he intoned. 'Now where's your fucking brother?'

'He'll kill you.'

'He'll try. The address?'

'There are some flats in Dalton Road,' she said through clenched teeth. 'He uses one of them. Number forty-four.'

'You'd better hope that checks out,' said Doyle. 'Because

if it doesn't, I'll be back to see *you*. And if I do have to come back, by the time I've finished, you'll be putting your make-up on with a fucking spoon for the rest of your life. Got it?'

'I hope he fucking kills you,' Shonagh shouted.

Doyle took a step towards her and, moving with incredible speed, he struck her across the temple with the butt of the Beretta.

Shonagh dropped like a stone.

Doyle swept her up in his arms and deposited her on one of the kitchen chairs, her head lolling on her chest.

He pulled out several drawers until he found what he wanted.

Cutting several lengths of nylon string he quickly bound Shonagh's wrists and ankles to the chair.

Satisfied she would remain secure he took one last look at her then strode towards the kitchen door. On his way out, he tore the phone from the wall. It shattered easily.

Doyle glanced at his watch. He might not have much time.

11

Doyle blasted on the hooter as he drove, clearing any idle pedestrians out of the way.

The mobile was wedged between his shoulder and his ear as he guided the Orion along the streets that led to Dalton Road.

'Yes, I'm sure,' he snapped. 'Tell Robinson he'll need a couple of armed units.'

The voice at the other end asked the address again.

'Flat in Dalton Road, number forty-four,' rasped Doyle. 'Got it?'

The voice wanted to know if either Finan or Leary were there.

'How the fuck do I know? It's possible, that's why I think Robinson will want armed units with him. But you tell them not to make a move until I arrive.'

He ended the call and dropped the phone on to the passenger seat.

As he turned left two men stepped into the road. Doyle hit the hooter and narrowly avoided them.

He pressed down harder on the accelerator.

The flats in Dalton Road were of a depressing uniformity. Here and there residents had attempted to individualise their humble dwellings with a lick of paint on the front doors and window frames but, for the most part, the peeling flesh of neglected council gloss was the only colour visible.

Graffiti on the walls. Lifts that didn't work. The residents were in no position to complain. The council had no inclination to improve their plight.

Some of the windows were boarded up. Some of the flats empty. Most had sustained broken windows at some time and there was still shattered glass on the walkways.

Along with the dog shit, the used condoms and the empty hypodermics.

Number 44 had once sported a blue front door but the paint was now scratched and scabrous. It lay at the top of four flights of precipitous stone steps. Even young men sometimes had to stop and draw breath during the climb.

Men like Matthew Finan and Declan Leary.

A dustcart was collecting rubbish down the street, the workers swarming around it like ants around a queen. One of them dropped a refuse bag as he hauled it up to deposit it in the back of the dustcart. The bag split open, spilling its reeking contents across the pavement. A chorus of jeers, curses and laughter greeted the mishap. Two of the men began scooping up the rubbish in their gloved hands and shoving it back into the torn bag.

Inside the cab another man sat motionless, his eyes fixed on the wing mirror of the vehicle. Through it, he had a perfect view of the entrance to the flats.

Two teenage girls left, both jabbering away into mobile phones. But apart from that very little moved.

No one, so far, had entered apart from an old woman with a shopping trolley.

PC Adam Sweetman of the Royal Ulster Constabulary kept his gaze fixed firmly on the wing mirror and watched.

And waited.

Doyle brought the Orion to a halt in the street that backed on to the Dalton Road flats.

There were three boys, no older than ten, standing close to the side of the road, kicking a punctured football back and forth, occasionally bouncing it off the other parked vehicles in the street. One was wearing a Manchester United shirt.

Doyle ignored them and reached for his mobile. He punched in a number and waited.

'I want to speak to Chief Inspector Peter Robinson,' he said. 'Tell him it's Sean Doyle of the Counter Terrorist Unit. It's important.'

There was a buzz of static then Doyle heard Robinson's voice. 'I've got one unit in position already at the north end of Dalton Road,' the policeman told him. 'There's another on the way.'

'Anybody know if Finan or Leary are inside?'

'How can they? No one knows what they look like.'

'Have any of your men been up to the flat to check it out?'

'Not yet.'

'Fuck it. Leave it. I'll do it myself.'

'Doyle. If they're in there, use the back-up. Understand?'

'You just be ready to move when I shout.'

'I mean it. Don't try being a bloody hero. If they're in there, use—'

Doyle cut him off. 'Bollocks,' he murmured, swinging himself out of the car.

One of the three kids kicked the ball in his direction. Doyle stopped it with the inside of his left foot then rolled it gently between his heel and toe.

'Manchester United supporter, eh?' said Doyle to the oldest boy.

The boy nodded.

'Great, aren't they?' he beamed.

Doyle flicked the ball up with his toe then volleyed it perfectly, watching as it sailed halfway down the street.

'You'll grow out of it,' he muttered as he watched them chase off after it, the one in the shirt sticking two fingers up at him.

Doyle dug his hands in his jacket pockets and hurried towards the corner of Dalton Road.

Shonagh Finan had no idea how long she'd been unconscious. All she was aware of as she blinked her heavy lidded eyes was the thumping pain inside her skull.

She tried to rise, forgetting that she was still firmly tied to the chair.

She strained against the restraints for a moment, feeling the nylon string cut into her wrists.

'Bastard,' she hissed under her breath.

She could see the phone shattered on the floor in front of her. If she could get free she had a mobile in her handbag upstairs.

Once more she began to strain against her bonds.

A VISIT

Ward had used the girl before. Her name was Jenny. At least that was what it said in the contact magazine where he'd first seen her photo and phone number.

Age: 24. Vital statistics: 32B, 23, 33.

She arrived in a taxi, as she always did, carrying a small, black holdall.

He sat gazing at the television screen until he heard the doorbell ring then he got to his feet and wandered through to the hall.

Jenny was wearing a short, black dress. Balanced on her open-toed high heels she was just under five-two. Her hair was brown, streaked with blond. Her face was round, her lips full. She was wearing too much make-up, some of it to conceal the two spots on her left cheek, but Ward was unconcerned. He ran appraising eyes over her and ushered her in.

She looked around the spacious hallway of the house and smiled professionally.

'Beautiful house,' she told him.

'You always say that,' he reminded her.

'Well, it is.'

She knew who he was. What he did for a living. The first time she had told him she'd read a couple of his books.

Ward had been unimpressed.

'Do you want a drink first?' he wanted to know.

'Brandy and coke.'

'You go up and get ready, I'll bring it.'

She turned and made her way upstairs.

Ward wandered back into the sitting room, poured her a

drink and had another himself, then he switched off the TV and made his way slowly back through the hall, pausing at the bottom of the staircase.

'You can come up,' she called.

He made his way almost wearily up the stairs and across the landing to the main guest room.

Jenny was now naked. She was sitting on the bed with her legs tucked beneath her. On the duvet before her lay two vibrators and a tube of KY jelly.

He nodded approvingly.

'Can we get the money out of the way first?' she said apologetically.

'How much?'

'Same as before.'

He fumbled in his pocket and pulled out two twenties and a ten. He laid the notes on one of the bedside tables and began to undress.

She took the larger of the vibrators and smeared it with lubricant, then she began to trail it over her neatly shaved pubic mound. It left several glittering trails on her thighs and belly as well as her vagina.

Ward was already erect. He stood beside the bed, his penis gripped in his right fist, his gaze travelling slowly up and down her body.

She was murmuring quietly now. Little gasps punctuated the increasingly deep breathing.

Ward had to admit it was a reasonably convincing performance.

She pushed the first of the vibrators into her vagina.

He could hear the buzzing of the batteries as she increased the speed.

Then she reached for the other one. Lubricated it and also smeared some of the clear fluid around her puckered anus.

He nodded.

Jenny pushed the thinner of the two sex toys slowly inside herself, wincing slightly as it penetrated her more deeply.

Ward clambered on to the bed beside her, his erection now throbbing in his hand. He pointed his penis in the direction of her face and increased the speed of his hand.

'Open your mouth,' he told her.

She did as she was instructed, closing her eyes as she heard him grunt. Two or three small spurts of oily white fluid streaked across her face. She murmured encouragement as he finished his ministrations.

As he stood up, she prepared to wipe the semen from her face. 'Leave it,' he told her. Again she did as she was instructed.

Ten minutes later, she was gone.

DREAMS

Ward awoke in a sweat.

He rolled over and looked at the clock. 3.11 a.m.

It was hot. There wasn't a breath of air in the bedroom.

He hauled himself out of bed and crossed to the window, pushing it open. The darkness was almost as total as the silence. He drew in a deep breath of warm air and rubbed a hand through his hair.

As he peered at the garden he heard rustling in the bushes, then the high-pitched yowling of two fighting cats. They continued their noisy combat for a few more seconds then silence descended once again.

Ward looked in the direction of the office. There was a silver-grey light coming from inside.

He exhaled wearily. He'd left earlier that day without switching off the monitor.

For long moments he considered what to do. If he left it on, what was the problem? It wasn't going to blow up or catch fire, was it?

Was it?

He decided to leave it and clambered back into bed, sliding over to avoid the sweat-drenched area he'd been sleeping on previously.

Whenever he woke at night he found it difficult to get back to sleep. He wondered if a drink might help.

Ward swung himself out of bed again and crossed to the window.

The silver-grey light inside the office had gone. There was only darkness.

He must, he told himself, have been dreaming.

Ward headed towards the stairs.

RAGE

On days when Ward couldn't think straight he was filled with conflicting emotions. There was the ever-present feeling of desolation. Of wasted time.

And there was the anger. The fury that came from sitting staring into empty air or at a blank screen without finding the will or the strength to write.

For those who didn't make their living in his business, it was difficult to explain how difficult it was.

From the outside, Ward realised how easy it must appear. Work from home. Sit behind a keyboard all day. Work when you wanted to. All the attendant bullshit that any self-employed person had to endure.

But this was different. Creativity couldn't be forced.

Self-employed bricklayers could make themselves work. Plumbers could force themselves to fix leaky taps. Decorators could will themselves to complete one more wall.

It was not so with writing.

No matter how hard Ward tried to make himself think, no matter how many times he shouted at himself in frustration, if the words wouldn't come then that was it.

On the wall in front of his desk there was a quote from Nietzsche: WILL A SELF AND THOU SHALT BECOME A SELF.

Nietzsche, he reminded himself, died insane.

The clock was showing 10.49 a.m. when he began to write.

12

Doyle jabbed the call button on the lift and muttered irritably to himself when nothing happened. He turned and headed for the stairs taking them two at a time to begin with. When he reached the second landing he slowed his pace, sucking in breath more raggedly.

He paused and lit up a cigarette before negotiating the next two flights.

The counter terrorist emerged on to the fourth-floor landing, walked to the parapet and gazed down into the street. The dustcart was still in position at one end, the men moving back and forth, emptying rubbish into the back of it. To his left, Dalton Road was still open.

He drew slowly on the cigarette as he watched a car pull up on the opposite side of the road. A man in his twenties got out and headed towards a house.

Doyle wondered, for fleeting seconds, if Shonagh Finan had given him a false address.

Only one way to find out.

He sucked on the cigarette once more then dropped it and strode towards the door of number 44.

He slowed his pace as he drew nearer, allowing his right hand to brush the butt of the Beretta inside his jacket.

There was another pistol strapped to his ankle in a small holster. The Smith and Wesson .38 Bodyguard held five rounds in its cylinder and was only slightly bigger than the palm of Doyle's hand. Hammerless, it was perfect for concealment and the counter terrorist had personally cut crosses in the tips of each bullet, ensuring they exploded on impact.

The third pistol he carried was in another holster beneath his right arm. A .50 calibre Desert Eagle. An automatic weapon capable of spewing out rounds at a speed in excess of 2,500 feet per second.

Tools of the trade.

Doyle looked at the doors as he walked past them.

Number 40. Boarded up.

Number 41. The window in the front door was cracked.

Number 42. There was a battered kid's tricycle outside.

He slowed his pace even more.

Number 43. As he reached the green painted door, it opened.

The man who emerged was in his early thirties. He glanced at Doyle then turned his attention back to the occupant of the flat.

The woman was roughly the same age. Auburn hair. Jeans. White T-shirt. She was barefoot.

She looked at Doyle then at the other man who rushed away.

'You've frightened him off now.' The woman smiled. 'He might not come back.'

'Sorry about that,' Doyle said, switching to his impeccable Irish accent with ease.

She began to close the door.

'Have you got a minute?' he wanted to know.

The woman eyed him warily, her smile fading.

'Maybe. What do you want?'

'I want to know when you last saw your neighbour,' he said, nodding in the direction of number 44.

'Why should I tell *you?* Who are you anyway?'

'I'm a friend of his. He owes me money. I think he's been trying to avoid me. If you know what I mean.'

'I haven't seen anyone go in or out of there for a couple of days.'

'Have you been here all the time?'

'More or less. I work from home.' She lowered her gaze momentarily.

'And the guy that just left was the first job of the day, right?' grinned Doyle.

She looked at him and the smile returned. She nodded.

'I think my friend's due back this morning but I don't want to miss him,' Doyle lied. 'He never answers his phone either.'

The counter terrorist held the woman's gaze with his piercing grey eyes, a slight smile touching his lips. 'It's a raw morning to be waiting about,' he said quietly, rubbing his hands together.

'Do you want to come in?'

'How much is it going to cost me?'

'That depends.'

Doyle grinned and stepped inside.

Matthew Finan saw the dustcart blocking Dalton Road and sighed irritably. He banged his hooter but the driver could only shrug.

Finan realised he'd have to either wait for the vehicle to move or drive around the block and come in from the other direction.

He stuck the Renault in reverse, swung it into the next street and guided it around the rear of the flats. As he drove, he reached for his mobile phone and worked his way through the call index until he found the number he wanted.

It was answered on the second ring.

'Declan, it's me,' he said. 'I'll be there in about five minutes. How long will you be?'

'About a half an hour,' Declan Leary told him.

'See you then.'

Finan ended the call and parked the car.

13

The flat smelt of cheap perfume. The scent grew stronger as Doyle stepped into the small sitting room. There was a low coffee table in the centre with a large ashtray and four plastic coasters. Guests obviously didn't bother with them because there were several circular marks on the surface of the scratched wood.

The single window was above a radiator shelf which sported several small ornaments, one of which, a ballerina, had an arm missing. Through the window, Doyle could see straight out on to the parapet. The walls were thin, and no one could pass the flat without him hearing.

As long as someone passed, of course.

He sat down on the mustard-coloured sofa, smoothed one hand over a cigarette burn in its arm and looked at his host.

'So, what do you want to do?' she asked, brushing her auburn hair behind her ears and moving towards Doyle.

'What did the last guy do?' he asked.

'The usual.'

'Which was?'

'Same thing he always does when he comes here. Empties his balls into a Durex while he's inside me. What do you think he does? What do you think they *all* do?'

'What's your name?'

'Whatever you want it to be.'

'I'm serious.'

'So am I. *You're* paying, I'll be whoever you like.'

Doyle looked around, his gaze alighting on some photos

on a sideboard to his right. One of them showed the auburn-haired woman and an older couple.

'Your parents?' he wondered.

She nodded.

'They must be very proud.'

'They're both dead,' she snapped.

'Mine too. Seems like we've got something in common.'

'Listen, if you're interested in spending some money then fair enough. If not, there are other guys who are.'

Doyle pulled out his wallet and pressed two twenties on to the coffee table.

'What'll that buy me?' he wanted to know.

'Whatever you want,' she smiled.

'Tell me your name.'

'Karen,' she said, reaching for the twenties.

Doyle shot out a hand and caught her wrist, pulling her towards him.

'Just leave them there for now,' he said. 'I just want to talk.'

'Oh, that's your thing, is it?' she purred, resting one hand on his thigh. 'Okay, shall I tell you how I want your cock inside me?'

Doyle shook his head. 'I'm paying for your time, not your fanny,' he said flatly.

She sat back, withdrawing her hand.

'Who the fuck are you?' she snapped. 'If you're a fucking copper, this—'

'I'm not a copper. I'm just a poor cold soul paying for your time, keeping a roof over my head while I wait for a friend. That's it. If you don't want the money then fine.'

He reached forward to snatch up the notes.

'No,' she blurted. 'All right, if you want to talk we'll talk.'

Doyle settled back on the sofa.

His gaze moved occasionally in the direction of the window.

14

Matthew Finan paused as he reached the staircase and pulled the mobile phone from his pocket. He found the number and as he began to climb pressed call.

The ring tone buzzed in his ear as he made his way up the first flight of steps.

Still ringing.

He wondered if his sister was still out shopping. But he'd spoken to her the previous day and told her he'd pop in and see her towards lunchtime.

He reached the second flight and continued his climb, sucking in deep breaths every so often.

Still no answer.

He wondered if she was okay. He'd always looked out for her ever since they were kids. That was what older brothers were supposed to do for their little sisters his parents had told him. It was a credo he'd always lived by.

He and Shonagh were close. Even when they'd been growing up together, there had been little of the sibling rivalry that normally blights brother–sister relationships.

Perhaps, over the years, he'd been a little over-protective (using a length of lead piping on a man he'd suspected of getting her pregnant when she was nineteen may have been a touch excessive) but, what the hell, he loved her and he wasn't about to see any harm come to her.

He knew that one of her neighbours had a key to her house. He could always call *her*. Get her to check on Shonagh. If he could just remember the bloody number.

He began to climb the third flight of stairs.

* * *

Doyle held the mug of tea in both hands and looked again at the window.

'How long are you going to be?'

Karen Mercer's voice seemed to echo inside the small flat.

The counter terrorist heard but didn't look at her.

'What would you be doing if I wasn't here?' he asked.

'Earning money.'

Doyle pulled another twenty from his wallet and slapped it down on the coffee table.

She regarded the cash for a moment then sat back in her chair.

'You're not waiting for any friend, are you?' Karen murmured.

'I told you, he owes me money.'

Doyle sipped at his tea. He heard footsteps on the parapet. Heard them stop outside the flat next door. Heard a key turn in the lock.

About fucking time.

'Put another sugar in there, will you, Karen?'

He handed her the mug then got to his feet, reaching in his jacket pocket for his mobile.

As she padded off to the kitchen, Doyle pressed the number he wanted.

'Give me Robinson,' he snapped before the voice at the other end even finished speaking. 'It's Doyle.'

Karen stood watching him from the living-room door.

'Someone's just gone inside the flat on Dalton Road,' said Doyle. 'Are the rest of your men in position?'

Robinson said that they were.

'I want to wait until both of them are inside,' Doyle continued. 'If we take one of them out we'll lose the other. Wait for my signal.'

'You're a fucking copper,' Karen said. 'I knew it.'

Doyle finished the call and turned to face her.

'I'm a guy who's given you sixty quid to keep your fucking mouth shut. I suggest you do it. I'll be out of here soon and you can get back to work. For the time being just sit down.'

She held his gaze for a moment then stepped forward into the living room and did as he instructed.

Shonagh Finan gritted her teeth and finally eased her left hand free of the nylon string. It had cut deeply into the flesh of her wrist and she gazed angrily at the red welts that had risen there.

She had no idea how long she'd been straining against the tightly fastened bonds. There was perspiration on her face from her struggles and both her hands felt numb.

She undid the string around her other wrist then freed her ankles.

As she got to her feet, she swayed uncertainly for a second or two, then headed towards the kitchen door and the stairs beyond.

Reaching the landing she saw her handbag lying on the bed. The mobile was in view.

Shonagh snatched it up and began dialling.

15

Doyle wandered across to the window of Karen Mercer's flat and peered out on to the parapet. He looked at the flat next door then at his watch.

The counter terrorist didn't want to move without Leary being present too but how long was Finan going to stay put?

Come on, think.

Karen sat watching him.

Take one of them or possibly risk losing both.

Doyle jammed a cigarette between his lips.

Shit or bust?

Footsteps outside.

Doyle stepped back from the window but kept his gaze firmly fixed on the man who had walked past.

About twenty-six. Five-ten. Light-brown hair, cut short.

Declan Leary?

Time to find out.

He reached for his mobile, and turned to face Karen.

'When I walk out of here, you stay put, got it?' he snapped.

She nodded. 'What about the money?'

'Keep it.'

'Doyle,' said a voice at the other end of the phone.

'Robinson. I think Leary's just arrived. Get your men to seal off both ends of the street.'

'I've got snipers in position too. You can leave it to us now.'

'Not a chance. I found these fuckers. I'm bringing them in.'

'I'll send men—'

'You send nothing. Just be ready to grab them if they get past *me*.'

'We need them alive, Doyle.'

'I'll do my best.'

He dropped the mobile back into his pocket then headed for the door of the flat.

'Thanks for the tea and shelter,' he said.

She raised one middle finger in his direction.

'Remember what I said?' he told her. 'You keep your fucking head down, right?' He slid a hand inside his jacket and pulled the Beretta from its holster. 'Otherwise you're likely to get it blown off.' He eased open the door. 'See you around.' And he stepped outside. Doyle heard her shout something as he went but he wasn't sure what it was.

Who cared anyway?

No one else was on the walkway.

He glanced across to the buildings opposite wondering if, even now, RUC snipers were drawing beads on him.

When you shoot, just make sure you shoot the right fucking person.

The dustcart was still at one end of Dalton Road. At the other end there was a large white Transit and a Land Rover.

Doyle peered down at the activity below for a second longer then turned his attention back to the door of flat number 44.

He had the Beretta held down low beside his leg as he edged forward.

How many times in your life have you been in this position?

Wondering if the men on the other side of that door know you're here. Are they standing there now with weapons waiting for you?

There was no reason why they should be, Doyle reasoned. As far as they were aware, no one knew their whereabouts, least of all the RUC and the Counter Terrorist Unit.

Doyle took a step closer.

The choices now were fairly simple. Kick the door down and go in blasting. Wait for them to come out and hope they wanted to give up instead of fight.

Your choice.

Something glinted across the street. Sunshine on glass. The

rays of the sun on a scope? If Doyle had seen it, perhaps Leary or Finan had too.

No reason to be expecting it.

He was less than a foot from the door now, pressed tight to the brickwork. The snipers would be watching him, relaying his progress to Robinson by two-way.

Go in blasting?

He knew there was no back door and if Finan and Leary were going to get away, they'd have to come straight through him.

He raised the butt of the automatic and prepared to bang on the door.

As he did he heard the high-pitched burr of a mobile phone from inside the flat. There was a moment of silence then some muted voices.

Doyle raised his hand again to hammer with the gun. He was about to strike when part of the door exploded outwards.

16

It was a shotgun. No mistaking the thunderous roar. Doyle had heard the sound enough times.

He stepped away from the door and pressed himself up against the wall, turning his face slightly as lumps of wood and metal erupted into the air, propelled by the force of two massive impacts. Several shotgun pellets rolled across the walkway and the counter terrorist smelled the all-too-familiar stink of cordite.

He worked the slide on the Beretta, chambering a round, his heart thudding more quickly against his ribs, adrenalin pulsing through his veins like heroin through a junkie.

What was fear to some men was close to exhilaration for Doyle.

He looked around. No cover on the walkway. If the fuckers came out shooting, it'd be messy.

Further down the walkway a door opened.

'Stay inside,' Doyle roared and the door slammed quickly.

There was another massive roar as the shotgun was discharged again. Another piece of the door was obliterated, tiny cinders and splinters spiralling into the air.

For one ridiculous moment he thought about telling them to put down their weapons and come out.

Yeah, right.

What else had they got in there with them? More guns? Explosive?

Come on, think.

One way out. One way in. Snipers across the street. Armed RUC men at both ends of the road.

Step back. Let them rot inside there. They're going nowhere.

He gripped the Beretta more tightly, aware now of the unearthly silence that had descended after the barrage of gunshots. The only activity was below in Dalton Road itself as plain clothes RUC men did their best to keep the thoroughfare clear of passers-by.

Doyle backed off slightly and dropped to one knee, steadying himself. He raised the Beretta and squinted along the sight.

The advantage was his. Finan and Leary had no idea how many men awaited them.

The counter terrorist wondered how they'd discovered they were under surveillance.

Finan's fucking sister. Little bitch.

He nodded as if to confirm his own suspicions. She must have warned them.

'Finan,' Doyle roared. 'Can you hear me?'

Silence.

'You and your fucking friend can stay in there as long as you like. You're covered on all sides. You're going nowhere.'

Still no reply.

'Personally, I couldn't give a flying fuck whether you come out with your hands up or you come out blasting,' Doyle continued. 'Either way you're going down. You either walk out of that flat or they carry you both out in body bags. Got that?'

He moved a little closer to the door, his eyes never leaving the sight of the Beretta.

'Pity about your sister,' he called, a slight smile on his face. 'She's an accessory now. I know she was the one who tipped you off. You'll do time and so will she. But before I arrest her there's something I want to give her. And I'm sure I won't be the first.'

Doyle heard sounds of movement from inside the flat. Muted voices.

'Pretty little thing,' he continued. 'You should have kept your business to yourself. You made *her* fair game too. After I've put you and Leary in the fucking ground I'll go back and pay her a visit. She looked like she was gagging for it when I was there this morning.'

'Fuck you,' roared a voice from inside the flat.

Bingo.

There were more sounds of movement. Doyle steadied the automatic.

'Nice arse,' he called back. 'Something for me to grip on to when I'm fucking her.'

'You fucking bastard,' bellowed the same voice.

Doyle smiled. 'Now, are you coming out while you still can?'

Silence.

Doyle stepped back slightly.

Across the street the snipers kept their eyes pressed firmly to their scopes.

'Come out now and I might only fuck her once,' Doyle shouted.

A small package, no larger than a man's first, rolled from inside the flat. It bumped against the parapet then lay still.

Doyle saw the detonator jammed into it.

He knew he had just seconds.

17

Doyle half ran, half threw himself to one side as he saw the package. It probably weighed less than a pound but he knew the damage a pound of plastic explosive was capable of.

As he spun away he gritted his teeth and hurled himself down, scraping the elbows of his leather jacket on the concrete.

The blast was deafening.

Doyle covered his head, the thunderous explosion tearing away part of the parapet and sending lumps of concrete spiralling into the air. Pieces of debris were flung out into the street and those below ducked or ran for cover as chunks of stone rained down like shrapnel.

A great cloud of smoke engulfed the walkway and Doyle found his lungs clogged by the noxious fumes. He rolled on to his side and squinted in the direction of number 44.

Through the smoke he saw two figures.

The bastards were making a run for it.

Doyle swung the Beretta up and squeezed the trigger. The burst-fire mechanism sent three bullets from the barrel milliseconds after each other. Two sang off the stonework, another cut through the fume-filled air.

The smoke was still thick and Doyle waved a hand angrily in front of his face as if to clear it. He fired again into the choking fumes. Shots were returned.

He heard a bullet part the air no more than six inches from his left ear.

Opposite, two of the RUC snipers opened up. Doyle heard

the loud crack of the HK81s. 7.62mm slugs struck the brick-work.

Finan and Leary were already hurtling along the walkway towards the stairs at the far end. It was their only escape route.

Doyle scrambled to his feet and squeezed off four more rounds. Empty shell cases spun into the air and the recoil slammed the butt of the 9mm against the heel of his hand. But he remained steady, pumping the trigger.

One of the bullets caught Finan in the shoulder, blasted through his right scapula and erupted from his chest just above his nipple. Gobbets of flesh, pulverised bone and pieces of clothing spewed into the air, propelled on a gout of blood.

Finan stumbled.

Doyle fired again. His next shot caught the Irishman in the thigh. Moving at close to 1,700 feet a second, the bullet fractured the left femur and sent Finan sprawling.

He dropped his weapon and Doyle saw Leary grab it and swing the Ithaca pump-action shotgun up to his shoulder and work the slide.

Doyle hurled himself to one side as the discharge dug a crater in the concrete close to his left foot.

By this time Leary had reached the stairs.

Doyle paused beside Finan for a moment, pressing two fingers to the jugular vein of the motionless younger man. There was a faint pulse but looking at the amount of blood spouting from the Irishman's leg wound, Doyle wondered if his bullet had cut Finan's femoral artery. If it had, he had about two minutes before his life fluid finished jetting from him.

There was already a huge puddle of it around him, and Doyle could hear the liquid spurts, like a conduit firing thick crimson from an unattended garden hose.

Doyle left the man and ran on in pursuit of his other quarry.

One down. One to go.

As he reached the top of the stairs another blast from the shotgun shattered the bevelled safety glass in the double doors.

Doyle saw that the slide on his automatic had shot backwards. He fumbled in his pocket for a fresh clip and slammed it into the butt.

His breath coming in gasps, he put his shoulder to the door and crashed through.

18

Fragments of shattered glass cut Doyle's cheeks and chin but the counter terrorist kept going. He stayed low in case Leary decided to let loose another blast.

Doyle could hear footsteps pounding down the concrete steps and he chanced a look over the metal banister. There was a deafening blast, amplified by the stairwell and a portion of the handrail simply disintegrated as the buckshot destroyed it.

He stuck the 9mm over the rail and fired three times. Another wave of sound shredded the eardrums of those on the stairs. Bullets screamed off concrete and the smell of cordite grew more intense.

Doyle dashed down the next flight, taking the stairs two or three at a time. He hit the landing hard and rolled, hauling himself upright as he charged on after Leary.

He could now hear his quarry breathing. The man couldn't be more than one flight ahead of him.

As he ran the counter terrorist holstered the Beretta and dragged the Desert Eagle from beneath his right arm. Even in Doyle's hand the pistol looked huge. Its triangular barrel was as distinctive as its incredible destructive power.

The breath searing in his lungs, he swung himself round on to the final flight of steps.

Leary was rushing for the main doors to the flats.

Doyle swung the Desert Eagle up and squeezed off two shots. The massive recoil was mostly absorbed by the weapon's mechanism but Doyle still needed all his strength to control the pistol.

One bullet punched a hole in the door, the second powered

into a wall, shattering brickwork and sending a fine cloud of reddish powder into the air.

Leary ran on and out into the street.

Doyle vaulted the last handrail, dropping the twelve feet to the ground. He hit the concrete hard, rolled over and dragged himself up, wincing from a pain in his left ankle.

Might have sprained it. Fuck.

But the pain was secondary and he ran on, bursting out into the street.

He looked to the left and right and saw Leary running towards the far end. There were men spilling from the Land Rover parked there.

Leary raised the shotgun and fired twice at the vehicle. The first blast sent the RUC men scurrying for cover. The second punched several holes in the chassis above the front offside wheel.

'Stop him,' roared Doyle, swinging the Desert Eagle up once again.

Leary was already pulling open the driver's door and clambering behind the wheel of the Land Rover.

Doyle fired. The bullet stove in most of the windscreen and Leary ducked down as fragments of glass showered him.

The driver of the Transit was attempting to manoeuvre into the path of the Land Rover but Leary jammed it into reverse and slammed into the larger vehicle with such force that he cleared a way through for himself.

'Shoot him, for fuck's sake,' Doyle bellowed as he charged at the reversing Land Rover.

'We can't open fire on a street,' one of the armed RUC men shouted back.

'He'll get away,' snarled Doyle.

He squeezed off two more shots from the Desert Eagle. The first of the .50 calibre shells drilled into the spare wheel, tore through the chassis and buried itself in the back of the passenger seat. The second ripped off a wing mirror.

Leary stepped on the accelerator. The back wheels spun madly for a moment then gripped the tarmac and the Land Rover shot forward as if fired from a catapult.

Doyle pulled open the passenger door of the Transit and climbed in.

'Get out,' he rasped at the driver.

'What the fuck are you doing?' asked the startled man.

Doyle pressed the Desert Eagle to his cheek. 'Get out, now,' he hissed, practically pushing the man out into the street.

He stuck the Transit in reverse, crashing into two parked cars as he struggled to bring it under control. He spun the wheel and floored the accelerator. The van sped off after the fleeing Land Rover.

The radio hissed and crackled. 'Panther Two, come in. Over,' said a metallic voice.

Doyle kept his eyes on his prey. He knew that if Leary made it to an open stretch of road he'd leave him standing. As long as he was in the narrow, busy streets of the city, it was a more even contest.

Doyle wondered if he could level it even more.

'Panther Two, come in,' the radio crackled again. 'What is your position and your situation? Over.'

Doyle grabbed for the two-way. 'Block all the fucking roads within a two-mile radius of Dalton Road,' snarled the counter terrorist. 'Do it now.'

'Panther Two, identify yourself,' the voice on the radio demanded.

'I'm the man who's doing your fucking job for you,' snarled Doyle and hurled the radio down.

Up ahead the Land Rover turned right, narrowly avoiding a Fiat.

Doyle caught the Fiat on its nearside wing and sent it skidding into a parked car at the roadside. He gripped the wheel more tightly as if urging extra speed from the Transit.

The traffic up ahead was fairly light.

If Leary gets a clear stretch of road he'll leave you standing.

The Land Rover was weaving in and out of the cars, overtaking and undertaking as Leary tried desperately to put distance between himself and his pursuer.

Doyle had already forced the accelerator to the floor. The needle of the speedo touched sixty-five.

There was a junction ahead. The Land Rover hurtled across it. Doyle followed, narrowly missing another car that came from his right, and striking the hooter hard. Those cars that didn't heed his warning were simply shunted out of his way.

'Fucking move,' he roared as he drove.

The Land Rover shot between two cars, paint scraping from both wings. Doyle followed, ramming one vehicle aside. It careened up on to the pavement, the driver stunned by the impact. Broken glass was spread across the road.

Doyle saw two women preparing to cross the street. The first was pushing a pram.

If Leary saw them, he made no attempt to slow down, and the Land Rover roared on doing over sixty.

19

D oyle gripped the wheel of the Transit with one hand. With the other he fired the Desert Eagle straight at his own windscreen. The noise was deafening.

The heavy-grain slug blasted a hole in the glass the size of man's fist. Shards of crystal sprayed in all directions.

Doyle fired again, struggling to control the recoil of the weapon. This shot hit the rear of the fleeing Land Rover.

Shoot the tyres out.

For fleeting seconds he thought about it.

And what if the car goes out of control and swerves up on to the pavement?

He aimed higher.

The two women preparing to cross leapt back from the kerb, one of them screaming in terror as the two vehicles roared past.

Traffic lights ahead. They were on amber but Doyle wondered if they'd hold.

Fifty yards. The traffic seemed to be more dense now.

Forty yards. Leary guided the Land Rover around a Renault.

Thirty yards. Traffic further ahead was slowing down.

Twenty yards. The lights flickered. Leary put his foot down.

Ten yards. Doyle imitated his action.

Red light.

The Land Rover hurtled across the junction. Doyle followed, steadying the Desert Eagle once more.

A metallic voice was whining from the radio but the counter terrorist had no idea what it was saying.

On the right there was a garage. Doyle could see several cars filling up.

And a motorbike.

Leary suddenly wrenched the wheel of the Land Rover to the right and the car shot across the forecourt of the garage. He slammed on the brakes and clambered from the driver's seat, the Ithaca still gripped in his fist.

Doyle followed, ducking low behind the wheel as he saw Leary raise the shotgun to his shoulder. He fired twice.

Both discharges thudded into the radiator grille of the Transit. Doyle saw steam rise from the ruptured bodywork. He struggled with the wheel for a moment then stepped hard on the brake.

The Transit skidded, kept sliding and slammed into several cars parked outside a glass-fronted showroom. The vehicles were shunted into the huge expanse of crystal and the jangling sound of smashing glass filled the air for long seconds.

Doyle gritted his teeth and slid from the cab, glass crunching beneath his feet.

Leary was already running towards the motorbike. The rider stared at him then backed away from this madman with a shotgun. He raised the weapon, pointed it at the motor-cyclist and squeezed the trigger.

The hammer slammed down on an empty chamber.

The Irishman hurled the empty shotgun aside then swung his leg over the seat of the Honda 600 and revved the engine.

Doyle sighted the Desert Eagle.

If you shoot you'd better hit the bastard.

He hesitated.

Even if he did hit Leary, from such close range the bullet would go straight through him.

Strike a petrol pump?

Doyle holstered the weapon and ran towards the motorbike. The front wheel left the ground as Leary gunned the throttle.

Doyle launched himself at his quarry. He slammed into Leary and both of them crashed to the ground. There were several small puddles of petrol on the forecourt and its smell was strong in their nostrils.

Doyle fixed his hands around Leary's throat and smashed his head down sharply on the concrete.

The counter terrorist was aware of Leary reaching for something. Seconds later he felt a cold punch in his side, then his thigh and left buttock.

Doyle grunted in pain as the knife was driven into him. He felt blood burst from the lacerations and released his grip on Leary's throat, trying to grab the man's wrist to prevent him stabbing again.

Leary brought his head up hard into Doyle's face and managed to roll from beneath him, his clothes spattered with petrol and Doyle's blood.

Doyle fumbled for the Desert Eagle. Saw Leary clamber on to the motorbike and work the throttle. The bike roared out of the garage into the street.

Doyle fired once but the bullet tore through the air six feet from its target.

The counter terrorist tried to rise, aware of the burning pain from his wounds. He put one hand to the deep puncture in his side and saw blood running freely through his fingers.

'Call the police,' he rasped at several onlookers.

Someone already had.

Doyle heard sirens approaching, and hoped one was an ambulance.

The counter terrorist tried to rise again but his leg buckled beneath him. Leary had driven the blade deep.

Cunt.

Doyle sat with his back against a petrol pump, the Desert Eagle still gripped in one fist. With his free hand he pulled a handkerchief from the pocket of his jeans and applied pressure to each wound in turn. The one in his buttock hurt the most.

More pain.

He felt dizzy. A combination of the petrol fumes and the stab wounds, he told himself. He closed his eyes so tightly that white stars danced behind the lids.

Don't pass out.

He could hear the motorbike receding into the distance. Leary was away.

For the time being.

'Bastard,' he hissed under his breath.

The first of the police cars screeched to a halt on the fore-court.

EXHAUSTION

Ward slumped back in his chair, eyes closed.

4.06 p.m. He took out the disk and switched off the computer. That was it for the day.

Enough was enough.

As he got to his feet he felt something he had not experienced for a long, long time. It was a sense of pride.

He set the alarm in the office, locked up then stepped on to the back lawn and stood with his hands on his hips taking deep breaths of the still air. His head was spinning.

In one of the gardens nearby, a dog was barking. He could hear kids playing noisily.

Ward waited a moment longer then wandered back to the house. As soon as he stepped inside the phone began to ring. He wondered about answering it then decided to leave the call to be collected by the answerphone.

He walked into the sitting room, heading for the drinks cabinet. Holding his glass of Jack Daniel's, he sat down in one of his armchairs.

Within minutes, he was asleep.

RUNNING ON EMPTY

The glass fell to the floor and bounced once on the carpet. Ward woke with a start, staring around the darkened room. At first he could see nothing.

Not a hand in front of him.

For one second of madness he thought he'd gone blind. Then he realised that night had descended. How long had he been asleep in the chair?

He sat up, looking down at the dropped glass as he slowly became accustomed to the gloom. He rubbed his eyes and squinted at his watch. 8.56 p.m.

Ward hauled himself out of the armchair and stumbled backwards and forwards turning on lamps. Their welcome glow spread through the darkness, banishing the blackness like an unwanted dream. He finally switched on the television, not caring which channel he found, wanting only the familiar sight and sound. He drew the curtains and shook his head.

There was a gnawing pain in the pit of his stomach and he realised how hungry he was. He hadn't eaten since lunchtime, over seven hours ago.

He picked up the glass he'd dropped, thankful that it had been empty, and made his way to the kitchen, switching on lights in his wake. The fluorescents buzzed like somnolent bluebottles and he winced as their brilliant, white light seemed to sear his eyes. He crossed to the fridge and took out a bottle of milk, drinking straight from the bottle in an attempt to quench his raging thirst. Then he studied the contents of the fridge.

Some tomatoes, a cucumber, lettuce that was beginning to turn brown, cheese and a couple of yogurts.

He exhaled wearily.

There was a frozen meal in the freezer, he remembered. It took less than ten minutes in the microwave. That would do.

He stuck the meal in the oven and made his way back into the sitting room where he poured himself a drink and waited for his dinner to cook.

He noticed there were three messages on his answerphone. He chose to ignore them for the time being. He would eat first and they couldn't be that important anyway. Not much *was* these days.

He watched a little of the news while he waited. A plane crash in India. An earthquake in Mexico.

He flicked channels. There was some American sitcom on Channel 4. A programme about World War II on BBC1. He watched that until his meal was ready.

And he drank.

ELECTRICAL PROBLEMS

Ward woke again at 12.15. He rubbed his eyes and moved quickly around the room switching off lights and electrical appliances, then he made his way up the stairs to bed.

As he set the alarm he glanced again at the answerphone and decided to check his messages the following morning. He was too tired now.

Undressing quickly, he climbed into bed without brushing his teeth. He hoped that he would fall asleep quickly. He didn't.

He tossed and turned for over an hour before dragging himself irritably to his feet.

The moon, despite the abundance of cloud, was bright and cast a cold, white glow over everything. Ward stood looking out into the night. He opened the window and sucked in several deep breaths.

His head was throbbing. A combination of drink and insomnia. He decided his prolonged naps during the day and evening must have caused his inability to sleep.

Ward looked at his office and saw the now familiar silvery grey light. He must have forgotten to switch off the monitor again.

One part of him said leave it, the other that he was up, he was awake, why not switch it off?

He pulled on a pair of jogging bottoms and a sweatshirt and headed for the stairs. He pressed the four-digit number to neutralise the alarm then passed through the kitchen to the back door.

The moon emerged from behind a bank of dark cloud just as he stepped out into the garden so he didn't bother switching on the outside light.

He made his way quickly towards the office and let himself in. He climbed the stairs and stood in front of the monitor. It was, indeed, still on.

Ward switched it off, muttering to himself, then turned and wandered back down the stairs and out into the garden. As he did so the moon retreated behind the clouds, plunging him into darkness.

Ward hesitated as he heard rustling sounds. One of the many cats that infested the neighbourhood, he told himself. He bent down, picked up a small stone and threw it in the general direction of the noise.

There was a loud yowl and Ward smiled. That might keep some of the cat shit off his lawn, he thought as he opened the back door.

He looked back at the office. Everything was in darkness. As it should be.

THE SLEEP OF THE DEAD

It was almost daylight by the time Ward finally drifted off to sleep.

He didn't hear the alarm clock when it rang three hours later.

He slept on.

MAKING AN EFFORT

Ward woke at 11.30 that morning. He showered, dressed and wandered out to the office, not hopeful of being able to write but anxious to make an effort.

There was a dead bird on the lawn. Probably killed by the cat he'd thrown a stone at the previous night. He made a mental note to move it when he'd finished for the day.

As he entered the office he shivered. But it was always cool at the bottom of the stairs, no matter what the time of year.

He climbed the stairs to the office.

The monitor was switched on.

A MYSTERY

He *knew* he'd turned it off. He would have sworn on a Bible if he'd had one handy.

He sat before the blank screen, gazing at it. Some kind of electrical fault, perhaps? A power surge in the night?

That had to be the answer. Either that or his memory was worse than he thought.

Had he dreamt coming out to the office the previous night? It was possible.

He rested his fingers on the keys, sucked in a deep breath and began to type.

20

Doyle hated the smell of hospitals. The cloying, antiseptic odour made him feel nauseous.

He wondered why. He'd been inside enough of the fucking places in his life. He should be immune to it by now. And the Royal Victoria Hospital in Belfast smelt the same as all the others.

He blinked hard, trying to clear his vision. He couldn't remember if he'd passed out in the ambulance or if his drowsiness was the result of anaesthetic.

He tried to move and felt pain in his side and left leg. 'Shit,' the counter terrorist murmured and pushed the sheets down.

All the old, familiar scars were there. The ones that crisscrossed his body like a street map. The result of bullet wounds, explosions. Whatever the weapon, Doyle bore a scar as testament to an encounter with it.

He looked down at his heavily bandaged torso and leg.

More to add to the collection.

A doctor had once told him that with the amount of injuries he'd received, he had no right to be alive. That he should be grateful. He looked down again at the scars on his body and shook his head.

Grateful?

He almost laughed.

The door of his room opened and a nurse entered.

'Mr Doyle,' she said. 'How are we feeling?'

'*We've* felt better,' he answered.

'I'm not surprised,' she told him, crossing to his bed and feeling for his pulse, checking it against the watch fastened to her tunic. 'They had to put thirty stitches in you. And you lost a lot of blood. Half an inch to the left and that knife would have cut a major artery in your leg.'

She let go of his wrist and scribbled something on his chart.

'When can I leave?' he wanted to know.

'When the doctor gives you the all-clear.' She took his temperature and wrote something else on the clipboard.

'Your records indicate multiple injuries over the years,' she said. 'Any residual effects?'

He shook his head.

'Do you get pain from any of these?' she wanted to know, running appraising eyes over his scars.

'Some stiffness every now and then but nothing to shout about,' he told her. 'That's probably my age, not the scars.'

'You're in good shape,' she smiled, pulling the sheet up around his chest.

Doyle met her gaze, watching as her cheeks reddened slightly.

'I'll be back with your lunch,' she told him, heading for the door.

'Stick a packet of fags on the side, will you?'

She paused.

'You've a visitor. Shall I send him in?'

Doyle nodded.

He heard voices outside then a familiar figure strode into the room.

Chief Inspector Peter Robinson removed his cap and ran a hand across his bald pate.

'What the hell happened, Doyle?' he said angrily.

'Nice to see you too. Pull up a chair. Or, better still, fuck off and leave me in peace. What do you mean, "what happened"? It's pretty obvious, isn't it? Leary got away.'

'Because you didn't follow procedure.'

'Because *your* men fucked up. You had snipers covering that flat, why didn't one of the dozy twats shoot him when he came out?'

'We didn't have positive ID.'

'Jesus Christ, some cunt comes rushing out into the street with a fucking shotgun in his hand and starts shooting at a police vehicle. I'd have thought that would have narrowed it down a *bit*.'

Robinson drew in a deep breath and met Doyle's furious gaze.

'What about Finan?' the counter terrorist wanted to know.

'He died before we could get him to hospital. You killed one of our main leads.'

'Shit happens,' Doyle said flatly. 'Any word on where Leary's gone?'

'Probably back into the Republic. We've more than likely lost him for good now.'

'He'll turn up. Trust me.' Doyle ran a hand through his hair. 'What did you find inside the flat?'

'Fifteen pounds of Semtex. Detonators. Weapons and ammunition.'

'What kind of weapons?'

'Mainly handguns. There were half a dozen automatics and revolvers. Four AK47s and a couple of Ingram Mach 10s.'

'Any other fingerprints apart from Finan and Leary?'

'If there are we haven't found them yet. It looks as if they were operating alone.'

Doyle nodded and silence descended on the room. It was finally broken by Robinson.

'You're lucky Leary didn't kill you,' the policeman offered.

'Yeah, so people keep telling me. Well, I'm telling you now, next time I run into him, *he* won't be so lucky. I'll kill *him*.'

'You've got to find him first. You're not going to do that lying in here are you?'

'I'll be out by tomorrow.'

'Have the doctors told you that?'

'*I've* decided.'

'And then what?'

'I'll take care of Leary once and for all.'

21

DOWNING STREET, LONDON:

Cigarette smoke had gathered beneath the high ceiling of the room and it hung there like a man-made rain cloud. Every now and then the air-conditioning would send ripples through the grey curtain and it would shimmer like a spectre in a fading dream.

Only one of the men in the room was smoking.

Bernard Wolfe was forty-eight years old and he'd been on twenty a day since he was thirteen. The Irishman enjoyed a cigarette, and the feeble intrusions of political correctness were of no interest to him. Neither were the occasional, exaggerated coughs of the men who sat opposite him.

Neville Howe was a year his senior. A tall man with pinched features, he had unusually lustrous brown hair for someone approaching their half century. There wasn't so much as a trace of grey at his temples, leading some people to wonder if he was immune to the onset of age or knew a very capable barber.

Howe stared alternately at Wolfe and the papers spread before him on the large, polished oak table at which they sat. He had held the post of Secretary of State for Northern Ireland for less than three months. This was his first meeting with anyone from Sinn Fein or any of the other parties embroiled in the mess that was Northern Ireland politics.

He wore a perfectly tailored charcoal-grey Armani suit, which he brushed constantly with one hand as if to remove some flecks of dust.

Beside him sat Sir Anthony Pressman. He was three years older than Howe, bespectacled, white-haired and had the kind of ruddy cheeks that suggested joviality. But if the Home Secretary *was* familiar with levity, then it was nothing more than a passing acquaintance. His heavily lined forehead was the legacy of six years in the job.

Pressman was no stranger to meetings such as these, whether the venue was London, Belfast or Dublin. Certainly since the Good Friday Agreement, he had been at more of these summits (as the press liked to call them) than he cared to remember.

Present at most of the meetings were Wolfe and his colleague Peter Hagen.

At forty-two Hagen was the youngest man in the room. He was also one of the youngest men ever to have been appointed to Sinn Fein's ruling body. It was rumoured that prior to this position, he had spent five years in an active IRA cell, operating everywhere from Londonderry to Birmingham. Amiable but occasionally short-tempered, he was as adept at the negotiating table as he had, allegedly, been with an Armalite.

Hagen reached for a jug of water and refilled his glass.

Bernard Wolfe was speaking. 'We feel that the action taken in Belfast was,' Wolfe paused as if searching for the word, 'excessive.'

'Certainly excessive force was used,' Hagen concurred, sipping his drink.

'The incident was regrettable, I agree,' Pressman offered. 'But you must see it from *our* point of view. Finan and Leary were both considered dangerous. Something proved during the incident, I hasten to add. Having said that, I agree that the measures taken against them were somewhat extreme.'

Wolfe blew a stream of smoke into the air. 'The fact is that neither Finan nor Leary were affiliated to *our* organisation,' he observed.

'Our concern is for the people of what we all want to regard as a united Ireland,' said Hagen. 'Innocent bystanders' lives were put at risk. Catholic *and* Protestant. Put at risk by a member of your security forces.'

'If the reaction of the security forces was extreme,' Howe interjected, 'it was because the situation they found themselves in was extreme.'

'Steps had already been taken by our organisation to prevent any further activity by Finan and Leary,' Wolfe continued. 'We view the activities of the Continuity IRA and the Real IRA with as much disapproval as you, Mr Howe.'

The Secretary of State nodded sagely and smiled a practised smile. 'We understand that, but the fact remains that neither Sinn Fein nor the military wing of your organisation has been able to control the activities of men like Finan and Leary. Also, most members of the Continuity and Real IRA are known to have been members of your organisation at one time.'

'That's open to question,' snapped Wolfe, grinding out his cigarette.

'But steps *were* taken to communicate with them,' Hagen said, sharply. 'We realise such men pose a threat to the peace process. We're as anxious to see peace in our country as you are.'

'A great many compromises have been made to hasten a complete end to the situation in Northern Ireland,' Howe said. 'Most of them, I might add, by this government.'

'Are you implying that your government are more anxious for peace than we are?' snapped Hagen.

'My colleague was implying nothing of the kind,' Pressman offered, raising a hand as if in supplication. 'We are committed to finding a peaceful solution to the problems in Northern Ireland. I find what happened in Belfast as shocking as you.'

'How can you guarantee it won't happen again?' Wolfe wanted to know.

'With the greatest of respect, Mr Wolfe,' said Howe almost apologetically, 'how can *you*?'

'Certain measures *will* be undertaken,' Pressman assured the men seated opposite him. 'This government will continue to support and encourage a peaceful settlement that is acceptable to all parties concerned. You have my word on that.'

'It's a matter of trust,' Howe echoed.

'So, what do you intend to do?' enquired Wolfe.

Pressman sipped from his glass and cleared his throat. 'I feel an example must be made,' he began.

For the first time during the meeting he smiled.

22

SEPTEMBER 5th, 1994:

The headstone was black marble. The rain that had been falling for most of the day trickled down it like tears as if imitating those that had been shed at the graveside earlier.

In the damp, night air the smell of flowers was still strong. They lay in their cellophane-wrapped bundles around the graveside, the falling rain beating a tattoo on the clear covering.

The smell of freshly turned earth mingled with the sickly sweet aroma and, through the stillness of the night, the scraping of metal on wood sounded.

A spade had connected with the wood of the coffin.

One of the two men standing inside the hole pulled a torch from his jacket pocket and aimed it at the top of the box. The light reflected off the brass nameplate.

The man sought out the six screws that held the coffin lid in place and bent to the closest of them. His companion, still sweating from his exertions, nudged him and shook his head.

No need to open the fucking thing.

There was more movement from the graveside. Something heavy was being dragged across the wet earth. Two of the bouquets were crushed beneath it.

The body was wrapped in plastic bin liners, wound around with gaffer tape. It resembled the cocoon of some huge, malevolent butterfly. But there would be no hatching from this plastic pupa.

The heavy form was tumbled into the grave and it landed

with a dull thud on top of the coffin. It took less than half an hour to refill the gaping hole.

The bouquets were placed back on top of the mound. The men prepared to make their way back to the car which awaited them just beyond the low stone wall that marked the perimeter of the cemetery.

One of them paused a moment longer and glanced once more at the headstone.

DOUGLAS WALSH
BELOVED HUSBAND AND FATHER
ASLEEP IN THE ARMS OF GOD

He nodded, almost reverentially. Now Douglas Walsh had someone to share eternity with him. The man looked up at the clouds and lit another cigarette.

The rain continued to fall.

23

BELFAST:

'Mr Doyle, I cannot stress strongly enough my disapproval at what you're about to do.'

Doctor Simon Bellamy watched in exasperation as Doyle hauled himself out of the hospital bed and carefully put his weight on his bandaged leg. The counter terrorist winced at the first contact then seemed to become accustomed to the pain.

'The wounds are not sufficiently healed,' Bellamy stressed.

'They're fine, doc,' Doyle told him, searching in the bedside table for his clothes. He was relieved to find they'd been washed. Although walking (or hobbling) out of the hospital with bloodstained gear wouldn't have bothered him.

He began to dress.

'You need at least three more days under observation,' Bellamy insisted. 'What the hell are you trying to prove?'

'I'm not trying to prove anything. Now, if there's some piece of paper you want me to sign, clearing you of responsibility, then great, give me the bloody thing. But I'm not staying in here a day longer.' He pulled on his T-shirt, feeling the tear where Leary's blade had sliced it.

'What's your hurry?'

'I've got work to do.'

'You're not going to be in a fit state to do anything if you leave here like this.'

Doyle eased his jeans carefully up his bandaged leg and fastened them. Then he pulled on his socks and stepped into the worn cowboy boots he'd also pulled from the locker.

He put more weight on his injured leg and gritted his teeth.
More pain.

'What's the worst that can happen, doc?' he asked, conver-
sationally.

'Your stitches could open.'

Doyle shrugged, pulled on a denim shirt and tucked it into
his jeans. 'I'll see my own quack when I get the chance,' he
said, as if that was meant to make Bellamy feel better.

'Mr Doyle—'

'There are people who need these beds more than I do,'
Doyle snapped, cutting him short. 'I'm doing you a favour *and*
some other poor sod. Look at it that way if it makes you
feel better.'

'Right now, *you* need to be in that, bed,' Bellamy answered.

Doyle pulled on his leather jacket and dug in the pockets
for his cigarettes. He was out.

'No good asking *you* for a fag is it, doc?' he smiled.

Bellamy shook his head resignedly.

Doyle's phone rang. He looked at the doctor, the only
sound in the room the shrill tone of the mobile.

Bellamy held up his hands as if in surrender and stepped
out of the room.

Doyle answered the call.

'How are you feeling?' said the voice.

He recognised it immediately. Well spoken, calm, measured
tones.

'Not bad,' he said.

'I had a full report on what happened.'

'Yeah, I bet you did. Listen, I had Leary. He—'

'Then why are *you* the one in hospital?'

There was a moment's silence then the voice continued, 'I
understand the injuries you received were severe.'

'A knife's better than a car bomb,' Doyle replied.

'I'm glad you're okay, Doyle.'

'Am I supposed to say thanks for the call?'

'You're not supposed to say anything, just listen to me. I
want you to take the first flight out of Aldergrove back to
London.'

'What for? I got Finan but Leary's still on the fucking loose. What's the point in me flying back to London now? The business is here.'

'It wasn't a request, Doyle. I'm giving you an order. I want you out of Belfast as quickly as possible. Do you understand? I want to see you in my office the day after tomorrow at ten o'clock.'

'Are you sending someone else after Leary?' Doyle snapped.

'Leary isn't your concern any longer. Just get on that bloody plane.'

'You know I'm the only one who can find him.'

'My office. Ten o'clock, the day after next.'

Doyle was about to say something else but Jonathan Parker, Director of the Counter Terrorist Unit in London, ended the call.

'Shit,' Doyle hissed.

He gazed at his mobile for a few seconds more then switched it off.

He looked into his locker again and saw a plastic bag, sealed at the top with Sellotape.

The counter terrorist smiled as he lifted it.

His guns felt comfortingly heavy.

CALLING CARDS

Ward sat back in his chair and stared at the screen. He re-read what was there, changed the odd word then rested his fingers on the keys once more.

He waited.

Nothing came. Nothing clicked into place. No further sparks of inspiration.

He muttered to himself and got to his feet.

He looked out of the window into the garden. The sun was shining and the sky was cloudless.

Ward looked back to the screen then got up and made his way down the stairs to the office door. He stepped out into the garden, breathing deeply.

Some ants were busying themselves around the cracks in the stonework beneath his feet. Ward watched them for a moment then walked slowly on to the lawn. It needed cutting and the grass almost reached his ankles. Daisies and buttercups sprouted abundantly and bees moved lazily from flower to flower.

Everyone was busy except him it seemed.

He could hear the sound of children's voices away to his left. He wondered why the little bastards weren't at school. A little further away, a dog barked.

Ward crossed to the large, rambling hedge that formed one boundary of his garden and looked at the blackberries growing there.

There was a sticky mound of glutinous matter close to his left foot. At first he thought it was half-eaten fruit, then he knelt to inspect it more closely. The stench made him recoil. It was excrement.

Fucking cats must have been in the garden again. He made a mental note to put some pepper down or, better still, slide three or four razor blades into the dirt around the holes in the fence where he knew they entered. Perhaps they wouldn't feel so much like shitting in his garden with their paws cut to shreds.

Ward smiled at his ingenious sadism, then the smile faded.

He looked again at the lumps of excrement, covering his face with a handkerchief to protect his nostrils from the foul odour.

This wasn't cat shit. It was too big. The stools too large.

Something glistened in the second pile. Ward reached for a twig to disturb the faecal mess. He prodded it carefully and managed to dig out the gleaming object.

He almost overbalanced when he saw it.

Another hallucination?

Were his eyes going?

The gleaming object he had prised from the excrement looked like a human tooth. He flicked at it with the stick but caught it too hard and the fragment flew into the hedge.

Ward cursed and tried to find it but it was useless. He got to his feet. Perhaps he'd look again later. Perhaps he'd forget about it.

He headed back towards the office.

UPHILL STRUGGLE

The words came slowly. Almost painfully. Ward tried to force himself to concentrate but it was difficult.

He got up and looked out of the window again, gazing in the direction of the mounds of excrement he'd found earlier. Dried by the the sun they had turned to dust.

Ward frowned. How was that possible? And what about the tooth?

He shook his head. It made no sense. But, then again, not much in his life *did* any more.

He sat down at his desk again.

24

LONDON:

The flat was cold. Doyle shivered as he walked in and closed the front door behind him.

How long since he'd been home? Three weeks? A month? Longer? Time didn't seem to matter much these days.

Come to that, what did?

There were some envelopes scattered across the mat and Doyle bent stiffly and picked them up, scanning the postmarks. Most of it was junk. Loan offers. Reader's Digest bullshit. Credit card promises. Doyle dumped them in the nearest bin.

He wandered through to the sitting room and switched on the TV and the stereo. Wondering why he was bothering, he looked at the answerphone. No messages.

Doyle didn't like silence and music soon filled the flat.

There was some shit Aussie soap opera on the TV but thankfully the music drowned it out.

'Lost in your dreams, nothing's what it seems . . .'

There would be no complaints from neighbours living in the flats above and below him. They were out at work from seven until five every day and Doyle hardly saw them. He'd lived in this part of Islington for over ten years now, shared this building with half a dozen other souls and yet he was no closer to them than he had been when he'd first moved in. A nod of acknowledgement was the extent of his community spirit.

'Searching my head, for the words that you said . . .'

He made his way into the kitchen and switched on the

central heating, hearing the radiators bump into life. Then he spun the cold tap and let it run for a while.

His leg ached. More from hours of sitting than the wounds themselves, he told himself. First the plane then the taxi from Heathrow. He'd normally have taken the tube but, much as he hated to admit it, his injured leg was giving him more pain than he'd anticipated. The doctor had given him some painkillers and he fumbled in his pocket for them, washing down two with a handful of cold water.

Getting old?

He drew a deep breath and filled the kettle, blowing the dust from a mug on the draining board.

Of course there was no milk in the fridge.

Shit.

He'd nip out later and get some. The counter terrorist had been relieved to see his car parked outside. Delighted, too, that it still had all its windows. The odd extra scratch here and there was hardly a problem. And the likelihood of theft was small. Who, he reasoned, would want to nick a seven-year-old Astra?

As well as milk he needed food. His cupboards were never exactly well stocked but then, as Doyle reasoned, why bother when he was hardly ever at home.

Fuck it. There was a KFC round the corner.

He left the kettle to boil and headed into the bedroom where he changed into a sweatshirt and a pair of jogging bottoms.

The bandages around his leg and side would need changing. He made a mental note to pick up some fresh ones from the chemist's at the bottom of the street when he went out for the milk.

He knew how to redress the wounds. He should do after all these years. He'd had enough of them.

Doyle went back into the kitchen and poured boiling water on to the tea bag. As he stood stirring it he wondered why Jonathan Parker wanted to see him. What could be so fucking important that his boss had pulled him off a case like Leary's?

Wait and see.

He fished the tea bag from the mug with a spoon, dropped it in the sink then drank.

The painkillers should start to take effect soon.

The music was still thumping away in the living room.

'My body aches from mistakes, betrayed by lust . . .'

He'd finish his tea and have a sit down before he went out.

'We lied to each other so much, now in nothing we trust.'

There was a more important job he had to do before it got dark.

25

No matter what the season, Norwood cemetery always seemed cold to Doyle.

Now, as he made the long walk from his car to the grave he sought, the wind whipped across the vast necropolis, blowing his long, brown hair around his face and making him pull up the collar of his jacket.

The trek took longer than usual because he was unable to maintain his usual brisk stride. Despite the painkillers, he was slowed down by the stiffness. Muttering under his breath, he forged on.

The drive had taken less than an hour. He'd been relieved that his car had eventually started, and that driving was less uncomfortable than he'd anticipated.

There were other people visiting the cemetery. Doyle saw two older women wandering back along one of the many gravel paths that criss-crossed the huge resting-place like arteries. One of them nodded at him as he passed.

He returned the cursory greeting and gripped his bunch of carnations more tightly. As usual they were red.

Like blood?

It had been her favourite colour. He always brought red flowers.

There was a slight rise ahead and Doyle gritted his teeth as he walked up the incline, the wind cutting into him as he reached the top.

The grave lay to his right at the base of the reverse slope.

He swallowed hard and dug in his jacket pocket as he approached the headstone.

The plinth was dirty. There were dead leaves and withered petals lying on it. Some bird shit on the stone itself. Doyle pulled the cloth from his pocket to clean the headstone.

Before he began he stood motionless by the grave and read the inscription:

GEORGINA WILLIS
AT PEACE

She had been just twenty-eight when she died.

He closed his eyes for fleeting seconds and her image danced before him.

The blond hair. The finely chiselled features.

Was it really more than ten years since her death?

So much pain.

Had time passed so quickly? So meaninglessly?

What was it people said? That you should let go of the past? Fuck that. Why let go of the past when there was nothing in the future?

He ran a hand through his hair and looked again at the stone.

'Hello, babe,' he murmured.

Doyle knelt and began cleaning, spitting on the cloth. He did the same with the metal vase that stood on the plinth, and then he placed the carnations carefully inside and set it back in position. He balled up the cellophane and stuffed it into his pocket.

For what seemed an eternity, the counter terrorist stood beside the grave, the cold wind gusting around him. His eyes were fixed on the stone and its gold letters.

You should be in there with her.

'I've got to go,' he said finally.

You should be the one who's dead. Not her.

He kissed his index finger and touched it to the headstone.

'I'll see you soon.'

Doyle turned and headed back up the gently sloping path. He didn't look back.

26

The building in Hill Street was a magnificent edifice. A three-storey monument with a walled garden to the rear. It had once been the town house of millionaire John Paul Getty.

Doyle drove past the dark, brick structure once, searching for a parking space. There were half a dozen large, black cars already nestled around the building like huge, black beetles around carrion. He could see chauffeurs seated inside. Two of the uniformed men were outside their vehicles, chatting in the warm early morning sunlight.

Doyle reversed then spotted an empty space right in front of the imposing oak doors of the building.

Fuck the double yellow lines.

He guided the Astra into the gap then fumbled in his glove compartment for the orange disabled sticker. He pressed it to the windscreen and swung himself out of the car, still clutching the remains of an Egg McMuffin in one hand. He quickly swallowed the last mouthful.

Doyle walked up to the door and pressed the buzzer beside it. The intercom hissed.

'Can I help you?' said a metallic-sounding female voice.

'Doyle, 23958,' he said into the grille. 'I've got an appointment with Parker at ten.'

There was a loud buzz and the door opened.

Doyle stepped inside, his footsteps immediately muffled by the thick carpet that covered the reception area of the London headquarters of the Counter Terrorist Unit.

The woman who'd buzzed him in was in her late twenties.

Short, dark hair. Of slight build. She was wearing a dark-blue two-piece and a white blouse and looked the epitome of efficiency. Probably hand-picked by Parker, Doyle thought. He liked his staff to be immaculate at all times. The counter terrorist glanced down at his own battered leather jacket and worn jeans and smiled to himself.

A large reproduction of Pietro Annigoni's portrait of the Queen hung on the wall behind the receptionist. It regarded Doyle balefully.

'Can you tell Parker I'm here, please,' Doyle said, reaching for a cigarette and lighting it.

'It's a no-smoking building,' the receptionist told him reproachfully.

'I'll try to remember that,' Doyle smiled.

He looked around the reception area and saw three men seated at various places around it. All were dressed in dark suits and all three never allowed their gaze to leave him the entire time he remained at the reception desk.

Doyle took a long drag on his cigarette.

Security?

The portrait of the Queen was giving nothing away.

'Mr Doyle is here,' he heard the receptionist say.

'Send him in,' Jonathan Parker instructed.

Doyle hesitated a moment, still inspecting the three besuited individuals seated nearby.

'If you go up the stairs, Mr Parker's office—'

Doyle cut her short. 'I know where it is,' he informed her, and she watched him as he headed for the staircase at the rear of the reception area. He occasionally winced as he felt the stiffness in his left leg.

The counter terrorist reached the landing and headed for the second door on his right.

Two more of the suited men were standing outside. They weren't CTU, he was sure of that. One took a step towards him as he approached the door.

'I've got business in there,' Doyle said, fixing the man in an unblinking stare. 'If I was you I'd move.'

The man hesitated a second then backed off.

Doyle knocked on the door once then walked in. He recognised Jonathan Parker immediately.

The Commander of the Counter Terrorist Unit was seated behind his antique desk sipping from a bone-china tea cup. Only his eyes moved in Doyle's direction as the younger man entered the room.

'Have a seat, Doyle,' said Parker, setting down his cup.

Doyle did as he was instructed, his attention now drawn to the other individual in the room who was sitting on a large, leather sofa to the right of Parker's desk. He was holding a manilla file on his knee.

There was something familiar about him.

Parker nodded in the other man's direction.

'Doyle, I'd like you to meet Sir Anthony Pressman, the Home Secretary.'

That's what the pricks in the suits were here for.

Pressman ran appraising eyes over the counter terrorist but his expression remained indifferent.

'Do you want to tell me what's going on?' Doyle said to his superior.

Parker took a deep breath.

27

'It's about what happened in Belfast,' Parker said quietly.

'Which is where I should be now, not here discussing it,' snapped Doyle.

'I know how good you are at your job, Doyle. That's why I've overlooked certain aspects of your behaviour over the years. You're the best we've got and I don't mind saying it.'

Doyle waved a hand in front of him. 'Did you pull me off a fucking case to give me a testimonial?' he said. 'Because if you did, thanks a lot but put it in writing and let me get back to work.'

'What you did in Belfast was unacceptable.'

Doyle turned slightly in his seat. The words had come from Pressman who was flicking through the file before him.

'What I did in Belfast was unavoidable,' the counter terrorist said sharply.

'Have you any idea the damage you caused? The cost of your actions?' Pressman continued.

Doyle smiled humourlessly and shook his head. 'I couldn't give a fuck about the cost,' he said. 'I was trying to neutralise two known terrorists. In case you hadn't noticed, they've already killed ten people in the past three months.'

'"Neutralise",' Pressman mused. 'What a quaint term. The problem is, Mr Doyle, that your actions caused more than a million pounds worth of damage to property and endangered countless innocent lives, not including those of the men you were attempting to "neutralise". One of whom, I hasten to add, is now dead. Killed by you.'

'They both would have been if I'd had my way,' hissed Doyle.

'The peace process between Great Britain and Ireland is continuing as we would wish. Action such as yours will only jeopardise an already unstable situation.'

Doyle got to his feet. 'This is bullshit,' he said dismissively. 'What am I supposed to do? Slap them on the wrists and tell them not to be such naughty boys?'

'Sit down, Doyle,' Parker told him.

The counter terrorist hesitated a moment then slumped back into the chair.

'It isn't as if this is an isolated incident, is it, Mr Doyle?' Pressman said. 'Your record with this organisation is littered with insubordination, disobedience and a complete disregard for the nature of your position.'

'The nature of my fucking position is that I get paid for tracking down and removing terrorists,' Doyle rasped. 'People who are a threat to this country.'

'Do you see yourself as a patriot, Mr Doyle?'

'I've never thought about it. I'm just doing a job.'

'How many people have you killed during the course of your duties?'

'What the fuck has that got to do with anything?'

'Your record,' Pressman held up the file. 'Includes your psychiatric report. I'm not an expert, Mr Doyle, but from what I've read, some of your behaviour has bordered on the psychotic.'

'You're right. You're *not* a fucking expert. You know nothing about me *or* the way I work.'

'Sean Doyle,' Pressman read. 'Only son of Irish parents. Both dead. You live alone. Never married. Borderline alcoholic. Sociopathic tendencies. You have a problem with authority. You've been injured on numerous occasions, two of them almost fatal. After both you were offered retirement but refused. May I ask why?'

'Is it important?'

'I'm curious. I can't understand why a man would want to continue in a line of work that guarantees his being put at risk on a regular basis. Is there so little in your life, Mr Doyle, that you're prepared to jeopardise it so easily?'

'Someone once said to me that a man with nothing to live for has no fear of death,' Doyle observed.

'Very profound. Where is that man now?'

'I shot him.'

A silence descended, finally broken by Pressman. 'It says in your file that you were involved in the death of a fellow counter terrorist agent some years ago,' the Home Secretary noted. 'Georgina Willis.'

Doyle glared at the politician. 'We were working together when she was killed,' he said.

'In the Republic of Ireland.'

'Spot on.'

Another long silence.

'You may or may not be aware, Mr Doyle, that my government is presently engaged in talks with Sinn Fein with a view to ending the violence in Northern Ireland once and for all,' said Pressman. 'Incidents such as those precipitated by you in Belfast recently are hardly conducive to the fulfilment of such a peace.'

'You're not negotiating with the IRA,' Doyle said disdainfully. 'You're *surrendering* to them. What have they contributed to this so-called peace? Nothing. What about decommissioning?'

'That will come,' Pressman interjected.

'Bollocks,' snapped Doyle. 'How many of the fuckers have you released from prison?'

'That is a necessary step agreed to by both sides.'

'Five more of them are released at the end of the week, aren't they?'

'That is the plan.'

'This fight isn't with the guys *you*'re talking to. The men I was after in Belfast are a new breed. They couldn't give a fuck about your talks and your promises. They couldn't even give a fuck about Sinn Fein.'

'I assume you mean the so-called Real IRA?'

'That's *exactly* who I mean.'

'Real IRA. Continuity IRA. They're a very small fringe operation.'

Doyle shook his head. 'In three years they've already been responsible for twenty-eight bombs in Ireland and five over here. If decommissioning *does* ever happen, there'll be plenty more of the Provos wanting to join them. This problem isn't going to go away.'

'Well,' said Pressman, closing the file. 'Whatever happens, it won't concern *you* any longer, Mr Doyle.'

The counter terrorist shot Parker a look.

'If it's any consolation, Doyle, I'm against this,' said the older man.

'Against what?' Doyle snapped.

The Home Secretary pressed his fingertips together and regarded Doyle evenly.

'You're being removed from the Counter Terrorist Unit,' he said.

28

'Removed!' Doyle rasped.

'Your methods are unsuitable,' Pressman continued. 'And, quite frankly, so are you. Your behaviour in Belfast proved that beyond question.'

'I was doing a fucking job. For *this* country.'

'A job you are now considered unfit for,' Pressman observed.

Doyle looked at Parker.

'I had nothing to do with this, Doyle,' said the older man.

'Mr Parker fought for your position,' said the Home Secretary. 'He doesn't want you removed. However, government policy dictates that we cannot tolerate a repetition of what happened in Belfast and your record seems to suggest that there's a strong possibility of that.'

'You gutless bastard,' hissed Doyle, glaring at the politician. 'You're giving in to them, aren't you? The IRA. This is another concession you're making.'

'There are certain criteria—'

Doyle cut him short. 'Fuck your criteria,' he snapped. 'You've got your head so far up Sinn Fein's arse you'll be cleaning shit out of your ears for months. Why don't you just wave your white flag now and get it over with.'

'The matter is closed,' Pressman stated. 'Your career with the Counter Terrorist Unit is over, Doyle.'

'And you're going to sit still for this?' Doyle asked Parker.

'Mr Parker has little choice, I'm afraid,' Pressman said, a slight smile on his face. 'The CTU receives more than ten million pounds a year in government subsidies. The organisation couldn't operate without that money.'

'You sold me out to a bunch of fucking politicians,' Doyle said angrily.

'I haven't sold you out to anybody, Doyle,' Parker replied. 'An example had to be made. Sinn Fein wanted proof of our good faith.'

'More proof? What are you going to give them next? The names of every agent working undercover in Ireland? You fucking prick.'

'People are tired of this conflict, Doyle,' said Pressman. 'They want an end to it, one way or the other.'

'What the fuck do you know about *people*, you're a politician,' snapped the counter terrorist.

'I need your ID and your guns, Doyle,' Parker said quietly.

Doyle hesitated for a moment then got to his feet. He dug in his pocket for the small leather wallet that contained his ID. For long seconds he held it in the air then threw it down on Parker's desk.

'And your guns,' the commander said.

'Forget it,' Doyle told him. 'Those are mine.'

'In case you'd forgotten,' Pressman cut in, 'it is now a criminal offence to own a handgun of any calibre larger than .22.'

'You want the guns then you come and take them,' Doyle snarled.

He slid his hand inside his jacket and pulled the Beretta from its holster. He worked the slide, chambered a round, then levelled it at the Home Secretary.

'Come on,' he said quietly. 'Take it.'

Pressman paled, his eyes fixed on the barrel of the automatic. He looked as if all the blood had suddenly been drained from his body.

'I have bodyguards outside,' he said breathlessly, his eyes widening.

'Big deal. I'll empty this magazine into you before they can get that fucking door open.'

'Doyle, put it down,' Parker said wearily.

Pressman sat motionless. 'It's all you know, isn't it? Violence. Threats,' he said, his voice cracking. 'The country will be better off without men like you, Doyle.'

Doyle took a step towards the politician.

'You *make* men like me,' he growled.

Pressman dropped the file he'd been holding and tried to push himself further back into the chair.

Doyle finally eased the hammer of the automatic down and holstered the weapon.

'As of now you are officially dismissed from the Counter Terrorist Unit,' Parker told him.

Doyle looked at him briefly.

'Stick it,' he snarled. 'Stick the whole fucking lot up your arse.'

He moved towards the door then turned and looked at Pressman.

'Tell your friends in Sinn Fein you did what they wanted,' he said. 'I hope they appreciate it.'

Doyle slammed the door behind him.

'The man's psychotic,' said Pressman, his hands shaking as he reached for his glass of water. 'I'd go as far as to say he's insane.'

'Well, that doesn't matter any more does it?' Parker said, looking at Doyle's discarded ID wallet.

Pressman thought about getting to his feet but his legs were still shaking too much.

'Fighting the Provos, the Real IRA, Continuity IRA, what-ever they call themselves,' Parker continued. 'We needed men like Doyle. He was dangerous. *That's* what made him the best.'

'That time has passed. *His* time has passed.'

Parker looked down at the ID once again.

'I hope to Christ you're right,' he said quietly.

THE PHONE CALL

W ard usually unplugged the phone while he was working so that it wouldn't disturb him. Wouldn't break his
train of thought. It took very little to break his concentration
and this meant one less distraction.

However, as very few people rang him these days, he had
taken to leaving the contraption alone. So it was a shock when
the strident ringing cut through the stillness of the office.

He finished the sentence he was typing then reached for
the receiver.

'Hello,' he said.

'Chris, it's me.'

He recognised the voice immediately. Martin Connelly had
been his agent for the past five years. A born-and-bred
Londoner, Martin was sometimes abrupt, sometimes brusque.
There were those who called him rude but he had always done
his best for Ward and the two men had a good working rela-
tionship.

'How are you?' asked Connelly.

'I feel like shit. What the hell do you expect?'

There was a moment's silence.

'Look, Chris, I won't beat about the bush. It's not good
news.'

Ward kept his eyes on the screen. On the words he'd just
written.

'They don't want to know,' Connelly continued. 'I've tried
five publishers and none of them are interested. But that's not
to say that someone—'

'Fuck them,' Ward interrupted. 'Fuck them all.'

'I can speak to a couple of other people and—'

'Forget it, Martin,' Ward said, cutting him short again. 'It's over. I know that. I'm going to put the house on the market.'

'You don't have to do that.'

'Don't I? Then tell me what the fuck I *am* supposed to do? I'm a writer who no one wants to publish. I write books that no one wants to read. This is all I know. It's all I've ever done. I can't just say, "Oh, okay then, I'll pack up writing full time and go back to the day job." There isn't a fucking day job. This is it. This is all there is. And now you're telling me it's gone.'

'There are other things . . .'

'No there aren't. There's nothing else you can do. Just admit it, Martin. We're both fucked. The only difference is you've got other clients. You can still collect your twenty per cent from half a dozen other people. I've got nothing else.'

Again there was a silence.

'What did they say?' Ward finally wanted to know.

'That sales on the last few books haven't been good,' Connelly told him. 'That their production costs are too high. That they can't afford to pay you what you want.'

'Bastards. If they'd given me some fucking support they might have got their money back. Where was the advertising? Where was the fucking publicity?'

'They say they did all they could.'

'Well, they're fucking liars,' roared Ward furiously.

'Listen, I know this must be a blow. I'll call you back in a day or two and we'll talk about what we can do—'

'Don't bother, Martin,' Ward said coldly. 'Don't call me back. There's nothing more to say.' He hung up.

Ward stood up and walked out of the office, slamming the door behind him.

DESOLATION

The drive to the local shops took less than five minutes. Ward found the off-licence and bought two bottles of Jack Daniel's, a bottle of Smirnoff and a bottle of Glenfiddich. Then he drove home.

He carried the bottles into the sitting room, sat down in one of his armchairs and set about the first bottle of Jack Daniel's. Less than thirty minutes later, it was empty.

Another hour and Ward was unconscious.

REALITY

C linical depression sometimes causes the sufferer to sleep for abnormally long periods of time. The desire to escape from the cause of that depression is overwhelming and the best way to escape is in the oblivion of sleep. Combined with alcohol or some other form of drug, this state of mind can be dangerous.

Christopher Ward was in danger.

He woke briefly at around 11.30 p.m. but immediately fell back into a deep, almost comatose sleep.

THE END

Ward sat in front of the blank screen. His head was throbbing, his mouth was sour. He hawked and spat on the carpet beside him.

If he had been in a position to appreciate it, the irony of the situation might have amused him.

The character he was writing about had lost his job. Ward himself had lost his job.

He rested his fingers on the keys.

Ha, ha. Very funny.

Ha ha.

He began to hit the two letters with increasing force.

hahahahahahahahahahahahahahahahahahahahahahahahahaha
hahahahahahahahahahahahahahahahahahahahahahahahahaha
hahahahahahahahahahahahahahahahahahahahahahahahahaha
hahahahahahahahahahahahahahahahahahahahahahahahahahah
hhhhhhhhhhhhhhhhhhaaaaaaaaaaaaaaaaaaaaaaaaaaaaaaaaaaaaa
aaaaaaaaahhhhhhhhhhhhhhhhhhhhhhhhhhhhhhh

He slumped forward on to the keyboard.

THE BEGINNING

I t was dark inside the office.
    Ward lifted his head slowly from the desk and blinked in an effort to clear his blurred vision. The only light was the silvery-grey glow coming from the computer screen.

Ward looked at the clock on his desk. 3.11 a.m.

He groaned, his gaze drawn to the screen. The print icon was showing: Print 1 to 30.

Ward pressed the return key and the printer whirred into life.

Pages began to spew from the machine.

29

Doyle watched as the steam rose slowly from his coffee. The cafe in Dorset Street was barely large enough to accommodate ten people but, at present, only the former counter terrorist and two members of staff were inside.

Doyle looked down at the scratched surface of the table where he sat. Obviously no one from the Environmental Health Department had put this place on the list for a visit lately.

A heavily built woman emerged from the kitchen carrying a bucket of soapy water and proceeded to wash the tiled floor with a mop.

The cafe now smelt of soap suds and frying bacon.

The former counter terrorist looked around for any No Smoking signs, saw none and lit up.

So that's it. You're finished.

He drew heavily on the cigarette.

Out of work. Discarded. Unwanted. Sacked.

It didn't matter which description you used, it amounted to the same thing.

Game over.

He glanced at his watch, wishing the pubs were open. Wishing he could walk into one, sit himself at a bar and drink until the world disappeared in a haze.

Why not just drive home? There's booze there.

The initial feeling of fury he'd felt upon leaving CTU headquarters had subsided into something he'd experienced only once or twice before in his life. A feeling of utter helplessness.

He knew that no matter what he did or said, there was nothing he could do to change his fate. It was over. Everything he had ever known. Everything he'd trained, suffered and sweated for had been taken away from him at the whim of some fucking politician.

Had all the pain and loss over the years been for this? To be told he could no longer do the job he loved. The job he was made for?

The only job he could do?

He took another drag on his cigarette, the knot of muscles at the side of his jaw pulsing angrily.

The woman mopping the floor moved to his table. She reached for the small disposable ashtray but Doyle shook his head and she moved away.

No one had ever beaten him in his life. Every man or woman he'd ever set out to hunt down, he'd caught. All those who'd tried to kill him he'd killed first.

He'd survived bomb blasts, bullet wounds, knife cuts and God alone knew what else. But what weapons could not achieve, a few words had. They had destroyed him more completely than a bullet in the head.

Where do you go from here?

He looked at the woman with the mop.

Cleaning fucking floors?

Doyle drew on his cigarette then ground it out in the ashtray. He lit another then ordered more coffee.

No rush. He had nowhere to go and the pubs didn't open for another half hour.

30

Daniel Kane drove the white into the triangle of pool balls and watched as they spun off in all directions. The sound reverberated around the inside of the pub for a moment. Seeing he hadn't potted anything Kane took a step away from the table and reached for his drink.

The Huntsman had only been open for an hour or so and aside from Kane and his three companions, there were just two customers. One was sitting at the bar running a nicotine-stained index finger over a copy of *Sporting Life*, the other was sitting in one of the booths near the main doors sipping at a pint of Murphy's.

'They're making fools of us,' Kane said, his face set in hard lines.

'They have been ever since that fucking Good Friday Agreement,' Ivor Best added, walking around the pool table, trying to spot his next shot.

At thirty-two, Best was four years Kane's junior. A tall, wiry individual with jet-black hair which was receding rather too quickly for a man of his age.

Kane was shorter but more powerfully built. Apart from his cleft chin the most immediately noticeable thing about him was the scar that ran from just below his left earlobe along the line of his bottom jaw. The result of a car accident twenty years earlier. Kane, however, was content to allow those who believed it to be the legacy of a fight to cling to their illusion. In the part of Belfast where he'd grown up reputations were respected and if some of his own was built on hearsay then so be it.

Like Best he had been active within the Ulster Volunteer Force for the past twelve years. Unlike his other three companions he had yet to serve a prison sentence. Some thought he was just lucky. Kane put it down to his intelligence and organisational abilities. Things that made him valuable in his chosen field.

He watched as Best took and missed his shot.

'Five more of those Fenian bastards are released at the end of the week,' Best hissed. 'And they expect us to accept it?'

'What choice have we got?' The question came from a chair pulled close to the pool table. Jeffrey Kelly picked at fingernails already bitten to the quick and waited for an answer.

'We might not have a choice but nobody says we have to fucking like it,' Best replied.

'Which prison are they being released from?' George Mcswain wanted to know, rolling himself a stiletto-thin cigarette.

'Maghaberry,' Kane said quietly, potting a ball. He walked around the table and chalked the end of his cue.

'Look, I don't agree with it any more than the rest of you,' Kelly said. 'But if it brings peace then what the hell.'

'You think the fucking IRA will stop just because their men are being released from prison?' Best snapped. 'All the British government is doing is giving them back their best fucking soldiers.'

'I agree, look what they did to that bus earlier in the week,' Mcswain noted.

'That wasn't the Provos,' Kelly offered. 'That was the Real IRA.'

'What fucking difference does it make?' snarled Best. 'People were killed. *Our* people.'

'Whose side are you on anyway?' Mcswain wanted to know.

Kelly glared at him and got to his feet. 'Fuck you,' he roared, his gaze fixed on Mcswain.

The man seated at the bar turned and glanced briefly in the direction of the raised voices.

The barman also looked across as he dried glasses.

'They won't stop,' Kane mused, lining up another shot and sinking the ball.

'The ceasefire, giving up their weapons. It's all bollocks. You all know that,' snapped Best. 'The only ones who *can't* see it are the fucking politicians.'

The other men nodded in agreement.

'Well, I'm not giving in to a bunch of fucking Fenians,' Best continued.

'Quite right, Ivor,' Kane murmured, surveying the remaining pool balls contemplatively. 'What do *you* think we should do?'

Best could only shrug. 'What *can* we do, Danny?' he wanted to know.

Kane drew back the cue and prepared to take his shot. 'We can hit back at the IRA the only way they understand,' he said.

He struck the white ball with incredible power. When it slammed into a red, the noise was like a gunshot.

Kane stood up slowly and looked at his companions one by one. Something unspoken passed between them.

Kane smiled malevolently.

31

LONDON:

Doyle could barely open his eyes. He groaned and attempted to sit up.

'Fuck,' he croaked, his throat feeling as if it had been rubbed with sandpaper.

It felt as if someone was trying to batter their way out of his skull using a pickaxe, and for fleeting seconds he had absolutely no idea where he was. But he didn't really care.

Only gradually did he realise that he was home. Somehow (Christ alone knew how) he'd made his way back to his flat the previous evening (afternoon, evening, night?) and obviously blacked out in the chair.

There was a bottle of Jack Daniel's on the floor close to him; some of it had dripped out on to the carpet.

What a waste.

Again he tried to open his eyes, this time to slightly better effect.

The thunderous headache intensified as he got to his feet and blundered towards the kitchen. Only then did he realise he was still wearing his leather jacket and boots.

Must have crashed out straightaway.

Doyle tugged off the jacket and dropped it on to the floor then he stumbled into the kitchen and spun the cold tap. As the water gushed into the sink he cupped handfuls of it and splashed his face. It helped a little but he knew what he had to do to help clear this fucking hangover.

He walked to the bathroom and turned on the shower. Then he undressed quickly, catching a glimpse in the mirror of his heavily scarred back as he pulled off his T-shirt.

Doyle sucked in a deep breath and stepped beneath the cold water.

'Fuck,' he hissed, allowing the water to strike every part of his body. His healing wounds stung under the powerful jet. He stood beneath the shower head and tilted his face upwards. Water soaked his long hair and it hung down like a nest of comatose snakes. For interminable minutes he stood beneath the spray, gradually becoming accustomed to the cold water. Eyes still closed he leant forward, his forehead resting against the tiles.

He had no idea how long he stood under the shower. His muscles were numb by the time he finally stepped from beneath the spray and reached for a towel. He found two Nurofen in the bathroom cabinet and swallowed them dry as he wiped himself.

Doyle wrapped a towel around his waist and padded back into the kitchen where he filled the kettle and spooned Nescafé into a mug while he waited for the water to boil.

In the street outside a car hooter blared loudly. The sound seemed to penetrate his very soul. He wondered how the hell he'd driven home. If, indeed, he had. He had been drunk before, many times, but he couldn't remember ever having been so completely wrecked.

Supposedly one drink destroyed a thousand brain cells. If that was the case he'd done some real damage last night.

Doyle poured water on to the coffee and stirred it, sipping at the black fluid, ignoring the fact that it was so hot it burnt his lips and tongue.

Better get dressed.

Why?

He drank more of his coffee.

It's not as if you've got anywhere to go, is it?

Doyle carried his mug into the living room and set it down next to the television. He switched the set on and flicked channels.

Kids' programmes. Some chat show. A quiz. He found the news.

The usual shit.

Train delays. Problems on the roads. A famine somewhere. A couple of murders.

Doyle switched it off and sat in the silence.

32

HMP MAGHABERRY, NORTHERN IRELAND:

The early morning wind was cold and Vincent Leary shivered slightly as he stepped into the breeze.

The T-shirt he wore beneath his denim jacket offered little protection against the chill but he was more than happy to suffer the minor discomfort. It wouldn't have bothered him if there'd been six feet of snow. He was free again and that was all that mattered.

As he and the four others released with him made their way slowly towards the main gates of the prison, Leary glanced back at the place he had been forced to call home for the past three years. He'd spent his first night in a cell two days after his twenty-seventh birthday.

Maghaberry prison was unusual because it held both male and female inmates. The latter were housed in Mourne House, well away from the men who were incarcerated in four two-storey cell blocks bearing the names Bann, Erne, Lagan and Foyle. Each block contained one hundred and eight cells.

Leary had learnt that around four hundred and fifty men were currently serving or awaiting sentence inside the complex. Eight hundred and fifty staff ensured that the prison ran smoothly.

Ten of those officers were stepping briskly along with the prisoners now, one on either side of the men to be released. Leary looked at their faces but found no trace of emotion there.

The officer at the head of the column brought it to a halt

with some curt commands and Leary stood patiently as the doors were opened mechanically. They slid apart to reveal the car park beyond.

There were a number of vehicles there, including outside-broadcast units from television stations on both sides of the border.

But it was the large, white, twelve-seater mini-bus parked twenty yards away that caught Leary's eye. This vehicle would take him and his companions back across the border into the Republic.

Home.

He smiled to himself and gripped his holdall more tightly.

The formalities of release papers had already been completed within the complex itself, and the first man clambered up into the waiting mini-bus and took a seat at the rear.

Leary dug in his pocket and found a roll-up. He lit it and dragged heavily.

All the men except Leary were now on board.

'Come on, Leary.'

The voice came from behind him.

'Don't you want to go home?'

The prison officer was looking fixedly at Leary who merely took another drag on his cigarette.

'Think yourself lucky you're not spending another fifteen years inside like you should be,' the uniformed man told him.

'Like *you* will be?' Leary said. 'I mean, *you're* the one with the life sentence, aren't you? Sure, you go home every night, you're not locked up like I was, but you've spent all your working life inside this place and you'll finish it here too.' He nodded towards the officer's key chain. 'The length of that chain shows your seniority, doesn't it? It also shows you've spent your whole life keeping men from their freedom. Are you proud of that?'

The officer leant close to Leary, his voice low.

'I keep scum like you away from decent folk,' he hissed.

'Not any more.' Leary smiled and tossed away his cigarette. He clambered on to the bus and slumped into a seat on the right-hand side.

The driver waited a moment longer then guided the vehicle down the driveway that led away from the prison.

Leary was aware of the television cameras being turned in their direction. Some of the men near him covered their faces. Leary looked out of the window and smiled at them.

It would take a couple of hours to reach the border so he decided to get some sleep. He never had a problem dozing off and could snatch a rest anywhere. The low babble of conversation from the other men only served to hasten his oblivion.

Within ten minutes he was asleep, blissfully unaware of the countryside and ignorant of the towns and villages they passed through on the way to the border. The mini-bus bumped over a cattle grid but even that didn't wake Vincent Leary.

Two of the men on the back seat were playing cards, engrossed in their game. The others were either talking or lost in their own thoughts.

None of them had noticed the dark-brown Corsa that had been following them for the last fifteen minutes.

33

'What the fuck's going on?'
The shout came from one of the men on the back seat of the mini-bus.

The vehicle had stopped so suddenly that it had skidded for three or four yards, finally coming to a halt on a road that wound tortuously between high hedges and thickly planted trees. Beyond lay fields.

It was from one of these fields that the tractor had emerged. Masked by the trees and foliage, the farm vehicle had appeared as if from thin air, thick clods of mud falling from its huge rear tyres.

The bus driver had reacted quickly, slamming on the brakes as the Massey Ferguson rumbled on to the narrow thoroughfare, blocking the other vehicle's route.

High up in the cab, the tractor driver drew a deep breath, seemingly as shaken by the near collision as the men on the mini-bus had been.

Vincent Leary woke from his nap and peered at the tractor.

One of the men from the back seat of the bus was making his way to the door, gesturing angrily to the driver of the tractor.

'Tell him to get out of the way,' he hissed to the bus driver. 'Stupid bastard could have killed us.'

Leary looked on impassively as the tractor driver waved an apologetic hand and prepared to guide the farm vehicle off the road.

He turned the key in the ignition.

The tractor's engine sputtered and died.

He tried again. Nothing.

The Massey Ferguson remained immobile, a large, red barricade to the progress of the mini-bus.

'Jesus,' murmured one of the other men wearily. 'What's wrong with this fucking idiot?'

Vincent Leary sat up in his seat, looking first at the tractor then to his left and right. The thick hedges and dense trees made it difficult to see beyond the grassy fringe that ran along both sides of the road.

The tractor driver was still trying, vainly, to start his vehicle but it remained where it had stopped.

'Did anyone take a course in mechanics while they were inside?' called a voice from the back of the bus. 'It looks like this guy's going to need some help.'

The other men laughed.

Leary looked at the tractor driver again, his brow furrowing slightly. The man was looking beyond the mini-bus at the road behind them.

Looking for what?

Leary turned in his seat and saw nothing but when he looked back, the man was still staring agitatedly in that same direction.

Vincent Leary got to his feet and made for the rear of the bus, looking out of the large window. He was the first to see the dark-brown Corsa approaching.

'We've got company,' he announced.

The car slowed down then came to a halt about twenty yards behind the mini-bus.

'This bastard will have traffic backed up all the way to Belfast soon,' another voice called.

Leary looked at the car then the tractor. Its driver waited a moment longer then jumped down from the cab, sprinting off into the gap in the hedge from where he had first emerged.

Simultaneously, two men clambered out of the Corsa. Both were wearing woollen masks, only their eyes visible through small slits.

Both were carrying guns.

Leary recognised the weapons as Sterling AR-180s. Assault

rifles with twenty-round magazines. The two men swung the rifles up to their shoulders and aimed them at the bus.

From the dirt track ahead two other men stepped on to the road. They also wore masks. They were also armed.

'Get out of the fucking bus,' roared one of the men from the Corsa.

For interminable seconds those inside the mini-bus froze. Leary swallowed hard.

'What the fuck do we do?' one of the other men asked, his voice cracking slightly.

'Just what they tell us,' murmured Leary.

'Get off the bus *now*,' bellowed the man again, his finger now resting on the trigger of the assault rifle.

One by one, the men did as they were instructed.

'Line up there,' snapped one of the other men in masks and he jabbed the barrel of his weapon towards the bus.

'Get your fucking hands up,' another hissed, pushing the muzzle of his rifle towards the man nearest him.

Again the former prisoners did as they were instructed.

The bus driver hesitated, looking anxiously at each masked face.

'Get in the line,' one of the men told him.

Still the driver hesitated.

The man nearest to him stepped forward and, with incredible speed and power, drove the butt of his rifle into the driver's face. His nose burst under the impact and he dropped to his knees with blood spurting on to his shirt. He remained kneeling for a second longer then fell forward motionless.

Vincent Leary regarded each of the men before him, his gaze occasionally straying to the four automatic rifles now aimed at himself and his four companions.

'All right, you Fenian bastards,' snarled one of the masked men. 'Turn around and face the bus.'

'What's wrong?' Leary said. 'Haven't you got the guts to look us in the eye when you pull the trigger?'

The first burst of fire hit Leary, slamming him up against the side of the mini-bus. Within seconds all four weapons were spewing their lethal loads into the newly released men.

The peaceful silence of the country road was ripped apart by the staccato rattle of automatic fire.

When the first magazines were empty, the masked men reloaded and emptied more heavy-grain shells into the five bloodied and torn figures before them. From such close range the damage was enormous. Bones were pulverised by the high-powered bullets, internal organs were blasted to pieces.

Blood covered the side of the bus and spread seven or eight feet around the tangle of corpses. Empty shell cases rolled around, steam rising from them.

The hooded men ran back to the Corsa and clambered inside. The driver started the engine, turned the car swiftly on the road and headed back the way he'd come.

He pulled his mask off and threw it in the back, wiping sweat from his face. The others followed his example.

Daniel Kane glanced at his watch. In less than five minutes they would dump the Corsa and change cars.

It had all gone as smoothly as he'd planned.

A REFLECTION

Ward sat and watched as the paper spilled from the printer. What a joyous sight. He might have found it even more joyous had he been able to remember writing what was on those pages.

But, what the hell, it was appearing before him perfectly typed and, as he glanced at it, well written.

The printer continued with its mechanical litany.

Ward turned and looked out of the window. He saw his reflection in the glass staring back. For long seconds he stared at his own face then he blinked hard, as if to dismiss the image.

When Ward looked again the reflection, obviously, was still there. But its expression hadn't changed to match Ward's. It wore a stern, almost reproachful look.

Ward moved back slightly.

The reflection of his face remained immobile, as if it had been painted on to the glass. It was almost as if a face were staring in at him. Unblinking. Unmoving. Perched on one of the branches that tapped gently against his first-floor office window.

Ward closed his eyes tightly then looked again.

The face was still there. A severed head impaled on sharpened wood. Stuck there like a Halloween Jack-o-lantern.

He shook his head.

His reflection didn't move.

He looked more closely at the eyes. They were fixed on the printer, watching the pages churning out.

Ward raised a hand and moved it slowly back and forth before the vision of his own features. There was no change. The face remained. Immobile.

Ward swallowed hard and hauled himself out of his seat. As he did, the mouth of his reflection opened wide as if in a soundless scream.

There was a single tooth missing from the upper jaw.

Ward ran down the stairs and out of the office, turned the corner and looked up into the tree.

He didn't know what he thought he'd see, but there was nothing there. Just leaves stirred by the night breeze.

Ward stood gazing up for a moment longer then wandered back into the office.

The reflection was gone from the window. The printer had finished its work. The office was silent again.

34

LONDON:

The room smelt of gun oil.

Doyle took each of the weapons in turn and field-
stripped them. He cleaned each part carefully and then
reassembled the firearms. He checked the slides on the automatics, then he ensured that the cylinder turned smoothly
on the revolver.

*Why are you doing this? You're not going to need any of these
fucking things again, are you?*

There was a bottle of Smirnoff on the table in front of
him and he stopped periodically to fill his glass. The bottle
was already half empty.

The TV was on. Some twat talking about his new novel.
Laughing like a fucking idiot as he sat on the sofa opposite
the presenters.

The stereo was also on.

The last thing Doyle wanted was silence.

He glanced at the TV screen, but it was the music that
dominated.

'Fallen angel, ripped and bruised, think of better days ...'

Doyle finished cleaning the Desert Eagle and sat back in
his chair, the barrel pointed at the screen.

'Life is rude, treats you bad, tears your wings away ...'

He worked the slide on the automatic then aimed it at
the male presenter of the morning show.

*'Take your dreams, broken schemes and sweep the past
away ...'*

Doyle squeezed the trigger and the hammer slammed down on an empty chamber. 'Bang,' he murmured.

The news was coming up.

Doyle remained where he was in his chair, the Desert Eagle still cradled across his lap as he reached for the Smirnoff once more.

'Fly, lonely angel, high above these streets of fire . . .'

Captions came up at the bottom of each news story. Rwanda. Kosovo.

Northern Ireland.

Doyle grabbed for the stereo remote and shut off the music.

The news camera was already panning over a scene of bloodshed in Northern Ireland. A bullet-riddled mini-bus, spattered with blood. Great puddles of crimson fluid congealing on the country road. He saw RUC men moving around among members of the emergency services.

Doyle pressed the volume button and the sound of the news reporter's voice began to fill the room.

'. . . all five men, granted early release as part of the Good Friday Agreement, had been serving sentences for terrorist-related crimes.

They are thought to have been ambushed on this quiet road and all were pronounced dead at the scene.'

Doyle sat mesmerised.

'The men were being transported back to the Republic on what was thought to be a top-secret route. No statement has been made yet by either the RUC or any of the political or military organisations involved in what appears to be the most ruthless sectarian killing for some time.'

Doyle sat a moment longer then jumped to his feet. He crossed to his phone and punched out the numbers.

'Come on.'

When the receiver was picked up, he barely gave the voice at the other end the chance to speak.

'Good morning, this—'

'Listen, I need to speak to Jonathan Parker,' Doyle said.

'I'm afraid that won't be possible, Mr Parker is—'

'I've got clearance.'

'Go ahead.'

'Doyle. Sean Doyle. 23958.'

There was a moment's silence at the other end.

'I have no record of clearance for that name or that code,' the voice told him.

'Let me speak to Parker now.'

'I repeat, there is no clearance for—'

'Just fucking tell him it's Doyle,' snapped the former counter terrorist. 'He'll speak to me.'

'Mr Parker is in a meeting.'

'Bollocks. Get him to call me back. He's got the number.'

'That won't be possible.'

Doyle slammed the receiver down.

'Cunt,' he snarled and headed for the hall where he pulled on his leather jacket. He snatched his car keys from the small table by the front door and strode out of his flat.

This couldn't wait.

35

Doyle left the Astra outside the building in Hill Street. He fed a handful of coins to the meter then stalked across to the front door of the CTU headquarters and pressed his thumb on the buzzer.

'Identification, please,' said the voice from inside.

'Doyle,' he said curtly, '23958.'

There was a moment's silence.

'Could you repeat that, please?'

He did.

'Access denied,' the voice said finally.

Doyle sucked in a furious breath and pressed the buzzer again.

'Doyle, 23958. I need to speak to Jonathan Parker now. Open the fucking door.'

Silence.

He struck the oak door with one fist.

'Access has been denied,' the voice on the intercom said. 'Please step away from the door.'

Doyle hit the buzzer once more and kept his finger there.

Open the fucking door, you bastards. You can't get rid of me that easily.

The sound of the buzzer reverberated around the quiet street. An elderly woman passed by on the other side of the thoroughfare and looked over at Doyle.

'Move away from the door,' said the voice from inside the building. 'Access has been denied. If you do not move, I'll call security.'

'Do it,' snarled Doyle. 'Call who you fucking like. I'm staying here until Parker speaks to me.' He leant on the buzzer once more.

The door opened and two men stepped out on to the pavement. Both were dressed casually. Both were a good ten years younger than Doyle himself. He assumed they were counter terrorist agents.

As he had once been.

'Just do one will you, Doyle?' said the first.

'Fuck you.'

'We don't want any trouble,' the second assured him.

'Then get out of the way and let me talk to Parker.'

No one moved. The men remained motionless, but their eyes travelled up and down him. Watching. Trying to detect the first hint of aggression. Doyle knew they had been trained as meticulously as he had been. He also had no doubt that they were armed.

'Five minutes,' Doyle said. 'That's all I want.'

The first man shook his head. 'We can't let you in,' he said. 'You don't belong here any more.'

Doyle's expression did not change.

Never let your opponent see what you're thinking. Never let your feelings show on your face. Retain eye contact. If you look away, they'll know you're going to make a move on them.

'Let him in.'

Doyle recognised the voice.

Jonathan Parker stood just inside the reception area.

For long moments the two agents blocking Doyle's path remained where they were, then, as Doyle stepped forward, they moved aside and allowed him safe passage.

'You asked for five minutes,' said Parker. 'That's what you've got.'

36

'Make it quick, Doyle,' Parker said, closing his office door behind him. 'This could cost me *my* job, just having you on the premises.'

'Worried in case your fucking politician friend finds out I was here?' Doyle spat.

'Sir Anthony Pressman is no friend of mine, I can assure you. As you know, if I'd have had a choice you'd still be a part of this organisation.'

'You could have told him to fuck himself.'

'No I couldn't, Doyle.'

'Couldn't or *wouldn't*?'

'If you came here to discuss the merits or otherwise of your removal from this unit then you may as well leave now.'

'I came here to discuss what happened in Northern Ireland this morning. Five newly released IRA men ambushed and slaughtered on their way home.'

'I'm not at liberty to discuss that or any other matter with you, Doyle. Not any longer.'

'Who do you think killed them?'

'I can't discuss it with you.'

'One of the murdered men was Vincent Leary.'

Parker said nothing.

'He was due for release from Maghaberry, I know that. Obviously so did someone else. Someone who wanted him and four of his friends dead. My money's on the UVF.'

Parker crossed to the large window that looked out on to Hill Street, clasped his hands behind his back and stared off into the distance. He could see the green expanse of Berkeley Square from where he stood.

'If it *was* the UVF then you've got a problem,' Doyle continued. 'This so-called peace in Ireland is on a knife edge anyway. If both sides start hitting each other again, then you can kiss the whole fucking lot goodbye.'

'I can't discuss this with you, Doyle,' Parker repeated again.

'I didn't come here for a fucking discussion. I came here to tell you what's going to happen. Declan Leary's brother was one of those IRA men killed. Now if I know Leary he's not going to sit still for that. He's going to go after whoever did it. He's been in hiding ever since that business in Belfast. This'll bring him out, for sure. And when he sticks his head up over the parapet, someone should be there to put a fucking bullet in it.'

'Like you?' Parker said, finally turning to face his former colleague. 'You're not a part of this organisation any more, Doyle.'

'Reinstate me. You know I'm the only one who can get Leary.'

'I can't do that. I wish I could but I can't. I know what you're saying is right. I know that if anyone can find him it's you.' The older man sighed. 'My hands are tied.'

'I'll work without official clearance.'

Parker shook his head. 'You'd be arrested as soon as you set foot in Ireland,' he said.

'They've got to find me first,' Doyle assured him.

'I can't allow that, Doyle.'

'I'll find Leary. That's what you want, isn't it? Besides, I owe that bastard. He tried to kill me, remember?'

'He wouldn't be the first.'

'That's right. But I want to put him where I've put the others who've tried to kill me. Six feet under.'

A heavy silence descended, finally broken by Doyle.

'He'll go looking for the men who killed his brother. When he does, I'll find him.'

Parker shook his head again. 'I can't give you your job back, Doyle. That's the end of it.'

The former agent regarded the older man evenly. 'Fair enough,' he said, heading towards the door. 'But perhaps there's something else you should consider. That mini-bus was on a route known only to the driver and certain members of the RUC and security forces. Yet the guys who hit it knew exactly where and when to find it. They couldn't have known that without the right information.'

'You think someone tipped them off?'

'What the fuck do *you* think?' Doyle said quietly. 'You've got an informant somewhere, Parker. You'd better find *him* too.'

Doyle opened the door.

'Doyle. Wait a minute,' Parker called, stepping from behind his desk. 'What will you do now?'

'Now you've shit on me, you mean? Put me out of fucking work. What does it matter to you?'

Parker reached into his jacket pocket and handed Doyle a plain, white business card. 'Go and see this man,' he said, holding out the card. 'He might be able to help you.'

'I don't need your pity, Parker,' Doyle said dismissively.

'I'm not giving it. Stop being so pig-headed for once and take some help when it's offered.'

'I don't need any help.'

'No, Doyle, that's *exactly* what you need. Without this job you'll be sucking the barrel of a .357 within a month. Take the card.'

Doyle hesitated a moment then snatched it from his former colleague's hand and shoved it into the back pocket of his jeans.

'By the way, Parker,' he said standing in the doorway, 'if I do end up with a gun in my mouth, just remember, *you* were the one who put it there.'

He slammed the door behind him.

AN OVERACTIVE IMAGINATION

Thirty pages.

Ward counted them again. Thirty pages. No mistake. More than he'd written in the last five days.

He numbered the pages and placed them with the rest of his manuscript, wondering why his hands were shaking.

He re-read the words on the screen. He remembered none of them.

Had he been *that* drunk that he'd managed to write thirty pages without even remembering?

Ward rubbed his chin thoughtfully. His head was spinning. A combination of tiredness and the effect of so much alcohol was beginning to close in on him. He tried to rise but couldn't. He sat down again and breathed deeply.

Finally he shut off the computer. As the screen went black the office was plunged into darkness.

Ward tried again to get to his feet and this time he managed it. He negotiated the stairs with great care. He had little worth living for but he still didn't fancy slipping and breaking his neck.

He locked the office and stumbled towards the house. As he went he heard sounds of movement in the bushes. He wondered if it was the same cat that he'd frightened off the other night.

He grabbed a stone and hurled it in the direction of the sound. He heard the missile strike the wooden fence beyond but nothing else.

Then it came again. Closer this time. Near to the office door.

In the blackness of night it was impossible to see anything.

Ward took a step forward.

A shape passed close to the door of the office. Low to the ground. On all fours. Sleek, with a very large head.

Ward reached for another stone and prepared to throw it.

Was it a dog he'd glimpsed?

He shook his head.

It was . . . too big?

No. It was the wrong shape.

It moved too awkwardly, as if all its weight was on its front legs. It moved more like an ape.

Ward kept his eyes fixed on the door of the office and stepped backwards towards his house.

Drink. Tiredness. Depression. A powerful combination and one likely to stimulate an overactive imagination. Or hallucinations?

He smiled to himself.

The shape by the office had gone. At least, he couldn't see it any more.

Ward went inside the house, locked and bolted the back door and peered out through the glass.

He could see nothing. No shapes. No imaginary figures. No hallucinations.

He turned away from the window and made his way up the stairs. Had he looked back he might have noticed that there was a silver-grey light coming from inside his office.

As if the monitor were once again switched on.

IDLE HANDS

Ward slept wthout interruption that night. A sleep aided by half a bottle of Glenfiddich.

He didn't dream. Or if he did he didn't remember them.

He woke at ten the following morning, showered, dressed and, for the first time in several days, shaved. Then he wandered out to the office.

The printer was whirring away as he opened the door. He recognised the sound immediately and hurried up the stairs.

He stood motionless and watched as the machine printed off thirty more pages.

37

BALLYKNOCKAN, COUNTY WICKLOW,
THE REPUBLIC OF IRELAND:

Declan Leary was surprised at how many people turned out for the funeral of his brother. Sure enough, Vincent had been a popular man but Leary was pleasantly surprised at the amount of souls prepared to pay their respects to his dead sibling.

He stood on the hillside overlooking the cemetery, sheltering beneath some trees from the rain that had been falling steadily for the last two hours.

He'd stood like some silent sentinel, watching while the priest intoned words he knew only too well. Aware that his mother was shaking as she fought in vain to hold back her tears as she watched her eldest child being lowered into the grave.

Leary could see one of his aunts with her arm around the frail old woman. On her other side stood Leary's younger sisters. Patricia was twenty. Angela eighteen months older. They were also crying.

How he longed to stand beside them. To comfort his family. To toss a handful of wet earth on to the coffin. To say a final farewell to the brother he had loved so much.

To swear that he would find and kill those who had taken his life.

The village, like so many in rural Ireland, was a close-knit place. Almost an anachronism in an age of self-betterment and disregard for others. Within it, still flowed the kind of community spirit that saw neighbours genuinely caring for one another. Hence the large number of people prepared to brave the elements to bid a last farewell to Vincent Leary.

There were two guarda cars parked beside the cemetery gates, their occupants sheltering from the weather but also anxious not to intrude upon the scene before them.

Leary knew why they were there. He had been expecting them. That was why he had chosen his position high up on the hillside in the shadow of the Wicklow mountains.

Clouds were gathering ever more menacingly over those distant peaks, threatening to bring more of the rain that was still falling. Like tears from the heavens for his departed brother.

'We're very sorry for your trouble, Declan.'

The words made Leary spin round, his hand sliding inside his overcoat, fingers closing over the butt of the Glock 17.

'No need for that,' said Seamus Mulvey, patting the younger man on the shoulder.

Leary relaxed slightly and looked at the other man who accompanied Mulvey.

Raymond Tracey nodded almost imperceptibly. A gesture designed both as a greeting and a condolence.

'We thought we should pay our respects to your brother,' Mulvey continued. 'On behalf of the organisation.'

'And for your mother's sake,' Tracey added.

'Thank you,' said Leary quietly.

'It seems that over the years I've worn this suit to more funerals than I care to remember,' Mulvey mused. 'I was hoping I wouldn't have need of it again.'

Leary turned and gazed back down at the grave surrounded by mourners.

'I hope I don't need it for yours, Declan,' the older man continued.

'Why should you?' Leary wanted to know. 'I'm not planning on getting killed.'

'What *are* you planning?' Mulvey enquired.

'My brother was murdered. I want to know who by.'

'And if you find out?'

Leary looked at the older man but initially didn't answer. 'That's my business,' he said finally.

'No it's not, Declan. It's everyone's business. Myself, Raymond. Everyone in the organisation. Political *and* military.'

'Did you come here today to warn me off?' Leary demanded.

'We came to give you some advice,' Tracey offered. 'I don't blame you for feeling the way you do about what happened to your brother. I'd be the same if it was kin of mine. I know how you feel.'

'You've got no fucking idea how I feel, Raymond,' snapped Leary. 'I can only stand here and watch while my own mother and sisters cry their hearts out over the body of my brother. I can't even go down there and comfort them. The one thing I *can* give them is justice.'

'Killing the men who murdered Vincent wouldn't be justice,' said Mulvey. 'It'd be suicide. For all of us.'

'I'll take that chance,' Leary told him flatly.

'I'm advising you not to, Declan.'

'In Donegal, you *asked* me, now you're *advising* me. What's the difference? Does *advice* come from the barrel of a gun?'

Mulvey looked up at the rain-sodden sky. 'If it had been the other way round, what do you think Vincent would have done?' he asked. 'Run off to find the men who killed *you?*'

'I'd like to think so.'

'No he wouldn't have,' Tracey said.

'How the hell do *you* know what he would have done? He was *my* fucking brother.'

'He wouldn't have done it because he put the organisation first,' Tracey continued. 'He understood that what he'd fought for was more important than personal matters. He'd have realised that the kind of action you're proposing is useless.'

'Bollocks,' spat Leary.

There was a moment's silence, finally broken by Tracey. 'Think about what you're doing, Declan,' he said. 'Think about what Vincent would have wanted.'

'I *am* thinking about Vincent,' Leary hissed. 'That's why I'm going to find the bastards who killed him.'

'You're making a mistake,' Tracey told him.

'Am I? We'll see.'

'The RUC will be looking for you after what happened in Belfast,' Mulvey said. 'So will every fucking SAS and anti-terrorist operative working in the six counties. Look what happened to Finan. That could be you this time round. Whoever killed Vincent will be expecting you to come after them too. They'll be ready for you. Just let it go, Declan.'

'Thanks for coming today,' said Leary quietly. 'I appreciate your concern. For me *and* my family. We've got nothing more to say to each other.'

He turned his back on the two men and gazed down at the last resting place of his dead brother.

38

LONDON:

Doyle walked briskly up the steps from Notting Hill Gate Tube station. He paused at the top and dug in his pocket for what he sought. The business card bore an address and he regarded it indifferently for a second.

He'd spent most of the day and night thinking about whether or not it was even worth visiting the place. Finally he'd rung and made an appointment for ten o'clock the following morning. The remainder of the evening had been spent slumped in front of his television set.

His brain had felt like a washing machine (it still did). Thoughts spinning round. Visions forcing themselves into his consciousness like some kaleidoscopic acid trip.

Dead bodies. Blood. Pain.

Georgie.

Guns. Knives. Explosions.

He'd seen the faces of Parker. Of Sir Anthony Pressman. Finan. Leary.

Georgie.

She was always there, somewhere.

He'd succumbed to a headache and fallen asleep in the chair after downing half a bottle of Smirnoff and three Nurofen.

When he'd woken, the business card Parker had given him was still on the table beside his chair.

Doyle had spent a long time staring at it.

Now he looked at it again:

CARTWRIGHT SECURITY
36 CLANRICARDE GARDENS
NOTTING HILL

There was a phone number beneath.

Doyle wandered along the road, checking street names until he found the right one.

It was a narrow cul-de-sac of two-storey mews houses, mostly converted into flats or offices. The number of name-plates outside each electronically operated front door testified to that.

Number 36 bore the name of Cartwright Security. Doyle pressed the buzzer and waited.

Just like old times.

'Cartwright Security,' said a woman's voice.

'My name's Doyle,' he said into the grille. 'I've got an appointment with Mr Cartwright.'

'We're on the third floor, please come up.'

There was a loud buzz and the door opened. Doyle stepped inside and made his way up the plush stairs until he found it. He knocked and walked in. There was a door to his right which was closed and another to his left which was open. Through the open one he could see a desk and a young woman seated behind it. Early thirties. Shoulder-length auburn hair. Attractive. She was dressed in a dark two-piece suit and highly polished court shoes.

There was another door behind her. Also closed.

The office was airy and brightly decorated. There were leather chairs along two walls and a low table in the centre covered with orderly lines of magazines. Doyle noticed copies of *GQ*, *The Face*, *Maxim*, *Vogue* and *Cosmopolitan*. There were even editions of the *NME* and a number of film magazines.

The secretary smiled at him and motioned towards one of the leather seats. 'Would you like a drink, Mr Doyle?' she asked. 'Tea, coffee?'

'Tea, thanks. White. One sugar.'

'I'll bring it through,' she told him. 'Mr Cartwright is ready to see you.'

No hanging about.

Doyle stood back up and followed her through to the door on the other side of the narrow corridor. She knocked once then entered.

As she did, Brian Cartwright got to his feet. He extended a hand, which Doyle shook, surprised at the power in the other man's grip. He ran appraising eyes over Cartwright who was immaculately dressed in a dark-blue suit and black roll-neck sweater.

'Thank you, Julie,' said Cartwright.

'I'll bring you a coffee through,' the secretary said as she stepped out of the office.

'She looks after me,' Cartwright said smiling.

He was an amiable man. Late forties. Wide-shouldered and thick-necked.

Doyle took a quick look around the office. It was high-ceilinged. Recently decorated. A small flight of steps led up to another smaller area where Doyle could see a sofa, a television and a video recorder. There were several framed photos on the walls. He recognised one or two of them. Film stars. There was one of Robert de Niro.

'Some of our clients,' Cartwright said, noticing his interest. 'We look after all sorts of people. Pop stars, actors, politicians, businessmen. You name it.'

Julie returned with their drinks, set them down and left, closing the door behind her.

'I understand you're looking for a job, Mr Doyle,' Cartwright said, sipping his coffee.

'Who told you that?'

'Jonathan Parker. Your old boss. He had your file biked over to me. He didn't think you'd have much in the way of a written CV.'

'He was right. How do *you* know him?'

'I used to be a Special Branch officer. We've known each other for years.'

'Why did you leave?'

'I retired. I was hurt in a car accident. The money I got went into this business.'

'You're obviously doing all right,' Doyle observed, looking around the office.

'I employ the right people. And I've got a *very* good accountant.' Cartwright smiled.

Doyle managed a grin.

'Jonathan seems to think you'd be suited to this line of work,' said Cartwright. 'Do you?'

'Look, I appreciate you seeing me but don't give me a fucking job out of sympathy. Just because Parker binned me off doesn't mean I need help from his friends.'

'You arrogant bastard,' said Cartwright.

Doyle shot him an angry glance, surprised when the older man held his venomous gaze.

'It's you who needs this job,' Cartwright reminded him. 'You're the one on the scrapheap.'

'I'll find work somewhere.'

'Doing what? What kind of work *can* you do, Doyle? Remember, I've read your file. Who's going to employ a man as potentially unstable as you?'

Doyle got to his feet.

'Sit down,' Cartwright snapped.

'Fuck you,' Doyle rasped.

'Face it, you're low on options. You're not in a position to dictate what you want. Not any more. If I can help you I will but it's got nothing to do with favours or sympathy. My motives are purely selfish. If I didn't think it was worth seeing you, you wouldn't be here now.'

Doyle sucked in a deep breath and slowly sat down again.

Cartwright reached into his desk and pulled out a file. 'I won't bother reading this back to you,' he said. 'I'm sure you know what it says anyway.'

'I'm not very good at this interview shit,' Doyle told him. 'I suppose I'm out of practice. I didn't think the day would ever come when I'd have to do one. I thought I'd be dead long before that.'

'Well, you're not dead, you're here. So let's get down to business.'

39

'They offered you retirement twice,' said Cartwright, flicking through the file on his desk. 'Why didn't you take it?'

'Why didn't *you?*' Doyle asked him. 'You could have been living off your invalidity pension from Special Branch now.'

Cartwright smiled. 'You're right,' he acknowledged. 'I chose to use the money to put into this business. I built it up from nothing to what it is now.'

'Why?'

'I saw a gap in the market and, if I'm truthful, I couldn't stand the thought of sitting around twiddling my thumbs for the rest of my life, getting under my wife's feet.'

'Join the club.'

'You're not married, are you?'

Doyle shook his head.

'That's probably just as well,' Cartwright told him. 'Security work is no job for a married man.'

'What about you? You're married.'

'I own the business. I can go home every night if I have to. The people who work for me can't.'

'Where do you get your people? Are they all cast-offs like me?'

'I've got ex-coppers. Ex-army. Even a couple of guys who worked as mercenaries in Kosovo for a time. They all know how to handle themselves should the situation arise.'

Doyle eyed him indifferently.

'I know you can look after yourself, Doyle,' Cartwright said. 'But the question with this job is can you look after someone else? Would you risk your life for a total stranger, one you might not even think very much of, just for the money?'

'I haven't really got much of a choice, have I?'

'You can walk away now if you want to. No one's forcing you to take a job here. No one knows if you'll even be capable of doing it. What do *you* think this job entails?'

'Making sure the wrong people don't get hurt. The ones who pay for that privilege.'

'I know that if you're looking after one of my clients and someone has a go at them then you'll be able to do the job. I know they'll be safe under your protection. What I don't know is whether or not you'll be able to cope with the other side of the business.'

'Like what?'

'You have to be a diplomat in the security business, Doyle. Melt into the background. Be courteous at all times.'

Doyle raised an eyebrow.

'Do as you're told,' Cartwright continued. 'It must be a while since you did that.' He smiled.

'I could try.'

'If I employ you, the way you act and behave reflects upon my business and reputation. One mistake and you're out. Got it?'

Doyle eyed the older man impassively for a moment. 'Does this mean you're offering me a job?' he wanted to know.

'Look on it as a trial. If you do well on the first one, there'll be others. I know it's not what you want but what choice do you have?'

'Not much by the look of it.'

Cartwright looked at him. 'Have you got a suit?' he asked.

'I *did* have. I don't know whether it still fits.'

'Then get a new one. I want you at number twenty-six Upper Brook Street at twelve tomorrow.'

'So I've got the job.'

'Yes you have. Don't mess it up. For *your* sake.'

'Am I supposed to say thanks?'

'You're not supposed to say anything, Doyle.'

There was a heavy silence, finally broken by the former

counter terrorist. 'What about weapons?' he asked. 'Do I carry them?'

'It depends on the job. You'll be informed by me or by other operatives working with you.'

'Who's working with me tomorrow?'

'Two of my best people. They've been on this job for the last month. One's a driver. The other's a personal bodyguard.'

'Who's the client?'

'Sheikh Karim El Roustam and his family. You might have heard of him. He's a Saudi prince. One of the richest men in the world and paranoid about assassination. He's over here for talks with the owners of Aspreys, the jewellers. He wants to buy the company for his wife.'

Doyle smiled. 'Who's guarding him?'

'Melissa Blake and Joe Hendry. They've both been with me for over six years. They're two of my best. You'll take your instructions from them. You've got no problem working with a woman have you?'

Doyle shook his head.

It wouldn't be the first time.

'Stay in the background,' continued Cartwright. 'Do as you're told. And, Doyle, try not to shoot anybody. Especially the Sheikh.'

Doyle nodded. 'I've never done security work in my life and you're ready to let me walk into a situation like this?' he asked.

'You've got to learn somehow. All my operatives had to. Now go and get yourself a suit, some decent shirts and shoes and a bloody tie. Try Burberry's.'

Doyle got to his feet.

'You might want to get your hair cut too,' Cartwright added.

'I'll think about it,' Doyle told him.

Cartwright stood too and extended his right hand. Doyle shook it.

'Don't disappoint me, Doyle,' said Cartwright. 'You've been given another chance. Not many people get that. Take it.'

Doyle turned and walked out.

'Remember,' Cartwright called after him. 'Twenty-six Upper

Brook Street. Twelve o'clock. Don't be late.'

He heard Doyle's footsteps receding down the stairs.

Cartwright crossed to the window, wincing slightly from a recurring stiffness in his back and leg. He looked out into the street where he could see the former counter terrorist heading away from the building.

After a moment or two he turned back to his desk and reached for the phone.

40

DUNDALK, THE REPUBLIC OF IRELAND:

The woman who ran the guest house was a cheerful individual in her mid-forties. She had offered to help Declan Leary carry his two holdalls up to his room, shrugging her shoulders when he declined.

As he followed her up the stairs he supposed he could have allowed her to carry the sports bag with his clothes in. The plain black one he preferred to carry himself. He didn't want her asking what was in it even though he had the lie ready on his tongue. Just as he'd been ready to give her a false name and tell her what he supposedly did for a living.

She'd told him that there were two other permanant guests in the house. The other two rooms she kept for those passers-by who found themselves in need of rest and shelter for the night.

Leary listened dutifully as she led him on to the landing and pointed out the two toilets, the other guest rooms and her own room.

Her husband, she informed him, had died of a heart attack two years ago. She had one son who visited her with his wife and small baby every Sunday.

Leary smiled and nodded efficiently in all the right places.

She pushed open the door to his room and stepped aside to allow him in.

It was a reasonable size with a double bed (although she told him that she would prefer it if he didn't bring young women back with him) a dressing table, a wardrobe and a wash basin close to the large window that looked out on to a small garden. Beyond it was a field.

Beyond that lay the main road leading from the Republic into the Six Counties. Leary could make the drive to Belfast in under two hours if the conditions were right.

In and out quickly.

The guest house would be an ideal operations base for him. If the main road was closed or too congested then there were innumerable other routes by which he could find his way into the North.

He thanked the woman and reached for his wallet.

She told him she would take a deposit, if that was all right, and the week's rent would be payable in full every Friday night. No notice was needed should he want to move out but, she told him with a smile, she hoped that he would treat the place as a home and not *want* to move out too quickly. Dinner would be served at seven-thirty. She hoped he would enjoy meeting the other residents of the house.

Leary thanked her and held the door open for her as she finally left him alone.

He waited a moment then quietly turned the lock and began unpacking his clothes, sliding T-shirts and underwear into drawers, hanging shirts and jackets in the wardrobe.

Leary left the black holdall on the bed until he was ready then he unzipped it and reached inside. He laid each of the weapons on the bed and regarded them impassively.

The Glock 17 automatic. The Smith and Wesson M459 9mm automatic. The Scorpion CZ65 9mm machine pistol.

And the knives. One an 8-inch-long double-edged blade sharpened to lethal degrees on both sides. The other his ever-reliable flick knife.

He replaced all but the flick knife and the Glock in the holdall then stashed it carefully at the back of the wardrobe and laid a dark-blue fleece over it, happy that it was concealed.

As he left the room, he locked the door behind him.

Outside it had begun to rain.

Leary climbed into the Ford and started the engine, glancing at the dashboard clock. He switched on the radio, found some traffic news. No major delays anywhere. He should be in Belfast before dark.

41

LONDON:

Doyle felt as if he was being strangled. He pulled at the tie as he clambered out of the taxi, attempting to loosen it slightly. He tried to remember the last time he'd worn one.

Georgie's funeral? How long ago had that been? Ten, twelve years?

He looked around at the houses in Upper Brook Street. *You could almost smell the money.*

He glanced at his watch then at the door of number 26. *Plenty of time to spare.*

There was a Daimler parked immediately before the building. In front of it a Rolls Royce and behind it a black Ferrari F40. Doyle was fairly sure that these cars belonged to Sheikh Karim El Roustam.

He climbed the three steps that led to the front door and rang the buzzer. There was a small video screen above the panel and Doyle turned towards it.

'Yes,' said a metallic-sounding woman's voice.

'My name's Doyle. I was sent here by Cartwright Security.'

'Who's your contact?'

'Melissa Blake.'

There was a loud buzz and the door opened. Doyle stepped into the hallway of the house and waited.

He knew a little about art (he'd had a book when he was a kid called *World Famous Paintings*, or something like that, and certain images had stuck in his mind) and he was sure that one of the paintings hanging opposite him was a Gainsborough. Next to it was a Constable. He was pretty sure they weren't copies.

There was other stuff he didn't recognise. More modern. He didn't doubt for one second, however, that it was just as expensive. The marble floor he was standing on, he reasoned, probably cost more than he'd earned in his life.

It was across this marble floor that Melissa Blake approached him. He could hear her heels clicking on the polished surface as she descended from the staircase ahead of him.

Doyle watched her approvingly. She had blond hair, just past her shoulders. Deep-brown eyes. Finely chiselled features and cheek bones you could have cut cheese with. Doyle suppressed a smile. She was wearing a dark-grey jacket and trousers, and a crisply laundered and almost dazzlingly white blouse, fastened to the neck. Early thirties, he guessed. She shook his hand.

'I'm Melissa Blake,' she said smiling. 'My friends call me Mel.'

'I'm Sean Doyle. I haven't got any friends.'

She smiled even more broadly, revealing several hundred pounds worth of dental work and a previously unseen dimple.

She held his hand a moment longer then gently slid free of his grip. 'Mr Cartwright told me to expect you.'

'What else did he tell you?'

'What he felt was relevant. You used to be in the Counter Terrorist Unit, didn't you?'

Doyle nodded. 'What about you?' he wanted to know. 'How did you end up in this line of work? It's not the kind of thing you usually find women doing, is it?'

'You'd be surprised. The demand for women bodyguards has grown over the last four or five years. Some women clients feel more comfortable with another woman. I can earn more than most men.'

'So what did you do before this?'

'I was a policewoman. Undercover.'

'Why'd you leave?'

'I got involved in a sexual harassment case. My boss tried it on once too often. I went to *his* superior and reported him but nothing happened. Next time he tried it, I broke his nose. He had me transferred. I resigned.'

Doyle shrugged. 'Shit happens,' he murmured.

She smiled again. It was a warm, infectious gesture.

'Come on,' she said. 'I'll show you around.' She led him towards the wide staircase at the end of the hallway.

Doyle felt his shoes sinking into the carpet as he climbed. 'Where's the Sheikh?' he asked.

'He's out with my colleague, Joe Hendry. He should be back soon.'

'What about his wife?'

'She's in her room. First thing to remember is that when you're around them, you don't speak unless you're spoken to. Most of the servants speak some English but they tend to keep themselves to themselves.'

'How many are there?'

'Twelve.'

'Jesus, where do they all sleep?'

'On the upper floors. The Sheikh and his family have the entire lower and first floor.'

'What about you and Hendry?'

'We've got rooms on the second floor.'

She led him towards another flight of stairs, past more expensive paintings and sculptures.

'Cartwright said he was paranoid about assassination,' Doyle said. 'Does he have reason to be?'

'He's worth over fifty million. They say his oil wells pump out the stuff at about sixty-four grand a second. I'd say that was reason enough, wouldn't you?'

Doyle nodded.

'He's more worried about his son though,' Mel continued. 'Kidnapping.'

'I didn't know he had any kids.'

'One boy. He's eleven. Son and heir, that kind of thing. The Sheikh's very big on that. That's where *you* come in.'

Doyle looked surprised.

'You travel with him to school every day,' Mel said. 'Make sure he gets there okay. Then you go and pick him up.

Two of the Sheikh's attendants will go with you.'

'I didn't know I was being hired as a fucking babysitter.'

She turned and looked at him. 'Watch your language, Doyle. You never know who's listening.' Again that infectious smile.

He nodded and exhaled wearily. 'Shit,' he murmured, but under his breath.

42

BELFAST:

Declan Leary couldn't remember how many pubs he'd been in since arriving in Belfast two hours earlier. Five. Six. More?

He'd drunk pints in the first two then switched to still mineral water with ice. To anyone who cared to look, he might just as easily have been drinking vodka.

He knew that what he was doing wasn't exactly an ideal method of finding the killers of his brother but, at the moment, it was all he had.

He sat at bars and listened to conversations while he gazed blankly at his paper. He sat in booths and tried to pick up names, sometimes whispered. Anything that might point him in the right direction.

He moved around the Woodvale and Shankill areas without detection. A Catholic looked no different to a Protestant, he reasoned. They were all supposed to be human beings, divided merely by religion and beliefs.

That was the way it *should* have been. But it was not the case. It hadn't been for over four hundred years and, as far as men like Declan Leary were concerned, it would continue like this for *another* four hundred.

Despite the promises of the Good Friday Agreement, Catholics and Protestants, for the most part, still kept themselves to themselves. Proddies stayed away from the Ardoyne and Turf Lodge, just as *his* kind kept out of Woodvale and the Shankill.

Except tonight.

Leary wondered what the mathematical probability was of bumping into one of his brother's killers in these circumstances. He found it was best not to even consider the astronomical odds.

So, what are you going to do?

He sipped his mineral water and watched a group of men gathered around a pool table.

At the bar there was a television set perched high above the optics. Those seated opposite were watching, barely able to hear because of the noise coming from the jukebox and the incessant chatter inside.

Any one of you bastards could have shot my brother.

He saw two young women enter. The first was wearing a white mini-dress and attracted many admiring glances. She tottered uncertainly on precipitous high heels. Her friend, dressed in imitation-leather trousers and a top barely capable of containing her large breasts, crossed to the bar and ordered some drinks.

Normally Leary might have paid them more attention but tonight his mind was elsewhere.

He got up and moved towards the dartboard, sitting down at an empty seat, watching the two men engrossed in their game. When one scored a bullseye, Leary clapped and raised his glass in salute.

The man looked at him and managed a smile. 'Do I know you?' he said.

Leary shook his head. 'I was just admiring a good shot,' he commented, his voice slightly slurred.

Part of the deception.

'Here's to a good shot,' he said and raised his glass. 'As good as the ones that killed those five Fenian bastards the other day.'

The two players looked at each other then continued their game.

Leary watched the darts thudding into the board.

'Bang, bang, bang,' he chuckled. 'As easy as shooting Catholics, eh?'

'What the hell are you going on about?' said the first man, retrieving his darts.

'It's a pity there isn't a fucking Catholic standing in front of that board. That'd be one more out of the way.' He raised his glass again.

The two men carried on playing.

'Can I buy you a drink?' Leary persisted. 'To celebrate what happened to those fuckers the other day.'

'Just leave it, will you?' the second man said, taking a sip of his beer.

'What's the matter?' Leary wanted to know. 'Five IRA men were shot. If that isn't cause for celebration, I don't know what is.'

'You're drunk,' said the first man, throwing his darts once more.

'That I am. But then do you blame me? Five more of those bastards wiped out is worth getting drunk for, don't you think?'

'I think you've had one too many,' said the second man.

'Fuck it,' Leary burbled. He got to his feet and raised his glass.

'God save the Queen and God save the UVF,' he called loudly.

The two players looked at each other. A number of other heads turned in Leary's direction.

'Will anyone else join me in a toast?' Leary shouted. 'I'll buy anyone in here a drink if they'll celebrate the shooting of those fucking Fenian bastards with me.'

There were murmurs from all corners of the bar.

Leary lurched towards the two women who both giggled as he approached.

'What about you two young ladies,' he slurred. 'You'll have a drink with me to toast the UVF, won't you?' He thrust himself close to the one in the white dress.

'Lay off, will you?' said the barman, his face set in hard lines.

Leary raised his glass but stumbled against a nearby bar stool and spilled some of the contents on the girl with the large breasts.

'Fuck off,' she spat.

'Sorry,' said Leary, trying to wipe the water off, squeezing the girl's breast as he did so.

'I said fuck off,' snarled the girl, stepping backwards.

'Right, get out now,' said the barman.

Leary looked at him.

Do it.

'Ah, fuck you then,' he grunted and stumbled towards the door. When he reached it he paused and looked at the sea of faces gazing at him. 'God bless the UVF,' he shouted.

He crashed out into the street, sucking in a deep breath. *Shit. No takers.*

He set off down the street, glancing behind him.

No one emerged from the pub.

Leary walked on. Past boarded-up shops. Past a cat that was clawing at a bulging, black rubbish bag, pulling the rubbish out and scattering it across the pavement.

Past a giant mural on the side of a house with the caption beneath that read: WILLIAM III CROSSING THE BOYNE.

Orange bastard.

There was more graffiti: NO SURRENDER. It was faded. As though someone had tried to wash it off.

Leary wondered how far it was to the next pub. He was still wondering when the car pulled up beside him. He slid one hand into his jacket pocket, his fingers closing around the flick knife.

There was one man in the car. He leaned over and pushed the passenger door open, gesturing to Leary. 'Get in,' he said.

'Why?' Leary wanted to know.

'I heard what you were saying back there. I hear you've been saying the same thing all over Belfast. Word gets around. I want to talk to you.'

'About what?'

'Just get in,' the driver insisted.

'Fuck off.'

Leary saw the gun pointing at him.

'I won't say it again,' rasped Ivor Best.

43

Leary looked at the gaping barrel of the .38 for a second longer then took a step towards the car. Thoughts tumbled through his mind.

Who was this bastard?

Had his rant inside the last pub brought this newcomer to him?

'Listen,' Leary said, his voice more even. 'What I said back there—'

'Get in the fucking car,' Ivor Best snapped, waving the revolver towards the passenger seat.

What if he's one of your own? There'd be an irony, wouldn't there? Looking for Proddies to kill and ending up shot by one of your own.

Leary moved closer to the car.

He's not going to shoot you in the street.

Is he?

Leary touched the flick knife once more then slid into the passenger seat and shut the door behind him.

Best slid the gun into his pocket and guided the car away from the kerb.

Leary relaxed slightly and looked at the older man.

'Keep your eyes ahead,' Best told him as he drove. 'Just listen to me.'

The car smelled of fast food. Leary saw a McDonald's wrapper on the floor.

'What you were saying back there in the pub about those IRA men being killed, did you mean it?' Best asked.

Careful.

'A man's entitled to an opinion, isn't he?' Leary said.

'He is that. But some opinions are best kept to yourself.'

They drove in silence for a moment.

Leary had no idea where he was or where he was being taken.

Just be ready when he stops the car. You can use the knife before he reaches the gun if you have to.

'What's your name?' Best asked.

The lie was ready. 'Keith Levine,' Leary told him. 'What about you?'

'My name's not important now. I want to know if you meant what you said back there in the pub. About the UVF. Being happy that they killed five of the IRA.'

'I meant it. As far as I'm concerned there's still a war going on.'

Best smiled. 'A man after me own heart,' he said, glancing at Leary.

The younger man studied his companion's features.

You're a fucking Proddie all right.

'People are scared to say what they think any more,' Best continued. 'Even more afraid to *do* anything about it.' Again he looked at Leary. 'Are *you* prepared to do something, Keith? To back up your opinions?'

Leary regarded him warily. 'What kind of thing?' he asked.

'You tell me. How far would you go to support your opinions? Or are you just all mouth like so many of the others? They say what they'd do but when the time comes, they haven't got the balls.'

Leary shrugged. 'What kind of thing are you talking about?' he persisted. Best stopped the car. 'Get out,' he said.

Leary looked puzzled.

'Get out,' Best snapped, more forcefully. He watched as the younger man pushed open the door and clambered out on to the pavement.

'If you want to find out more then be here tomorrow night at eight,' said Best. 'If you're not here then I'll know you're all talk.'

He reached across, slammed the passenger door shut and drove off.

Leary squinted in the gloom and picked out the registration number of the car.

'Oh, I'll see *you* again,' he whispered as he watched the car disappear around a corner. 'Count on that.'

SEEING IS BELIEVING

Ward wondered, briefly, if he might still be drunk.
Perhaps in some alcohol-induced haze he had imagined watching the finished pages fall from the printer. Maybe he had dreamt the entire bizarre episode.

Failing that, there had to be an electrical fault of some description with the machine. But, if that were the case, why were the pages pouring from the printer filled with words? Lucid, perfectly formed prose the like of which he would have typed himself.

What the hell was happening?

He stood frozen until the printer had finished, then advanced slowly towards the desk, scanning the pages that had been vomited forth with such frenzy.

Ward sat down and picked them up carefully, scanning each one.

No spelling errors. Everything in context. These, surely, were not the fumblings of some alcohol-fuelled episode.

So, what were they? Where had they come from?

He had no answers to his perplexing questions.

Ward numbered the pages and added them to the rest of the manuscript. He was breathing heavily as he did so, squinting myopically at the numbers. On more than one occasion, his vision blurred and he was forced to stop. The beginning of a headache was gnawing at the base of his skull.

He looked at the blank screen almost fearfully. Very slowly, he rested his fingers on the keyboard. And began to type.

44

LONDON:

Doyle watched the knife as it whipped back and forth with dizzying speed. The cuts were uniform.

One of the three chefs who cooked for Sheikh Karim El Roustam was aware of his gaze but acknowledged it with only an indifferent glance.

'Mind your fingers,' said Doyle quietly.

The man looked at him again and returned to chopping shallots.

Doyle wandered out of the kitchen and towards one of the sumptuous reception rooms on the first floor. It smelt of air freshener and polish. The whole house smelt the same. As if the moment anyone touched anything, one of the hordes of cleaners descended to remove any trace of human contact.

He stood looking at one of the paintings that hung above the ornate marble fireplace then crossed to the window that looked out over Upper Brook Street.

Down below Joe Hendry was running a cloth over the windscreen of the Daimler, wiping away some of the rain that had fallen during the night, ensuring that he didn't get his navy suit wet.

Hendry was thirty-seven. A tall, broad-shouldered man with close-cropped dark hair and bags beneath his eyes.

Over the years Doyle had convinced himself that he could perceive a person's character within thirty seconds of meeting them. Instinct, he maintained, was as important as his ability with weapons. Those instincts had rarely been wrong.

With men he looked for the strength of their handshakes. Whether they held his gaze when they spoke to him.

Hendry had met both these criteria. He also had a good sense of humour and, another plus in Doyle's book, he didn't talk too much.

'Nothing better to do?'

The voice caused him to turn.

Melissa Blake was standing in the doorway of the reception room dressed in another of the dark suits she seemed to favour.

'Sorry, was I neglecting my newly found duties?' Doyle asked.

'Prince Hassim is ready for school,' Mel smiled.

Doyle nodded and followed her down the stairs to the hall where the boy stood obediently, flanked by two servants. Both were big men with swarthy features. One, Doyle noticed, had a deep scar on his left cheek.

The boy was dressed in his dark-blue school uniform, a brown leather satchel slung over one shoulder. He eyed Doyle as he descended the stairs then made his way outside.

'Set?' said Doyle, glancing up and down the street.

Hendry nodded and slid behind the steering wheel of the Daimler.

Doyle motioned towards the two servants and they walked out on either side of the boy who walked towards the rear door of the vehicle then stood still.

'Open the door,' he said, looking up at Doyle.

His accent was faultless. It should be, Doyle reasoned, it was an eight grand a term accent.

The former counter terrorist looked down at the boy.

'I said, open the door,' Hassim repeated. 'Now, you fool.'

Doyle clenched his teeth and did as he was instructed.

The boy smiled and climbed in.

Little shit. Eleven years old. Want to see twelve, you little bastard?

Doyle clambered into the passenger seat while the two servants arranged themselves in the back of the Daimler, one on either side of Hassim.

'Let's go,' said Doyle.

The Daimler moved out into the traffic.

The trip to Beauchamp Place took less than twenty minutes.

Hendry brought the Daimler to a halt ten or twelve yards from the main gate of the school and looked in the rear-view mirror at Hassim and the two servants. One of them, the man with the scar, made to scramble out of the vehicle but Hassim held up a hand.

'No,' he said. 'Let *him* do it.' He jabbed a finger into Doyle's back. 'Open the door for me,' the boy insisted.

The knot of muscles at the side of Doyle's jaw throbbed furiously but he swung himself out of the car and opened the rear door.

The boy slid out and, once more, looked up at Doyle with that supercilious grin on his face. He waited a moment longer then walked towards the gate of the school where several other children of all races and nationalities were gathered in front of a matronly looking teacher.

Doyle could see other cars parked around the entrance. Rollers. Jags. Land Rovers.

None of these little fuckers had to worry about waiting for buses, he mused.

He climbed back into the car and exhaled deeply. 'Fucking kid,' he murmured under his breath.

'Fancy a coffee?' said Hendry, barely able to suppress a smile.

'I was hoping for something stronger,' Doyle said, through clenched teeth.

'We go back now,' said one of the servants from the back seat.

'No,' said Doyle. 'Old English tradition. Bodyguards drink coffee. You sit in the car.'

Doyle shook his head almost imperceptibly.

Hendry chuckled.

BLOCK

Four lousy pages.

Ward looked at his watch. It had taken him three hours to write four pages.

Why not the outpouring of the previous night? Why not thirty pages?

He sat back and gazed at what he'd written.

A thought came unwanted into his mind. He was working on a book that no one wanted. Slaving over words that nobody would read. What was the point?

He placed both elbows on the desk and sat staring at the paper before him.

A book no one wanted to publish. The words hit him like fists. The realisation was as painful as a kick in the ribs.

He stood up and stepped away from the desk, leaving the keyboard and monitor switched on. It was 4.17 p.m.

A GATHERING STORM

The first rumble of thunder was so loud it woke Ward. He rolled over in bed and opened his eyes, looking towards the window in time to see the sky illuminated by the cold, white glow of a lightning flash.

It was followed immediately by another. A great fork that rent the clouds and stabbed towards the earth like a highly charged spear.

The thunder came again. A volley of cannon fire across the landscape.

He sat up, watching the celestial fireworks with the fascination of a child.

It had been a humid, unsettled day but there had been no hint of the ferocity of the storm that was now raging. Rain hammered against the window so hard it threatened to crack the glass.

For long moments Ward lay on his back staring at the ceiling, then he finally swung himself out of bed and crossed to the window.

He looked out at the storm, stunned by its power. The lightning was tearing across the sky with ferocious regularity, illuminating everything by cold, white light.

Ward saw something moving at the bottom of his garden. A dark shape. A large, four-legged shape that carried all its weight on its front two limbs. He blinked. The shape was still there. Then he saw another close by. A third near the door of the office.

Cats? Dogs? Too big for either. Just like the other night.

Was this a dream? Some bizarre hallucination?

The shapes were moving. They darted about the garden with almost obscene grace, moving effortlessly.

Ward swallowed hard.

The lightning stopped. The garden was plunged into darkness once more. He cursed under his breath, wanting the light. Wanting to see those three shapes once more.

There was another flash of lightning. In the momentary glare, Ward saw them again. They had gathered together close to the door of the office.

He cupped his hands around his eyes and pressed his face close to the glass. Through the blackness he could see six yellowish points of light. Their eyes?

They were motionless now. Ward felt the hairs on the back of his neck rise as he realised they were looking at him.

The lightning flashed again quickly, like a manic strobe, then faded. The darkness returned.

He continued peering in the direction of the office.

More lightning. No shapes. No strange visions. Only darkness and driving rain. Thunder rumbled menacingly.

Ward moved back from the window and sat on the edge of the bed. He glanced down at his clothes, wondering whether he should pull on the jogging bottoms and sweatshirt and venture out to the garden. See if he was indeed losing his mind.

There could be little other explanation for what he had seen. He was going mad. End of story.

He smiled to himself, shook his head and climbed back between the sheets.

The storm continued to rage. It was still roaring an hour later when he drifted off to sleep.

WARNINGS

I t was still dark when he woke.
   He felt something wet running down his face and sat up, wiping it away. His hair was drenched. So were his sheets. The dream must have been bad. The bed was sodden.

   He held out one hand and saw that it too was sheathed with moisture. It was also shaking.

   As he swung himself out of bed he stepped on his clothes. Both his jogging bottoms and his sweatshirt were soaking wet. As if he'd been standing, uncovered, in pouring rain.

45

The cafe in Sloane Street had only been open half an hour. Doyle went inside and ordered two coffees while Hendry parked the Daimler then followed him in.

The driver was constantly looking out at the vehicle. Doyle sat across from him, facing the door. He sipped his coffee and took a bite from his croissant.

'Haven't they got any sandwiches?' he said, looking disapprovingly at the pastry.

'They're not cut yet,' Hendry said.

'Waiting for the fucking organic baker to arrive, are they?' Hendry smiled then looked, once again, at the Daimler.

'Nobody's going to nick it, Joe,' Doyle said smiling. 'Not with those two twats in it.' He nodded in the direction of the servants who gazed out agitatedly from the back seat.

Hendry nodded and smiled. 'I suppose you're right,' he said.

'Anyway, even if they did, the Sheikh could run to a new one, couldn't he?' He lifted his coffee cup in salute. 'Cheers.'

Hendry chuckled and imitated the gesture.

They sat in silence for a moment then the driver spoke. 'Force of habit, is it?'

Doyle looked puzzled.

'Sitting facing the door?' Hendry elaborated.

'You could say that. Old habits die hard.'

'Why did you leave the CTU?'

'I didn't volunteer, I was invited. Didn't you know?'

'No one said anything to me but then, why should they? It's none of my business.'

'Does Mel know I was thrown out?'

'If she does she hasn't said.'

'What's the SP with her? Married? Boyfriend? You and her?'

Hendry grinned. 'Not a chance,' he said. 'We've worked together before but that's it. I don't know much about her background, except what she's told me, but I do know she's not attached. Why? You interested?'

'Just asking. I'm curious by nature.'

'Another old habit?'

Doyle sipped his coffee and nodded. 'So what about you?' he asked. 'How did you get into this line of work?'

'I've always been in the security game. Music business mostly. I used to look after AC/DC, Judas Priest, Iron Maiden.'

'My kind of music.'

'*And* George Michael.'

'Not much fucking difference,' Doyle snorted. 'What made you give it up?'

'I got sick of the travelling. Three hundred days a year on the road, it wears you down after a bit. It's great when you're a kid starting out but after a while it gets on your tits. It got me used to dealing with egos though. I had a spell as a chauffeur too.'

'Married?'

'No. What about you?'

Doyle shook his head. 'It's not for me,' he said.

'I'd like to get married and have kids one day. Run my own business, like Cartwright does.'

'He seems a decent enough guy.'

'He is. It's a good firm to work for. You were lucky he took you on.'

'I didn't feel very lucky this morning. That fucking kid . . .' He allowed the sentence to trail off.

'He's testing you. He did it to me when we first started working for the Sheikh. Little bastard took off a five-grand Rolex, dropped it in a dustbin and said I could have it if I fished it out of the rubbish.'

'What did you do?'

'I told him I already had a watch.'

Doyle smiled.

'He knows he's got the power and he likes to use it,' Hendry continued. He looked at his watch. 'We'd better make a move,' he said.

'Fuck it, let's have another coffee.'

'Didn't Mel tell you? We've got another job this morning. The Sheikh's wife wants to go shopping at Harrods. If we're lucky we get to carry her bags.'

'Jesus Christ,' Doyle sighed.

'Come on, it could be worse,' said Hendry getting to his feet.

'How could it be worse?' Doyle called after him.

The driver was already outside.

46

BELFAST:

Declan Leary took a final drag on his cigarette and looked again at the building before him.

Number 134 Tennent Street was one of the three RUC stations in the city that housed members of the law enforcement agency's 'D' Division. The divisional headquarters was in the Antrim Road. Another sub-divisional station, like this one in Tennent Street, was located in Antrim itself, close to the banks of Lough Neagh.

A, B and E divisions were served by divisional headquarters in Musgrave Street, Grosvenor Road and Strandtown. Each of those also had at least two sub-divisional headquarters buildings.

Like anyone fucking cares.

Leary ground out the cigarette beneath his foot and walked up the ramp that led into the main reception area of the building.

He had mixed feelings. Part of him felt uneasy. He knew he was taking a risk (albeit a necessary one) but he also felt a pleasurable *frisson* from the knowledge that he was in the very jaws of his enemies and, as far as he knew, none of the uniformed men moving officiously around the building were aware of who he was.

Were they?

He moved towards the counter and nodded affably at the duty sergeant busily scribbling on a sheet of paper.

'Morning,' said Leary.

'Good morning, sir,' replied the sergeant. 'If you can just give me a minute, I'll be with you.'

Leary nodded and continued glancing around him.

'Right,' said the sergeant finally. 'What can I do for you, sir?'

'I want to report a stolen car,' Leary lied.

The sergeant sighed and rummaged around for the necessary forms. One of which he handed to Leary.

'If you could fill that out please, sir.'

'Is that it? Fill a form in and hope for the best?'

'Sir, there were over three hundred instances of car theft reported at this police station alone last year. If you multiply that by the number of other stations in the city, you're looking at over five thousand vehicles a year.'

'So you're telling me I'm not going to get my car back?'

'I'd be lying if I said it was likely, sir.'

'Could you not run it through your computer or something? It was only taken last night.'

'Sir—'

'If I give you the details, can't you just have a look? There were needles and insulin and Christ knows what else in there. You know, for medical use.'

He looked hopefully at the sergeant.

'Well, that *does* make it a slightly different matter, sir. Could I have the make and registration number of the car, please.'

Leary gave it to him. Even down to the colour.

The sergeant's fingers moved swiftly across the keyboard. He hit the return key and glanced at the screen.

'And *your* name, sir?'

'Dermot Mallen,' Leary lied.

The sergeant frowned. 'The car you've described is registered to a Mr Ivor Best. Not Dermot Mallen.' The uniformed man regarded him with narrowed eyes.

'I know,' Leary said unfazed. 'He's my brother-in-law. That's why I need to get the car back as quickly as possible. He leant me the bloody thing. He'll be after going crazy when he finds out it's been stolen.'

'Who's the diabetic? Yourself or your brother-in-law?'

'What difference does it make?'

'You said the car was full of syringes. They could be taken and used for drugs and—'

Leary cut him short. 'Oh, right, sure. It's my brother-in-law. He keeps them in the glove compartment. In case of emergency.'

'You'll have to fill out the form, sir,' the sergeant said, preparing to press the delete key.

'Have you got a pen there?' Leary asked.

The sergeant nodded and ducked down.

As he did, Leary looked at the screen. There was no address listed beneath the name.

Shit.

The sergeant re-emerged from beneath the counter and handed Leary a Bic.

'Actually, I'll take this form home and fill it in,' Leary said as the details disappeared from the screen. 'Thanks all the same.'

The sergeant nodded.

Leary turned and headed towards the exit. When he got out on to the street he balled up the form and threw it to the ground. He reached for his cigarettes and lit one.

'Ivor Best,' he said under his breath. 'Time you and I had a chat.'

He turned and headed off down the street.

47

Declan Leary looked at his watch and ducked back into the phone box.

Five minutes to eight.

The light inside the box was broken, making it difficult to see the features of anyone inside. That suited Leary.

He'd been there for the last ten minutes, the phone pressed between his ear and shoulder so as not to look suspicious to anyone walking past.

Leary watched the corner of the street, waiting for the arrival of the car he was sure would come.

After leaving the police station earlier that day, he'd spent some time in the library scouring the Belfast phone book for Ivor Best. He hadn't been surprised to find that there were over three hundred entries under that name. Leary had eventually given it up as a bad job. If Best wanted to talk to him then he'd turn up on the street corner as promised.

Why hunt your prey when it was willing to come to you?

If, indeed, Best was one of the men he sought. Whatever happened, he intended to find out.

He slid his hand into his jacket pocket, his fingers brushing against the flick knife. Beneath his left arm, tucked snugly into a shoulder holster, was the Glock 17 automatic. The pliers were in his other pocket.

Leary chewed on a matchstick, his eyes ever alert for signs of movement.

When he finally saw the car he remained motionless.

Bang on eight.

Ivor Best cruised slowly down the road, turned the vehicle

at the far end then guided it back up towards the corner of the street opposite where Leary hid.

There was someone else in the car with him.

If you're going to do this, you're going to have to do it quickly.

The car was slowing down. Leary could see Best and his companion peering to the left and right, the second man gesticulating.

Leary leaned on the phone-box door and it opened slightly. The car was less than ten yards from him. He eased the Glock from the shoulder holster and took a step out on to the pavement.

Best brought the car to a stop and revved the engine once.

Leary ran across to the vehicle and tapped on the passenger-side window.

Jeffrey Kelly looked around at him.

Ivor Best smiled and nodded. 'Get in the back,' he called, motioning to the rear door.

Leary did as he was instructed.

'Nice to see you again, Mr Best,' said Leary smiling.

'How the fuck do you know my name?' Best began. Then he saw the gun.

Leary pressed it to the back of Kelly's skull. 'Just drive or I'll blow his fucking head off,' he hissed.

'He's bluffing,' Best said, seeing the look of horror on his companion's face.

'Am I?' Leary challenged, thumbing back the hammer of the 9mm.

'Who *are* you?' Best wanted to know.

'Drive. I'll introduce myself,' Leary snapped.

48

'So, who the fuck are you?'

Ivor Best glanced into the rear-view mirror and caught sight of Leary again. The young Irishman was still sitting with the Glock pressed to the base of Jeffrey Kelly's skull.

'RUC?' Best murmured. 'SAS?'

'What the fuck would the SAS want with *you*, you Proddie bastard?'

'What do *you* want?' Kelly asked, trying to keep his voice even.

'Information,' Leary said.

'About what?'

'Why did you pick me up last night after I left that pub?' Leary wanted to know.

Best regarded him in the mirror again but said nothing.

'Why were you there again tonight? You knew I'd show up, didn't you?' Leary continued.

'I was interested in what you had to say,' Best replied.

'About the UVF? Why?'

Another heavy silence filled the car.

'Why were you so fucking interested in what I had to say about the UVF?' Leary repeated.

Best watched the road ahead. There was a junction coming up. Perhaps if he turned the car sharply enough he could cause his new passenger to overbalance. Then he could reach over and grab the gun.

Maybe.

'How did you know my name?' Best wanted to know.

'Research,' Leary grinned.

'You're not RUC, are you?' Best said. 'You wouldn't have to use plain clothes.'

'So if I'm not RUC and I'm not with the fucking SAS, *you* work it out.'

'Fenian,' said Best and it was more a statement than a question.

'Maybe. Now I want to know what *you* know about the UVF.'

Another silence.

'I'm going to count to five,' Leary said, 'then, I'm going to spread your friend's brains all over that fucking windscreen. Understand? One . . .'

Kelly tried to turn his head slightly.

'Two,' Leary continued.

Best saw a set of traffic lights up ahead. They were on amber.

'Three.'

Hit the brakes hard.

'Four.'

'All right,' said Best irritably.

'What do you know about the UVF?' Leary said. 'And I mean *you.*'

'We know as much about them as the next man,' said Kelly, swallowing hard. He could feel the barrel of the automatic against his flesh.

'You know who they are, don't you?' snapped Leary. 'Every Proddie in this city knows who belongs with them.'

'Like every Catholic knows who's in the fucking IRA,' grunted Best.

'You know them, don't you?' Leary insisted. 'You know the men I'm looking for.'

'I don't know what the fuck you're talking about,' Best sneered dismissively.

Leary fired once. The noise inside the car was incredible. For fleeting seconds, Best and Leary both felt as if someone had ignited a charge inside their ears. The sound filled the space.

The bullet exploded from the barrel of the Glock, tore its

way through the base of Kelly's skull then travelled upwards. It ripped through the soft tissue of his brain and erupted from his forehead just above his left eye, carrying a reeking flux of pulverised bone, blood and macerated tissue with it. Most of it spattered the windscreen, some splashed Best. The bullet left an exit wound large enough for a man to push his fist through.

What was left of Kelly's head slumped back against the seat.

The air was filled with the stench of cordite, blood and excrement as his body voided itself.

Best almost lost control of the car but he gripped the wheel and guided the vehicle on, his hands now shaking. His ears were throbbing from the massive roar. His retinas seared by the muzzle flash that had filled the car like the flame from a welder's torch.

'Has that helped your memory?' Leary rasped. 'I want to know what you know about the UVF. Now.'

Best was breathing heavily. Sucking in the stench. It was like a mobile charnel house.

'Have you ever been approached by the UVF?' Leary continued. 'Do you know anyone *in* the UVF?'

Best nodded.

'Then fucking tell me,' Leary snarled, pressing the barrel of the Glock to the driver's head. 'And do it before you end up like your friend.'

49

'You hear things,' said Best, his voice cracking slightly. 'You know how it is.'

'Tell me.'

'People mouthing off. Rumours. You never know if they're true or not. Someone says they know someone who knows someone who's in the movement. That kind of thing.'

'Was *he* in the UVF?' Leary asked, nodding towards the corpse.

The coppery odour of Kelly's blood was growing stronger.

Best nodded.

'What about you?' Leary continued. 'You are too, aren't you?'

No answer.

'You wouldn't have followed me last night otherwise.' You thought you had a new recruit on your hands, didn't you? That was why you wanted to meet me again tonight. To see if what I said yesterday was bullshit.' He smiled. 'Well, now you know it is.'

Best continued driving, occasionally glancing at the glove compartment. Wondering if there was any way he would be able to reach the .38 Smith and Wesson revolver that was hidden in there.

'So, what are you?' he said finally. 'Fucking IRA or what?'

'Does it matter?'

'Not really. You're all the same. Murdering Fenian bastards.'

'Murderers is it? What was done to those five IRA men last week, doesn't *that* count as murder? You know the ones I mean?'

Best nodded almost imperceptibly.

'Did you know anything about that?' Leary wanted to know.

Best shook his head.

'Lying bastard,' snapped Leary. 'Who killed them?'

'Do you know what every member of *your* organisation is up to twenty-four hours a fucking day?'

'I just want to know if it was the UVF that killed them.'

'And what? If I tell you, you'll let me go?'

'Was it the UVF?'

'Yes it was, and I'm glad it was.'

'How did they know where that mini-bus was going to be? There were a dozen different routes it could have taken from Maghaberry to the border. Who had access to that kind of information?'

'It's fuck-all to do with me.'

'Just a soldier then, are you? Just do what you're told?'

No answer.

'Who told you to ambush that fucking mini-bus and kill all the men on it?' Leary snapped.

Best gritted his teeth.

'Who's your section commander?' Leary persisted, pressing the gun harder against Best's cheek.

'If you kill me, the car'll crash. We'll both die,' Best said.

'Stop the car. Now.'

Best continued driving.

'You heard me,' hissed Leary. 'Stop the fucking car.' He smacked the barrel of the Glock into Best's temple. Powerfully enough to hurt him but not so violently as to make him lose control.

He stepped on the brake and looked round at Leary.

'How many men took part in the ambush?' the younger man demanded.

'Four.'

'Including you and him?' said Leary, nodding in the direction of the bullet-blasted body of Kelly.

Best nodded.

'Give me the names of the other two.'

'Fuck you,' Best snarled.

Leary struck him hard across the face with the Glock. The

impact loosened two of his front teeth and burst his bottom lip. Blood ran down his chin.

Leary reached across the front seat and grabbed Best by the hair, hauling him upright. He pulled the flick knife from his pocket and freed the blade.

With surprising gentleness, he pressed the needle-sharp point against Best's left lower eyelid.

'The names of the other two men,' he hissed. 'Or I'll take your fucking eyes out, one by one.'

Best was breathing heavily now, his tongue occasionally flicking across his split lip to lick at the red stream flowing from the cut.

'Their names,' Leary snarled, pressing harder with the knife point. 'You think either of *them* would give a fuck about saving you if *they* were in this position?'

'I can't tell you. They—'

Leary pushed the knife forward. The point sliced through the soft flesh of Best's eyelid with ease then parted muscle and punctured the base of the eyeball itself. Blood and vitreous fluid spurted from the socket.

Best shrieked in agony and tried to escape the probing steel.

Leary held the weapon with remarkable dexterity and expertise.

As yet less than an inch of the blade had penetrated the lower part of the socket.

'Tell me,' Leary said more loudly. 'Another two inches and your fucking eye is out.'

'No,' screamed Best.

'Their names.'

'George Mcswain and Daniel Kane,' Best shouted frantically. 'For God's sake—'

Leary struck swiftly.

He drove the knife deep into the left eye, putting all his force behind it. Tore it free and did the same with the right orb.

Both blows penetrated to the brain.

Best's head slammed back against the side window with

each impact, the shrieks of agony dying in his throat.

Leary pressed the Glock to the man's temple and fired once.

He waited a moment then clambered out of the car, checking that none of the blood and pieces of brain matter had sprayed his clothes.

They hadn't.

He slid the Glock back into its shoulder holster then wiped the blade of the flick knife on his handkerchief, closed it and dropped it back into his jacket pocket. He turned and headed back down the street.

It was beginning to rain.

50

LONDON:

'This is bullshit.' Doyle stared angrily at Melissa Blake.
'It's the job,' she told him sternly.

He sucked in a deep breath.

'Prince Hassim has requested that you guard his room tonight,' Mel continued.

'He's doing this on purpose, the little bastard.'

'It doesn't matter why he's doing it, Doyle. If that's what he wants, that's what he gets. Like I said, it's the job. If you don't like it you know what you can do.'

'Thanks.'

She could only shrug.

'Where's the little prick now?' Doyle wanted to know.

'He's upstairs in his room.'

'Hendry said the little shit was testing me,' Doyle mused. 'It looks like he was right.'

'Perhaps he just likes having you around,' Mel smiled.

'Yeah, Mr Popularity, that's me. Is there anybody with him?'

'One of the servants.'

Doyle glanced at his watch. 8.30 p.m.

He made his way towards the flight of stairs that led to the first floor.

'I'll bring you some food and drink about ten,' Mel told him.

'I'll look forward to it,' Doyle called without turning round.

He turned left at the top of the stairs and made his way past several oak-panelled doors until he reached the one he sought. A single wooden chair had already been placed outside it. One of the Sheikh's servants was standing opposite the door. He regarded Doyle warily as he approached.

'You stay here tonight,' said the Arab. 'Guard Prince.'

Doyle nodded. 'Why can't *you* do it?' the former agent wanted to know.

'Prince ask for you.'

The door opened and Doyle saw the boy standing there. He looked Doyle up and down. 'You will bow in my presence,' he said quietly.

Doyle glared at the boy.

Don't push it, you little bastard. I might need a job but not that fucking bad.

'Bow,' Hassim repeated.

Doyle nodded his head swiftly.

'Come inside,' the boy said in his perfect English accent.

Doyle hesitated for a second then stepped into the boy's bedroom. It was vast and high ceilinged. The floor was covered in plush carpet. Doyle saw a stack system and a DVD player. Every electrical appliance imaginable. The television was on in the corner of the room, so too was the computer, its screen flickering. There was a large bed, several upholstered chairs and a chaise longue.

'These are only some of the things I have,' Hassim told him.

'Great,' said Doyle uninterestedly.

'My father is a very rich man.'

'I gathered that.'

'He is very powerful. I will be even more powerful when I am older. I have power already. The servants in this house must do whatever I wish.'

Doyle merely held the boy's gaze.

'*You* must do whatever I wish,' Hassim continued.

'That's not strictly true. Your father *owns* the servants. He doesn't own *me*. He just employs me. If I want to walk away I can.'

'You would not dare.'

'Wouldn't I?'

There was a moment's silence, broken by Hassim. 'I will show you how much power I have,' said the boy. He called something in Arabic. The words sounded harsh.

The servant who had been outside stepped into the room and bowed in the direction of the Prince. The boy snapped something else and the man stood in the middle of the room, arms at his sides.

Doyle looked on silently as Hassim crossed to his bedside table and slid open one of the drawers.

'Do you know what real power is?' Hassim said, his back to Doyle.

The former counter terrorist said nothing.

'I will show you,' said the boy.

Doyle could see that he had something gripped in one hand.

Only as he drew closer could he see that it was a Stanley knife.

PROGRESS

Twenty-two pages. Ward counted them, numbered them and placed them with the rest of the manuscript. He moved like a man in a trance, touching the pages almost warily, carefully scanning the words on each one.

Then he sat and gazed at the blank screen. And the keyboard. And the box of white Conqueror paper that fed the printer.

The top sheet was slightly discoloured. Crinkled at the bottom, like parchment. Ward picked it up and rubbed it gently between his thumb and forefinger. He gently folded it then dropped it into the waste bin beside his desk.

The bin needed emptying. There were pieces of paper, sweet wrappers and other discarded items spilling over the sides. Some of the rubbish even lay on the carpet around the bin. He looked down at the mess, realising that he should clear it up.

The waste bin near the sink was in the same state. Tidiness was not one of Ward's strong points.

Neither, it seemed, was memory. He could not recall having come to the office the previous night. Could not remember sitting and writing another twenty-two pages of his book. In fact, he had little recollection of much of what he'd produced during the past month.

Drink destroyed memory cells. Depression also interfered with the brain's recollective processes.

He looked at the manuscript, now swollen to almost three hundred pages. Was it possible he could have forgotten so much? If not, what was happening?

He ran a hand over cheeks that needed the attentions of a razor blade and gazed once again at the screen and the keyboard.

As he looked down at the squares and their letters and symbols he shook his head gently. He touched one of the keys and held it down.

aaaaaaaaaaaaaaaaaaaaaaaaaaaaaaaaaaaaaaaaaaaaaaaaaaaaaaaaaaaaaaaaa
aaaaaaaaaaaaaaaaaaaaaaaaaaaaaaaa

Ward ran his fingertips over several others, feeling the outline of the symbols as if he were working on some kind of braille machine.

He sat back in his chair and exhaled deeply. He closed his eyes.

The phone rang.

Ward jumped in his seat and looked at the device as if it were some kind of venomous reptile, then he shot out a hand and picked it up.

'Hello,' he said.

Silence at the other end.

'Hello,' Ward repeated.

Still nothing.

'You must have got the wrong number,' he said and hung up.

He sat at the desk a moment longer then got to his feet, switched off the monitor and made his way out of the office. As he paused to lock the door he looked down.

There were several deep furrows in the wood both at the bottom and around the handle.

They looked like scratch marks.

SEEKING OBLIVION

Ward slumped in the armchair with the bottle of Jack Daniel's in one hand and a crystal tumbler in the other. He poured himself a large measure and drank it in one fierce swallow.

Another followed. Then a third.

He switched on the television and gazed blankly at the screen.

It was another hour before he dragged himself to his feet and wandered out to the hall. He picked up the phone and jabbed out a number. It rang and rang until an answerphone clicked on.

Ward pressed down on the cradle and searched the small notepad beside the phone for another number. He dialled that and waited.

When the robotic voice at the other end informed him he had reached the voicemail of that particular mobile phone he almost hung up again but, despite himself, he hung on. 'Martin, it's Chris Ward. Call me when you get the chance. It doesn't matter what time it is.'

He hung up and returned to the sitting room. There was no telling what time his agent would ring back. If he did.

Ward poured himself another drink.

And waited.

WAITING GAME

It stayed light until well past nine o'clock. Ward finally got to his feet and drew his curtains at about 9.40.

A moment later the phone rang. Ward caught it on the fifth ring.

'Hello, Martin?' he said, expectantly.

'Yes,' Martin Connelly said. 'Are you okay, Chris? I just got your message. I would have rung earlier but I've been out for a drink with—'

'Just listen to me,' Ward interrupted. 'When was the last time we spoke on the phone?'

'What?'

'When was the last time we spoke on the phone? It's a simple enough question, Martin.'

'I'm not with you.'

'Today? Yesterday?'

'I called you two days ago. We were talking about work and—'

'But I haven't called you? We haven't spoken since then?'

'What's this about, Chris?'

'I need to know.'

'Are you pissed?'

'Not yet.'

'Listen, is everything all right?'

'My career's crumbling around my ears, my life's being destroyed. Why shouldn't everything be all right?'

'You know what I mean.'

'No, Martin. I'm not sure I know anything any more.'

'Listen, come down to London, we'll have lunch. I'll pay. I can't say fairer than that, can I?'

'Thanks for calling back,' said Ward.

A STRANGE CALL

Ward sat in his large kitchen and ate the sandwich he'd made from three-day-old bread and ham that was perilously close to its sell-by date.

Music drifted from the compact sound system that stood on one worktop. Ward hardly heard it. He finished his sandwich and put the plate in the sink.

The phone rang. As he crossed the room to it he looked at his watch. 6.15 p.m.

Who the hell would be calling him at this time?

He picked up the receiver. 'Hello,' he said wearily.

'Hi, Chris, it's Jenny,' said the voice at the other end of the line.

'Jenny?'

For a moment he could not recall.

'What time do you want me to come round tonight?' she asked him.

'What are you talking about?'

'You phoned and asked me to come to your house.'

'What the fuck are you going on about?'

'You rang . . .'

'When?'

'Earlier today.'

'What time?'

'I can't remember exactly. Does it matter? You just didn't say what time you wanted me—'

'What time did I ring?' he demanded.

'I said, I don't know.'

'Morning, afternoon? When?'

'It was this afternoon. Look, everything's all right. I spoke to one of the other girls and she said she'd come along. It's going to cost you though. A hundred for me and the same for her. Her name's Claire. She's gorgeous. Long, dark hair, slim. She's done this kind of thing before so—'

Again he cut her short. 'What the fuck are you talking about? I didn't ring you.'

He heard a deep sigh from Jenny.

'All right, just tell me what time, will you?' she said.

'I don't want you here tonight,' he said.

'But I've arranged it with Claire. I told her—'

He slammed the phone down. As he backed away, his heart was thudding hard against his ribs.

Ward turned and headed for the sitting room. He needed a drink.

NOWHERE TO RUN

Ward sat looking at the phone for what seemed an eternity.

Had he really called Jenny? Asked her to come to the house. And with another girl?

Making phone calls without being able to remember them. Writing lucidly and productively, then failing to recall doing so. What was this? Drunkenness?

Had he begun suffering from some kind of blackouts? But what manner of breakdown caused memory loss yet inspired creativity?

Ward shook his head as if to answer his own unspoken question. It was impossible.

And yet it was happening.

He drained what was left in his glass and decided to go to bed. No matter how long he sat up pondering on his current dilemma, it wasn't going to help.

He trudged through to the kitchen and took a couple of paracetamol. For fleeting seconds, he wondered about taking the whole bottle.

He drew the kitchen blinds slowly, peering out into the blackness of the garden. He looked towards the office. No silvery-grey light shining inside. Nothing.

He pulled down the blind and turned to leave the room. As he did, he heard the scratching. Loud at first but then dying away rapidly.

It was coming from the back door.

Ward stood where he was as the sound came again. Then silence.

He took a step closer to the door. The handle moved slowly. Ward swallowed hard.

Someone was trying to break in.

He crossed to the kitchen drawer and slid out a large kitchen knife. It was serrated with a wickedly sharp point and fully twelve inches long.

The door handle moved slowly up and down as whoever was outside stealthily attempted to gain access. Ward wondered how long it would be before they tried a more forceful method. He crept closer to the door, his eyes riveted on the handle. It had stopped moving.

The scratching sound, however, had begun again. More insistent this time. It continued for a full five minutes.

In the silence that followed he stood motionless. Waiting. Wondering what he was going to do if someone *did* get inside.

Ten minutes later he was still standing there.

The scratching had not recommenced and the door handle had remained still.

He shook his head. Another hallucination?

Ward clutched the knife as he made his way out into the hall. He set the alarm and climbed the stairs, hurrying to his bedroom, anxious to see if he could detect any signs of movement from a higher vantage point.

The garden was deserted. He looked in the direction of the office and saw nothing.

For a full fifteen minutes, Ward stood at the window, the kitchen knife gripped in his fist.

Finally he laid the weapon on the other side of the bed, undressed and slipped between the sheets. He fell asleep with his fingers still touching the handle of the knife.

SWEET DREAMS

3.11 a.m. Ward woke with a start. He reached for the knife, his breath coming in gasps, the last vestiges of the nightmare fading. The images were gone as soon as he opened his eyes. He tried to remember the dream but couldn't.

He put down the knife and tried to swallow but his throat was dry. He swung himself out of bed and stumbled into the bathroom where he spun the tap and scooped several gulps of water into his mouth.

Ward ran both hands through his hair and made his way back into the bedroom. He stood beside the window for a moment, gazing out into the night. The silence was overwhelming. He leant forward, pressing his forehead against the cold glass.

Something smacked into the window with such force he thought it was going to shatter.

Ward stumbled backwards, his heart thundering in his chest. He looked up.

Pushing against the window was a bird, its wings fluttering madly, its head flattened against the glass.

No, it wasn't a bird. The wings were leathery. The face was flat and rodent-like.

A bat? It was too large. Jesus, it was *much* too large. The fucking thing was the size of a hawk.

It hovered there for interminable seconds, its claws scratching at the pane.

Ward looked into its blood-red eyes and felt the hairs rise on the back of his neck.

There was crimson around its mouth. On its small, sharp teeth.

It finally wheeled away, disappearing into the blackness.

Ward sat down on the edge of the bed, his heart still pounding. He reached for the knife and found his hand was shaking. He got up again and drew the bedroom curtains shut.

Dawn seemed to be a long way off.

LIFE GOES ON

No marks on the back door. None on the office door. Ward sat down at the keyboard, pressed the power button and watched the screen light up.

He began to type.

51

'Sit down.'

The boy spoke with an authority beyond his tender years.

'No thanks, I'd rather stand,' Doyle told him, his gaze moving alternately between the boy's face and the glinting blade of the Stanley knife.

Hassim smiled and held the blade before him.

'You will never understand true power because you will never have it,' he said, looking at Doyle. 'I will show you what it is.'

He struck at the servant. The razor-sharp blade carved effortlessly through the material of the man's jacket, exposing the material of his shirt beneath.

Hassim continued to smile.

The servant remained motionless, his eyes looking over Hassim's head, as if he were studying the wall opposite.

'Whatever I want, this man must do,' said the boy. 'I tell him to obey me and he does.'

He used the knife again. This time he cut through the servant's shirt and into his flesh, just below the elbow. Blood burst from the deep cut and stained the material.

'I tell him he must not move and he obeys,' said Hassim.

He cut again. This time the blade hacked into the flesh and muscle just above the servant's wrist. More blood began to flow, some of it running down his arm and dripping from his outstretched fingers.

Doyle took a step forward. 'All right,' he snapped. 'That's enough.'

Hassim rounded on him, his face suddenly contorted with rage. 'No,' he hissed. 'I am the one with the power. I will decide when it is over.'

He cut the servant a third time. The wound was deep. It ran from just below the inside of the elbow to an inch or two above the wrist.

Doyle saw the servant sway slightly, his eyelids flickering. Blood was now pouring freely from the wounds. It splashed the expensive carpet beneath.

Hassim took a step back. 'He will not move until I say,' the Prince announced. 'He belongs to me. He serves me.'

'Because he *has* to,' snarled Doyle.

'Because he *loves* me and my family.'

Doyle took another look at the servant. His face was pale and there was a thin film of sweat on his skin. Another minute or two and he'd pass out.

'You've made your point,' Doyle said. 'Now let me get him a doctor.'

'I will decide when the time is right. You are only a servant like him. You do not tell *me* what to do.'

Little bastard. Sadistic, malevolent little bastard.

The servant wavered. Hassim barked something at him in Arabic and the man fought to regain his balance. Struggled to remain upright before the boy.

Blood continued to stain the carpet.

Hassim held up the crimson-smeared blade and smiled. 'My word is power,' he said. 'This knife is nothing compared to the one who uses it.'

Doyle glared at the boy.

The servant finally dropped to his knees. Hassim turned on him furiously. He swung the blade around and caught the man across the cheek, laying the flesh open to the bone. The boy snarled something else in Arabic and spat at the hapless servant.

Doyle turned and headed for the door.

'I did not give you permission to leave,' Hassim called. 'Stay where you are.'

'Or what?' Doyle said challengingly. 'Do you think *I'm* going to stand still while you do to me what you just did to that poor sod?'

'I will tell my father you disobeyed me.'

'Tell him. What's the worst he can do? Throw me out? Because if he does I'll tell *you* something *Your Highness*.' The last two words were spoken with distaste. 'I'll make sure that his worries about you are well-founded because *I'll* come after you. You want to see *real* power?' He slid his hand inside his jacket and pulled out the Beretta 92F. He aimed it at the boy.

'Now, you make one sound and I'll stick this fucking thing down your throat and pull the trigger. I couldn't give a flying fuck if your dad's the richest man in the world or Sinbad the fucking Sailor. Do *you* understand?'

'You dare to threaten *me*?' Hassim said, his voice cracking.

Doyle nodded. 'Fucking right,' he hissed. 'And you'd better get used to it. Do we understand each other?'

Hassim hesitated.

Doyle took a step closer, the barrel of the gun inches from the boy's head.

'Someone tried to break in,' Doyle said quietly. 'I tried to protect you. That's what I'm here for. Shots were fired. You got in the way. What a tragedy. That's what the police would hear and that's what they'd believe. Now, you wanted to test me. You've done that. Let's call it quits and let me get that poor fucker a doctor.'

The servant was lying prone on the bloodied carpet, his life fluid still pumping into the thick, expensive pile.

Hassim swallowed hard. 'You would kill a child?' he said softly.

'Try me,' Doyle told him.

'What kind of man are you?'

Doyle laughed humourlessly.

Hassim put down the Stanley knife.

Doyle holstered the automatic. 'What happened in here tonight,' he said, 'is between you and me.'

'If my father found out about this he would have you killed,' said the boy.

'And that's supposed to scare me, is it?' Doyle snapped.

'He'd be doing me a fucking favour. Now, are you going to keep your mouth shut or not?'

Hassim nodded.

Doyle turned towards the door.

'Excuse me, Your Highness,' he said quietly and stepped out into the corridor.

Hassim stood staring at the closed door. When he tried to move he found that his legs were shaking.

52

'What the hell happened in there tonight?'

Doyle took a bite of his sandwich and raised his eyebrows.

Melissa Blake nodded in the direction of Prince Hassim's room.

'The kid showed me something,' Doyle said. 'I showed *him* something.'

'What happened, Doyle? If you touched that boy . . .'

'I never put a fucking hand on him. Ask him. You know if I had he'd have come screaming to his old man.' He wiped some crumbs from his mouth. 'How's the servant?'

'He needed twenty-six stitches and a couple of pints of blood,' Mel said. '*He* won't say what happened either.'

'Has the Sheikh asked?'

Mel shook her head.

'He probably knows what that little bastard did anyway,' Doyle mused.

Mel glanced at her watch. 2.11 a.m. The house was silent. The Sheikh and his family were sleeping, as were those servants not needed for night duty.

'Do you want some company?' Mel asked.

Doyle stood up and offered her the chair.

She smiled and shook her head.

He watched as she sat down on the floor next to him, slipped off her shoes and drew her legs up beneath her.

'How are you coping?' she wanted to know.

'With sitting on my arse outside the bedroom of some

psychotic Arab kid?' Doyle said. 'I can think of better ways
to spend my time.'

'I meant with the job.'

'Like the man said, it ain't what it used to be, but it'll do,'
he murmured.

'We move tomorrow. All three of us. A new job. Cartwright
phoned me earlier.'

'What about the Sheikh?'

'He's going back to Saudi. His business here is finished.'

'And us?'

'Another client. You must have done okay, Doyle. I mean,
Cartwright hasn't sacked you.'

Doyle took another bite of his sandwich. 'Who made this?'
he asked.

'I did.'

'You're quite domesticated when you have to be, aren't
you?'

Mel smiled and shook her head. 'Domesticity isn't for me,
Doyle,' she told him.

'Career woman?'

'You could say that.'

'What about boyfriends? There must have been one or
two.'

'I didn't come up here to talk about my private life,' she
said a little warily.

'Fair enough. I was just making conversation.'

'Polite conversation?'

'About as polite as I get.'

There was a moment's silence between them finally broken
by Mel.

'Yes, there were boyfriends,' she confessed. 'A couple long
term but I've always been wary of getting too close to people.
My parents were both killed in a plane crash when I was
twelve. They were everything to me. I've always been frightened of getting close to anyone in case I lose them too. Does
that sound crazy?'

'I know exactly what you mean,' he told her.

'Blokes are always saying that women want commitment.

I must be one on my own. I'm as happy with a one-night stand as any bloke would be.'

He grinned.

'Does that make me sound like a tart?' Mel wanted to know.

'It makes you sound honest. Just give me a shout next time you fancy some uncomplicated sex.'

They both laughed.

Doyle watched as she stretched first one leg then the other out in front of her. She flexed her toes then returned to her sitting position.

'Please, Mel, sit on the bloody chair, will you?' he said, again getting to his feet.

'I'm fine, really. I shouldn't be here anyway. I just wanted to make sure you were okay.' She smiled that infectious smile at him.

'Didn't the Sheikh want to know how one of his servants got cut up?' Doyle asked.

She shook her head. 'It's not his concern,' Mel said.

'His kid is waving a fucking Stanley knife around and it's not his concern?'

'That's the way things are. It's a different culture. A way of life we'll never understand.'

'Good. I don't *want* to understand it.'

'But you wanted to understand the IRA.'

He looked at her, puzzled for a moment.

'You were undercover in the CTU. You infiltrated the IRA on a number of occasions. You must have had to understand them to do that.'

'That was different,' he said quietly.

'Who was Georgina Willis?'

The question took him by surprise. He looked angrily at Mel.

'What the fuck's that got to do with anything?' he snapped.

'Cartwright said she was your girlfriend. He said she was killed when—'

'Cartwright should keep his fucking information to himself.'

'I'm not prying, Doyle. I'm just making conversation. I'm interested.'

'In what?'

'In you. If we've got to work together then it's in my interests to know about you.'

'That depends what you want to know. Georgie's not relevant to this. Or what went on between me and her.'

They regarded each other silently for a moment, then Doyle took a sip of his tea. It was cold but he swallowed it anyway.

'Look, I said I wasn't prying,' Mel told him.

'Just forget it, Mel. I have.' He reached for his cigarettes but Mel shook her head. Doyle muttered something under his breath and shoved them back into his pocket. 'Right, no smoking, I remember.' He exhaled wearily. 'So, tell me about the next client.'

'His name's William Duncan. He runs a pharmaceutical company. He's rich.'

'Aren't they all? Who's after him?'

'Muslim extremists. A fatwa's been declared against him. His company was building a new factory in the Middle East, apparently they bulldozed some holy ground.'

'So we have to protect him from a bunch of religious nutters? Great.'

'This one will be different, Doyle. We'll all be armed twenty-four hours a day. It'll be dangerous.'

He looked down at her and shrugged. 'Life's looking up,' he said flatly.

53

BELFAST:

'Are you sure the fingerprints match?' Chief Inspector Peter Robinson ran a hand over his bald head and sat back in his chair.

'No doubt about it,' John Morris told him. 'The prints on the shell cases we found in Best's car match those taken from the flat in Dalton Road. There is no mistake. Declan Leary killed Ivor Best and Jeffrey Kelly.'

Robinson got to his feet and looked first at the coroner's report then at the man himself.

Morris was a stocky man in his late forties, a year or two younger than Robinson. He wore round glasses that were constantly sliding down his small nose. Each time they did, he pushed them back into position with his thumb.

'The question is, was the hit approved?' Robinson mused.

'Best and Kelly were known members of the UVF. It's possible. I would have thought the main question was *who* sanctioned it.'

'Provos or Real IRA,' said Robinson, not expecting an answer. 'It's unlikely to have been the Provisionals.'

'Have you any idea if Leary is part of a cell or working alone?'

'Up until the business in Dalton Road he was working with Matthew Finan. Just the two of them as far as we know. Until Finan was killed. It's my guess that now he's working without official clearance from the Northern Command. Also the nature of the injuries he inflicted on Best seem to indicate more than just a straightforward hit.' The policeman leant forward and flipped through the file on his desk. He paused at two photos of Ivor Best. 'I mean, why stab him in the eyes before shooting him? It's not very professional apart from anything else.'

Morris could only shrug. 'Best was still alive when Leary shot him,' said the coroner. 'The damage to the eyes looks as though it was intended as some kind of torture.'

'Why not just shoot him, like he did Kelly?'

Again Morris shrugged.

'Is Leary trying to start a war with the UVF?' Robinson wondered aloud. 'And if he is, why?'

'You're the policeman, Peter, not me. It's down to you and your boys to find out. I just get the feeling *I'm* going to be busy too.'

'If Leary's running wild, you can guarantee it.'

'So we should expect reprisals.'

'The UVF won't sit still for this. They'll want to hit back. I just hope to God they don't go after the Provisionals.' He sighed wearily. 'All these years of fighting. I really thought it was going to end.'

'It'll take time, Peter. You can't wipe out five hundred years of history with one agreement.'

'Do *you* agree with it, John?'

'With the Good Friday Agreement? In principle. But I think the IRA have come out of it better than most. There's a lot of people who aren't happy about that. I think we've given them too much.'

Robinson regarded his colleague silently.

Morris got to his feet.

'If that's all, Peter,' he said. 'I'll get back to work.'

Robinson nodded, his eyes still fixed on the photos of Ivor Best. 'Thanks, John.'

He heard his office door close as Morris left.

Ivor Best. Jeffrey Kelly.

Robinson shook his head. Was Leary still in Belfast? The policeman doubted it. He would know he was being hunted. He'd be aware that his identity was no longer secret.

Why didn't that bother him? Why leave prints on the shell cases and inside the car?

He looked at Declan Leary's name, scribbled on a sheet of paper. He found himself drawing lines beneath it, pressing ever harder on the paper.

'Where are you, you bastard?' he whispered to himself.

LOOKING FOR INSPIRATION

It was important to Ward to always end his work at a point where he could easily begin again the following day. If he had a starting point, it didn't make for such racked brains and sweat.

Ha ha ha.

2.20 p.m. He continued working.

54

DUNKALK, THE REPUBLIC OF IRELAND:

The 9mm rounds lay on the bedspread gleaming like metallic confetti. Declan Leary regarded the ammunition for a moment longer then crossed to the bed and sat down on the edge of it.

He picked up a handful of the shells and began feeding them into the first of the twenty-round magazines he had for the Scorpion machine pistol.

His room smelt of gun oil and metal. Leary was dressed in just jeans and a T-shirt, and was still too warm. The central heating was playing up, the landlady had explained. The thermostat was stuck on high and it would be a couple of days before an engineer could fix it. She had apologised to all her guests for the inconvenience. They had all accepted with good grace.

Leary continued pushing the bullets into the second of the Scorpion's magazines then, that done, he placed both of them to one side and turned his attention to the Smith and Wesson .459.

It held fifteen shots in its magazine and Leary filled two of those as well, slamming one into the butt of the pistol before working the slide to chamber a round and slipping on the safety catch.

He repeated the procedure with the Glock.

Once the guns were ready he crossed to the small wash basin and poured some oil on to the small stone block that lay on the porcelain. He picked it up and took the 8-inch double-edged knife from the the side of the sink.

With careful, measured strokes, he drew each cutting edge back and forth across the oiled stone, honing each to a razor finish.

He did the same with the flick knife.

Having done that he placed the Scorpion, the .459 and the hunting knife in his black holdall and zipped it shut. Then he spun both taps and filled the sink, washing oil from his hands.

Leary looked at his watch when he heard footsteps outside on the landing. 8.30 a.m. One of the other residents was making his way downstairs for breakfast.

Leary dried his hands, pulled on a sweatshirt and decided to join his fellow guest.

His stomach rumbled audibly and, as he emerged from his room, he smelled bacon and heard the chink of tea cups.

Leary smiled. A good breakfast was just what he needed before the drive to Belfast.

Daniel Kane felt something vibrating against the small of his back. He couldn't hope to hear the ringing of his mobile phone but the Nokia buzzed insistently in its clip on his belt.

Kane waited a moment, swinging the fork-lift around and guiding the two prongs beneath one of the huge crates stacked before him.

Elsewhere inside the warehouse, men moved back and forth, each concerned with his own task. Beneath the safety helmet Kane wore, the sounds were muffled.

The phone was still ringing.

He switched off the engine and reached for the mobile, pulling his safety helmet off as he pressed the Nokia to his ear. The noise inside the warehouse made it difficult to hear the voice on the other end.

'Who is it?' he said, straining his ears to catch the words.

The voice identified itself.

'What the hell are you doing calling me now?' Kane wanted to know.

The voice explained that there was a problem.

'What kind of problem?'

It was difficult to speak. They would have to meet.

'That's not convenient,' said Kane dismissively.

The voice insisted that it was a very important matter.

'Ah, come on, whatever it is it can wait a couple of days,' Kane snapped.

The person at the other end said something else.

'What?' Kane said, his expression darkening. 'Say that again? Declan Leary?'

Again the other voice proposed a meeting.

'Where?' Kane wanted to know.

A hiss of static.

'I didn't hear you,' Kane said. 'The usual place? All right. What's the hurry?'

The voice told him that Declan Leary was looking for him.

'What does he want with me?'

More static.

'Does he know I killed his brother?' Kane said.

The line went dead.

55

CHESHAM, BUCKINGHAMSHIRE, ENGLAND:

Doyle guessed that the driveway must be a good five hundred yards long. From the entrance, through the wrought-iron gates flanked by a ten-foot-high stone wall, it led past perfectly manicured lawns and landscaped gardens. He spotted what looked like an orchard off to the right, enclosed by a high privet hedge. To the left were some red-brick buildings that he guessed were stables. Beyond them were low hills and enough space to exercise the runners in the last three Grand Nationals.

As the car drew nearer the house, topiary animals (also immaculately trimmed and maintained) began to form a kind of honour guard on either side of the drive, which slowly widened into an arc before the house.

The building itself was grey. Whether it was brick or, as it appeared to be, simply hewn from one vast lump of stone, Doyle had no idea. The walls were seething with ivy and the weak sunlight sparkled on the dozens of windows at the front.

But, for all its splendour, there was little ostentation about the home of William Duncan. Multi-millionaire industrialist the man might be, thought Doyle, but the place had none of the outward vulgarity sometimes associated with those lucky enough to have more money than sense. The place looked, first and foremost, a functional home, rather than a status symbol.

The stables, the orchard and whatever other adornments

were contained within the grounds had, by the look of them, been there upon purchase rather than added in some self-conscious flourish. The fact that there was a heated outdoor pool, two tennis courts and a maze to the rear of the building came as no surprise to the former counter terrorist.

He perused the plans of the property that Mel had given him and shook his head.

'Plenty of places to hide,' he murmured as Hendry guided the Jag up the driveway.

Mel turned in the passenger seat and looked at him. 'What did you say, Doyle?' she wanted to know.

'I said there are plenty of places to hide,' he repeated. 'If a bunch of nutters want to kill Duncan then this fucking place is heaven. They could hang around the grounds for days without getting caught.' He shook his head. 'A fucking maze in the back garden. Jesus. How the other half lives.'

He looked at the building and, once more, shook his head.

'It's closer to London than I thought,' Hendry offered.

'Right at the end of the Metropolitan Line,' Doyle said. 'You won't have to drive him into his office in the mornings, Joe. You can just stick him on the fucking tube.'

Hendry chuckled.

'We'd better walk the grounds once we've met the Duncans,' Mel said. 'Check them out more thoroughly.'

Doyle nodded. 'Any kids?' he asked.

'No. Just Duncan and his wife.'

'How much do we know about them?' Hendry asked.

'What do we *need* to know?' Doyle asked. 'We're here to protect them, not make friends with them.'

Mel looked at him for a moment then back at Hendry.

'Duncan's in his fifties. His wife's twenty-six. I don't know if *that* tells you anything,' Mel smiled. 'He's a keen golfer and archer.' She raised her eyebrows. 'Mrs Duncan likes to ride.'

'I bet she does,' Doyle chuckled.

Hendry also smiled.

Mel shook her head. 'You're like a couple of kids,' she said, her attempts at chastisement failing as she also laughed.

Doyle reached for his cigarettes and lit one, taking a couple

of hasty drags before the car stopped. 'Who's guarding them
at the moment?' he wanted to know.

'Special Branch. They have been for the last two months,
ever since the fatwa was first passed.'

'Why the change?'

'The taxpayers are footing the bill,' Mel smiled. 'I think
Duncan's starting to feel guilty about it. That's why he called
in a private firm.'

'Too right. I mean, how much did it cost to guard bloody
Rushdie? Two million?' Doyle said irritably. 'It would have been
cheaper to let the fucker take his chances.'

'I agree,' Hendry said. 'I reckon he knew what he was doing
when he wrote that book. He knew he'd offend the Muslims
and how they'd react.'

Mel looked at each of the men in turn. 'Nice to see you
two share the same kind of compassion,' she said, shaking her
head.

'Fuck him,' Doyle insisted.

Hendry brought the Jag to a halt and all three of them
clambered out.

As they did, Doyle crushed the cigarette beneath his foot
and drew a deep breath. He ran appraising eyes over the
house then followed Mel towards the large oak front door.

There were CCTV cameras mounted on either side of the
porch. Doyle had seen more of them on the main gates and
also at strategic points along the driveway.

Mel rang the doorbell and waited.

After a moment or two they heard several bolts and locks
being unfastened, then a tall man in a dark-brown suit opened
the door and looked out at them.

'We're with Cartwright Security,' Mel told him. 'I'm—'

He cut her short. 'You're late,' he said tersely.

MISTAKEN IDENTITY

'Back again?' The girl behind the glass of the cash desk was in her early twenties. She wore a gold name-badge on her right breast that proclaimed: Teresa.

'Sorry?' said Ward. 'What did you say?'

'I said, "back again?"' she repeated. 'You were only here this afternoon. You should get a job here considering how much time you spend here.'

'What are you talking about?' Ward wanted to know.

The smile on the girl's face faded slightly. 'You came in this afternoon to see a film and now you're back again. Twice in one day. Most people don't come twice in a month.'

Ward swallowed hard. He looked at his watch. 7.46 p.m.

'Which film did I see this afternoon?' he wanted to know.

She looked bewildered.

'Which film did I see when I was here earlier?' he insisted.

'*Enemy at the Gates*,' she told him.

'What time was that?'

'I'm not sure exactly.' The smile had faded completely by now.

'What time was the performance?' he demanded. 'Check it on your sheet.'

She hesitated.

'Please,' he said.

'Two o'clock,' she announced finally.

Ward nodded. He stepped away from the box office and moved past the other waiting people. Some glanced at him in amusement.

He walked back to his car. Ten minutes later he was home. He headed straight for the office.

There was a small pile of paper near the printer. Ward picked up the sheets and put them in the right order.

Thirty of them.

56

If the outside of the house was impressive, the inside was nothing short of breathtaking.

Doyle looked at the plethora of *objets d'art,* the expensive fixtures and fittings, the furniture. Everything in the house smacked of impeccable taste. He wondered who had decided upon the interior decor. He also wondered how much it had cost.

As he stood in the hallway with its two suits of genuine medieval armour guarding the doorway leading to the main sitting room, he was aware of eyes upon him. Those of the man in the brown suit.

Detective Sergeant Mark Boffey was a powerfully built man in his thirties. He regarded the newcomers from Cartwright with a combination of suspicion and contempt. Something Doyle wasn't slow to pick up.

'How many men are with you?' Mel asked the Special Branch officer.

'Three,' Boffey told her. 'We set up a command post in one of the smaller rooms at the back of the house. All the closed-circuit stuff's in there. There are cameras inside and outside the house. The only place that isn't covered is the maze. Someone will have to watch twenty-four hours a day.'

'Just because *you* sat around getting piles doesn't mean *we* have to,' Doyle told him.

'This man's life is in danger. There are certain measures that must be taken to—'

Doyle cut him short. 'Yeah, we're aware of that,' he said dismissively.

'Has there been any activity while you've been here?' Mel wanted to know.

'If you mean has anyone had a crack at him yet, then no,' Boffey told her. 'But it's coming.'

'How can you be so sure?' Mel asked.

'There've been some threatening phone calls, hate mail. The usual thing.' Boffey looked at all three of the bodyguards. 'Are you armed?'

Doyle and his companions nodded.

'How are they coping?' Mel enquired.

'Pretty well. Business as usual, all that crap.'

'It might be an idea if we met them,' said Mel.

Boffey nodded, glanced once more at Doyle then led the trio towards a door on the right.

It was a smaller sitting room, furnished with leather sofas and chairs. Beyond it, through an open door, Doyle caught sight of a kitchen. Through the window to his left he could see out over the garden that seemed to stretch away as far as the horizon. The maze lay at the bottom of it. The glass-enclosed pool, about two hundred yards from the house, was reached via a narrow gravel path.

Doyle saw a man in a pair of black trousers and a roll-neck sweater walking along the path towards the house. He had a shoulder holster.

'One of my colleagues,' Boffey said, aware that Doyle had spotted the other Special Branch man.

'I didn't think it was one of the assassins,' Doyle told him.

'We do a two-hourly search of the grounds,' Boffey said, acidly. 'It's best to stay vigilant.'

'We'll bear that in mind,' said the former counter terrorist.

Mel shot him a questioning look but Doyle was still looking at Boffey.

There was another door adjacent to the one leading into the kitchen and it was towards this one that the Special Branch man ushered them. He knocked once and walked in.

As Doyle followed his companions inside, he wasn't sure where to look first.

'Jesus,' he murmured, under his breath.

57

It was like walking into an armoury.

Doyle allowed his gaze to move swiftly around the room, taking in as many details as he could.

The walls on every side were festooned with a dizzying display of ancient weapons: pikes, lances, spears, halberds.

He saw maces and battleaxes of various sizes. These were arranged amongst swords, sabres, scimitars and cutting weapons of such divergence Doyle wondered which historical wars they had come from.

And then there were the bows. Longbows and crossbows. Each one with at least six of its arrows or bolts.

The former counter terrorist could only begin to imagine how many lives had been taken by this massive array of antique killing instruments. The blades of some were polished, others rusted but still intact and wickedly sharp.

The room was a testament to the savagery of days gone by. A reminder that man's mind is never so fertile as when devising methods of butchering his own kind.

'Call it a passion.' The words came from William Duncan. 'I'm a collector.'

He noticed Doyle's inquisitive gaze and smiled as he stepped forward to shake hands.

Duncan was a tall man. Broad-shouldered and possessed of an easy smile that seemed to contradict the deep frown lines across his forehead. Doyle felt the strength in his handshake as the introductions were made.

Helen Duncan also extended her hand and Doyle shook

it more gently. He could smell her expensive perfume as she leant closer to him.

She was wearing tight black trousers and a dark-blue jumper that showed off her shapely figure to perfection. Her light-brown hair cascaded as far as her shoulder blades and, when she sat down again and crossed her legs, Doyle could see that the soles of her gleaming leather boots were barely marked. He could even see the size stamped there. The number thirty-seven was clearly visible. These were either new or she didn't do much walking in them, he decided.

Duncan gestured for the newcomers to sit down and all three did as they were instructed.

'I assume you know all the details,' he said. 'And you know what you have to do.'

'Stop you getting killed,' Doyle offered.

Duncan grinned. 'That would be most appreciated, Mr Doyle,' he said.

'If anyone comes at you, you should try using some of those against them,' Doyle said, nodding in the direction of the weapons on the walls.

Again Duncan smiled.

'The people before you stayed inside the house,' Helen Duncan said. 'You'll do the same. There are rooms for each of you.'

'Feel free to help yourself to food and drink,' Duncan told them. 'The kitchen isn't off limits.' He gestured over his shoulder. 'There's a games room along the hall. Should you need to pass the time then feel free to use that as well. I realise this job can become somewhat tedious.'

'Is there anyone else in the house other than yourself and your wife, Mr Duncan?' Mel asked. 'Staff of any kind?'

'We have a cleaner three times a week,' said Helen Duncan. 'Two gardeners once a week.'

'Would it be possible for me to have a list of all deliveries or visits you're expecting from day to day?' Mel continued.

Helen nodded. 'I'll see to that now,' she said, getting to her feet. 'In the meantime, I'll show you to your rooms.'

Doyle and his companions stood up and followed the shapely young woman towards the door.

As they reached it, Duncan also rose. 'I'll ask now,' he said evenly. 'And I'd appreciate an honest answer.'

The three security personnel turned to look at him.

'What are our chances of getting through this?' Duncan wanted to know.

Mel opened her mouth to say something but no words came.

Duncan held up his hand. 'It was an unfair question,' he conceded.

'Let's put it this way,' Doyle interjected. 'If they come after you, they'll have to be prepared to put their own lives on the line. If they get to *you*, that means they've got past *us*. It's not going to happen.'

Duncan attempted a smile.

'That's the most reassurance I can give you, Mr Duncan. If I said anything else I'd be lying.'

'I appreciate your candour.'

'Are either of you religious?' Doyle wanted to know. 'Because if you're not, now might be a good time to start.'

58

The faulty fluorescent in the kitchen buzzed like an irritated bluebottle. Doyle glanced up at it as he stood waiting for the kettle to boil. He made his coffee then sat down at the breakfast bar, pulling the newspaper towards him.

The clock on the far wall ticked loudly in the large room and the former counter terrorist checked his watch against the other timepiece. 2.03 a.m.

He'd walked slowly around the house, even venturing into the gardens after checking the banks of CCTV cameras set up at the rear of the building.

Nothing moving.

He slipped off his jacket and hung it on the back of the stool. The 9mm automatic was secure in his shoulder holster.

Mel would relieve him in two hours. Hendry had already done his shift and, besides, he had to be up early in the morning to drive Duncan into London. Mel had suggested that either she or Doyle should accompany them but they had yet to decide who.

Doyle sipped his coffee and scanned the paper. There was a small column on page five about two killings in Belfast. The police believed them to be sectarian. A suspect was being sought.

Just like old times.

'Anything interesting in there?'

If the voice startled him the surprise didn't register on his face. He looked up to see Helen Duncan enter the room.

She padded across the tiled floor wearing only a knee-length silk dressing-gown.

'Sorry if I woke you up,' Doyle said.

'You didn't. I can't sleep. I think it's a common symptom when your life's in danger.' She attempted a smile but it never touched her eyes. 'Would you object to some company?'

'Help yourself. It's your house.'

She made herself a cup of tea and perched on the stool next to him, her perfectly pedicured toes curled around one of the struts.

Doyle met her gaze. Her eyes were a piercing blue but at present the whites were somewhat bloodshot. However, even the dark rings beneath them and the fact that she wore no make-up did not detract from her exquisite features. She was indeed an immensely attractive young woman.

'I think my husband is adjusting to this better than me,' she said, almost apologetically.

'It's not an easy situation to be in, is it? But rich and powerful men tend to make enemies more easily than most.'

'William's made enemies before but never anything like this.'

'I should think the advantages outweigh the *dis*advantages, don't they?'

'What do you mean?'

'Well, the money, the lifestyle. *You* wouldn't change it, would you?'

'I suppose not. We have a good life together.'

'I bet you do.'

'I know what you're thinking. You and everyone who meets me. "She's half his age." "She only married him for his money." That kind of thing.'

'That's none of my business. I don't get paid to think. I get paid for doing a job. And, at the moment, that job's protecting you and your husband.'

There was a silence between them. She crossed her legs, the dressing-gown sliding up further to reveal a slim thigh.

Doyle looked and she was aware of his gaze but she didn't move.

'Are you married?' she wanted to know.

He shook his head.

'What about that woman you work with? Mel. Is there anything between you?'

Doyle regarded Helen silently for a moment then shook his head once more.

'She's a very attractive woman,' Helen noted.

'She's good at her job too.'

'My husband's very good at his job. Sometimes I think he's *too* good.' She sipped her tea. 'I hate it when he's away from home.'

'Is he away a lot?'

'At least four months of the year if you add it up.'

'And *you* obviously do.'

Helen smiled. A little more warmly this time. 'I have friends, of course, but it's not the same when he's not here. This lifestyle *is* wonderful, Mr Doyle, but it would be even more wonderful if I could share it all year round with my husband.'

'Swings and roundabouts. If he doesn't work, you don't have all this.' He gestured around him. 'You can't have it both ways, Mrs Duncan.'

'Call me Helen, please. I don't know how long you're going to be around. It doesn't sound so formal. It makes you sound less like some kind of hired hand.'

'Even though that's what I am.'

'You know what I mean.'

Doyle drained his drink and placed the mug on the worktop. 'Do you get lonely when he's not here?' he wanted to know.

'I miss him but, as I said, I have friends. All my needs are catered for.' She smiled and looked into his eyes. 'He knows what I do when he's not here,' Helen told him. 'How I entertain myself. He accepts it.'

'I've got to check the grounds again,' Doyle told her, preparing to get to his feet.

'Not interested in what I have to tell you, Mr Doyle?'

'It's none of my business.'

'Would it bother *you* if you were in my husband's position?'

'I'm not.'

'Hypothetically?'

'Would what bother me?'

'That I sleep with other women when he's away.'

Doyle regarded her silently.

'It isn't as if I'm cheating on him. He knows the truth. He even knows the women.'

'Like I said, Mrs Duncan, it's nothing to do with me. Don't feel you have to confess to me.'

She shot him an angry glance.

Doyle held her gaze. 'It's your life,' he said finally.

'Sometimes, when he's here, he watches.'

Doyle said nothing.

'Wouldn't you like that, Mr Doyle? To watch me making love to another woman. A beautiful young woman? Wouldn't you like to watch me make love to Mel?'

'I'm not a very good spectator, Mrs Duncan.'

'Would you like to join us? I expect you would. What man wouldn't?'

He shook his head again and got to his feet. 'Duty calls,' he said.

She stretched one leg out in front of him, as if to prevent him leaving.

Doyle looked down at the shapely limb, waiting until she lowered it.

What kind of fucking game was this?

'What do you expect me to say?' he murmured. 'That I envy your husband. He's got a ton of money and a beautiful wife who'll put on a show for him with another woman any time he likes. Am I supposed to be jealous?'

'Are you telling me you wouldn't want what he's got?'

Doyle shook his head.

Helen slowly withdrew her leg, allowing him to pass.

'Do you think the men who are trying to kill us are out there now?'

'I doubt it but I'm not going to take that chance.'

'What if they're watching or listening to us. The house could be bugged.'

Doyle shook his head. 'As far as we can tell there's no electronic surveillance,' he said reassuringly. 'The phone company have already done line sweeps. We've used RF detectors inside the house. No spycams either. Special Branch already had spectrum analysers in place so the men who are trying to kill you can't use laser bounce either. The place is clean.'

As Doyle reached the kitchen door he paused and looked back. 'These guys aren't interested in your conversations, Mrs Duncan, they just want you dead.'

59

BELFAST:

R ain hammered against the windows of the Fiat making it virtually impossible to see in any direction.

Daniel Kane checked his watch and tried to squint through the glass into the rain-drenched night beyond. Nothing but darkness.

From where he'd parked, he could see the lights of Belfast below him, twinkling in the foul night. He saw the landing lights of an aircraft as it swung low on its last descent into Aldergrove.

He'd parked just off the road on a narrow dirt track that led to open fields, water-logged by the last two days' persistent rain. The dirt track was rutted from the passage of farm vehicles and the ruts had filled with muddy water. The Fiat was approachable by that route but Kane knew from which direction the other car would come.

He checked his watch and murmured something irritably under his breath.

Another two hours and it would be light. The dawn would haul itself reluctantly across a sky swollen with dark clouds.

Still the rain fell.

Kane switched on the engine for a moment and allowed warm air to blow on to his windscreen. The inside of the car was misting up, thick with condensation. He wiped some away with his hand, the high-pitched squeaking filling the car.

Headlights cut through the darkness.

Kane sank further down in his seat, one hand sliding inside

his jacket to brush the butt of the Smith and Wesson 9mm, model 9 auto.

The headlights continued towards him.

Then passed by.

Just a small white van. He watched as its tail lights disappeared into the gloom then sucked in a deep, stale breath.

The tapping on the side window almost made him shout aloud in surprise. He tugged the 9mm free and pressed his face to the glass.

The figure standing outside the car was soaked. Clothes sodden by the pouring rain.

Kane hesitated a moment then reached back and opened the rear door. The figure clambered in and sat in silence for a moment.

'What the fuck are you doing?' Kane snarled. 'Why the hell didn't you park where you normally park?'

The figure in the back seat said nothing.

Kane could smell the dull stench of wet earth and something more pungent. 'Have you been walking through cow shit?' he demanded.

Still the figure said nothing.

'Come on then, get it over with,' Kane insisted. 'You were the one who wanted this fucking meeting. You told me that it was definitely Declan Leary who killed Ivor Best and Jeff Kelly. Where's the bastard now? If he's coming after me I want to know.'

He turned to face the figure. As the dark shape began to speak, a flash of lightning tore across the sky. The rain continued to hammer down.

In the back of the Fiat, the figure continued his speech.

60

CHESHAM, BUCKINGHAMSHIRE, ENGLAND:

'There's a van coming up the drive.'
Doyle touched the earpiece he was wearing as if unsure of the words he'd just heard.

When Mel repeated herself he peered through the privet hedge surrounding the orchard and saw the red vehicle making its way towards the Duncans' house.

Post van.

'I can see it, Mel,' he murmured into the pin-microphone attached to his lapel. 'Are they expecting any deliveries?'

'No.'

Doyle slid one hand inside his jacket, his fingers touching the butt of the Beretta.

Just in case.

'I'll follow it in,' he said. 'You watch yourself.'

He made his way quickly back along the narrow path that wound between the trees and opened on to a large expanse of lawn. He was two hundred yards from the house. If he moved now the occupants of the van would see him.

How many were there?

It was difficult to tell from his vantage point. He squinted and caught sight of one man.

There could be others in the back.

Doyle eased the automatic from its holster, gripping it in his fist.

The van came to a halt and the driver's side door swung open. The man who got out was dressed in the usual dark uniform of a postman. He stood looking up at the house for a moment then strode towards the front door.

Doyle slipped the safety catch off.

The newcomer rang the doorbell and waited.

'He's on his own as far as I can see,' Doyle said into his microphone. 'I'm on him. Just watch it when you open the door.'

'Got it.' Mel's voice filled his earpiece.

He saw her open the front door.

Doyle could hear snatches of their conversation through his earpiece but it was only the odd word here and there. He lowered the 9mm and began walking across the lawn towards the house.

He was halfway there when he saw the man return to the van and retrieve something. It appeared to be a box about 12 inches square.

Doyle moved more quickly now, watching as the man handed the package to Mel.

The former counter terrorist was less than a hundred yards from the van now. His eyes never left the uniformed man.

Seventy yards. Doyle was practically sprinting.

Fifty yards. The postman turned away from the door and headed back towards the van. He saw Doyle as he was preparing to climb back in.

'Hold it there,' Doyle said, raising the Beretta. He was advancing slowly now.

The man turned pale and his lower jaw dropped.

'What's in the box?' Doyle wanted to know.

The man tried to answer but all he succeeded in doing was shaking his head.

'It feels quite light,' Mel called.

'Any smell?' Doyle wanted to know.

Mel looked puzzled.

'Does it smell sweet?' Doyle snapped. 'Like marzipan?'

Like fucking Semtex.

Mel shook her head.

'What's in the fucking box?' Doyle said, his gaze still fixed on the terrified delivery man.

'I don't know,' he answered breathlessly. 'I'm only supposed to deliver what—'

'Did you bring that from the main sorting office?'

The postman nodded.

Doyle moved closer, the barrel of the Beretta still aimed at the man's head.

'What do you want to do?' Mel said, kneeling beside the package.

'Is there a sender's address on it?' Doyle wanted to know.

'No.'

Doyle took a step nearer then glanced at the postman.

'Go on, piss off, Postman Pat,' he snapped.

The relieved man clambered behind the wheel of the van and drove off, the vehicle disappearing down the drive considerably faster than it had approached.

Doyle holstered the automatic and looked first at the box then at Mel.

Her gaze was fixed on the package.

'What do you want to do?' she said again.

Doyle knelt beside the box too, scanning every inch of it for any tell-tale signs of something amiss.

Come on, you're the fucking expert. You've seen bombs close up before. Very close. Close enough to put you in hospital.

'If it *is* a bomb and it's on a timer then there's no way of knowing when it might go off,' he said. 'If whoever sent it can detonate it by remote then they could be watching us now. They could set it off whenever they like.' He looked at Mel who merely nodded.

'We don't know that it *is* a bomb,' she said, as if trying to find reassurance in her own words.

'No, you're right. And there's only one way to find out if it is or not. Open it.'

61

'Wait, let's think about this logically.' Mel stood up, her eyes never leaving the package.

'When it comes to bombs, there isn't much logic involved,' Doyle told her studying up too. 'They go off and people die. It's pretty simple.'

'And if we open that box and there *are* explosives inside then *we* die.'

'I'll do it, Mel. Just make sure that Mrs Duncan stays inside and you stay with her.'

'Doyle, you can't do that.'

He had already picked up the box and was walking across the drive towards the carefully manicured lawn.

'Get inside the house,' he shooted.

'Just leave it.'

'And what if it *is* a bomb and it *is* on a timer?' He shook his head. 'Get inside.'

She hesitated a moment longer then stepped back into the house and closed the front door.

Doyle continued across the lawn. A hundred yards from the house. He kept walking. Two hundred.

'Can you hear me, Mel?' he said, setting the box down.

Two hundred and fifty yards. That should do it. Even if the fucking box is full of explosive then the house won't suffer any damage. They'll only need a matchbox to bury you in too if it goes off.

'Mel?' he repeated.

'I can hear you, Doyle,' she said through his earpiece.

He looked back in the direction of the house. Then the

former counter terrorist regarded the object intently.

Fairly light. Nothing rattling about. Whatever was inside was either packed in something or secured to one side of the box. A couple of ounces of Semtex would be enough to destroy a car.

The box was sealed with masking tape.

'How are you going to open it?' Mel's voice sounded loud in his ear.

'Very fucking carefully,' he murmured, reaching into his jacket pocket. He pulled out a small penknife.

Come on. Get it over with. If it's going to blow, it's going to blow.

Doyle rested the blade against the tape and swallowed hard. He drew the cutting edge along the masking tape as slowly as he could, the blade slicing the tape easily.

'I'm opening it,' he said into the pin-mike.

Just like old times.

He dropped the penknife back into his pocket and slid his thumbs beneath the flaps of the box. With infinite slowness he began to raise them.

If there's a trigger attached you'll know about it pretty soon.

The flaps opened a little more. Doyle continued to raise them.

There was a smell coming from inside the box. It was rancid. Not the marzipan scent of plastic explosive. This was more pungent.

He wrinkled his nose as he opened the box wider.

There was tissue paper inside.

Doyle frowned. As he removed some of it he saw that the sheets further down were spotted with blood.

There was something at the bottom of the box. Something wrapped in sodden, red tissue paper.

Doyle retrieved the penknife and used the tip of the blade to remove the last few sheets. He gazed down at the contents of the package.

'It's not a bomb,' he said quietly.

'Thank God,' Mel murmured. 'What is it?'

'I'm bringing the box inside. I think Mrs Duncan should see this.'

CAUGHT ON CAMERA

Ward had bought the video camera in New York about eight or nine years ago. In the days when money was no object.

Now he set it up in one corner of the office, squinting through the viewfinder until he was satisfied that the cyclopean machine was trained on his desk. He readjusted the focus once again then pressed the red record button.

The tape inside the machine was a ninety-minute one. He'd return in an hour and a half and replace it. Check out what was on the first one.

He locked the office door behind him as he left.

It was 9.15 p.m.

PHOTOGRAPHIC EVIDENCE

10.50 p.m.

Ward got to his feet and made his way swiftly through the house to the back door. He paused for a moment, looking at the office.

In the darkness it seemed a hundred yards away. Almost invisible in the impenetrable gloom.

He made his way quickly along the path that connected the house to his place of work. His hand was shaking as he pushed the key into its lock and turned it.

Ward climbed the stairs and glanced at the monitor. It was blank. There were no pages overflowing from the printer.

He moved to the camcorder and checked the battery. There was still some power left in it. The tape had run out. He had a full ninety minutes to view.

But ninety minutes of what? Empty air?

As he took the camera from its tripod he wondered what he was really expecting to see on the tape.

He retreated back into the house and connected the necessary leads and wires from the camcorder to the television. Then he sat back on the sofa and pressed the play button.

For forty minutes he gazed at the screen, waiting for something to happen. He was still waiting twenty minutes later.

He fast-forwarded the remainder of the tape then slumped back wearily.

Nothing. Just an endless shot of his desk and computer. No words appearing mysteriously on the screen. No paper pumping from the printer with newly created chapters on.

Nothing.

He sucked in a deep breath.

The phenomenon, for want of a better word, seemed to happen more often at night. In the dead of night when he was sleeping.

He decided to set up the camcorder again. It was already after midnight. Whatever he imagined he might record on film, he might have a better chance of getting in the small hours.

He checked another battery for power then attached it to the camcorder and headed back out to the office where he went through the same procedure as before. He trained the lens on his desk, peering through the viewfinder like a scientist squinting through a microscope at some newly discovered organism. Then he pressed the record button and slipped quietly down the stairs.

It was 1.17 a.m.

MOVING PICTURES

Ward woke at 8.45 the next morning. He was lying on the sofa, still fully clothed, the television burbling in the background.

He could remember little of the previous night. Checking the camcorder the first time. Coming back inside the house. That was about it.

He had no idea what time he'd fallen asleep. Or blacked out. Whatever the hell he had done.

He got to his feet and wandered through to the downstairs bathroom where he splashed his face with cold water. It did little to clear his head but he could at least see a little better by the time he emerged.

With a mixture of trepidation and anticipation, Ward made his way to the back door, let himself out and made for the office. He ran up the stairs.

Sheets of paper had spilled from the printer. The screen still had words on it.

He swallowed hard and crossed to the camcorder.

The tape was still. There was nothing but blackness when he looked through the viewfinder.

He clenched his teeth, the knot of muscles at the side of his jaw pulsing. What time had the camcorder battery run out? How much did he have on tape? Thirty minutes? An hour? Had the unblinking eye of the camera caught what he wanted?

There was only one way to find out.

However, before he made his way back inside the house, he crossed to the desk, sat down and carefully numbered each newly printed page. There were over two hundred and fifty. The manuscript must be close to completion.

Ward wished he knew *how* close.

62

Helen Duncan sniffed back more tears and shook her head uncomprehendingly.

Doyle and Mel hung back, wondering whether or not to approach the woman who stood motionless inside the stable. She was gazing at a bay that was tossing its head agitatedly. Occasionally kicking out with one powerful hind leg.

'What kind of people are they?' Helen Duncan said finally.

'What I want to know is how the hell did they get inside the stables to do this?' Mel murmured quietly.

Doyle merely shook his head, his eyes fixed on the bay.

Both of its ears had been hacked off. The mane and coat around them were matted with dried blood. Flies buzzed around the horse, attracted both by the excrement in the stall but also by the open wounds.

'An animal that size isn't just going to stand there while its fucking ears are cut off, is it?' Doyle mused. 'They must have sedated it.'

Helen Duncan clapped ironically. 'You should have been a detective, Mr Doyle,' she said.

'When was the last time you were in here, Mrs Duncan?' Mel asked.

'Two days ago,' Helen Duncan said, her voice catching. 'Christ, you're meant to know where I've been, I can't move a fucking muscle without one of you following me.' She rounded angrily on the two bodyguards. 'Why did you let this happen?'

'We had no way of stopping it,' Mel answered.

'Someone breaks into my stables and cuts the ears off one

of my horses and you can't stop them. What makes you so sure you'll be able to stop them when they come after myself and my husband?'

The horse whinneyed as if in agreement.

'You'd better check the others,' Doyle said. There were two more horses in the stable. A grey and a chestnut.

Helen wiped her face hurriedly then moved to each stall in turn. The other two animals seemed unharmed although both were understandably skittish. The grey in particular tossed its head wildly as Helen reached out to touch its muzzle.

'I'll call the vet,' she said. 'He'll have to look at them. Just to be sure. They could have been given poison or anything.'

'You're lucky they didn't kill them,' Mel offered.

'They did it to show how close they can get if they want to,' Doyle said. 'How far's the stable from the house? Two hundred yards? Less? This was a warning.'

Helen Duncan glared at Doyle then stalked out of the stable and headed back towards the house.

Mel hesitated a moment then hurried after her.

Doyle remained in the stable, walking slowly back and forth between the stalls, peering intermittently at the bay. Or, more specifically at the bloodied stumps of torn flesh where its ears used to be.

He waited a moment longer then left the stable and walked slowly around the red brick house. Beyond, the fields and hills stretched away into the distance. He could also see the maze towards the bottom of the long garden. As he looked, his eyes narrowed.

'Mel,' he said into his microphone.

There was a crackle of static. 'What is it?' she asked, her voice clear in his earpiece.

'I'm going to walk around the grounds again. There's something I want to check out.'

He lit up a cigarette and began to stroll towards the maze.

63

BELFAST:

Declan Leary slid down in the driver's seat and turned up the heater, blowing more warm air into the car. The clock on the dashboard showed 5.09 a.m.

The sky was grey and smeared with banks of grubby clouds that promised more of the drizzle that had been falling since dawn first hauled itself reluctantly into the sky.

Leary watched as George Mcswain stopped the milk float, got out and took two bottles from the back of the vehicle. Mcswain hurried up the short path to the front step of the house and left the bottles then returned. He wrote something on a notepad then clambered back into the float and drove on, the engine making its familiar droning sound.

Glass clinked against glass as the float moved over several speed bumps.

Mcswain stopped the vehicle again and placed the required number of pints at the doors of each house.

Leary reached towards the passenger seat and picked up a bottle of his own. It was Lucozade. He swigged and wiped his mouth with the back of his hand.

One or two people were on the streets. On their way to work at this ungodly hour of the morning, Leary imagined. But, for the most part, Mcswain was alone as he manoeuvred along the narrow streets of the Woodvale area of the city.

Leary had been tracking him for the last two days. It had been easier than he'd thought. Once he'd found his man (courtesy of www.peoplesearch.com) it had been a small matter to keep a watch on him.

Planning. Waiting for the moment.

Leary was helped in this by the fact that Mcswain was so regimented in his movements. Driven, it seemed, by routine.

He began his milk round every morning at 4.15. It took him approximately three hours. When it was finished he would return to the depot, complete his paperwork and return home to the house he shared with his wife and two children. A boy of twelve and a girl of thirteen. He usually stayed in until six in the evening when he would go out for a drink. He returned around ten.

Like fucking clockwork.

If Mcswain knew he was being watched then he'd certainly given no indication of it.

Leary finished off his Lucozade and flipped open the glove compartment of his car. The Scorpion CZ65, a twenty-round clip already jammed into it, lay there until he needed it.

He had decided that it would be best to take the Proddie bastard out during his milk round. Early in the morning when the streets were at their most desolate.

On more than one occasion he had thought about completing the job this very morning but had finally decided against it. He could wait one more day.

Leary slipped the car into gear and, after allowing the milk float a minute's start, he followed, overtook it, then parked up once more. Just watching.

And waiting.

64

CHESHAM, BUCKINGHAMSHIRE, ENGLAND:

The sunset stained the sky crimson. It looked as if the clouds had been soaked in blood.

Doyle glanced across at the large garage as he made his way back to the house.

Joe Hendry was reversing the Mercedes 300SL through the doorway. Inside, Doyle could also see two other vehicles belonging to the Duncans. All would be checked before they were used the following day. Brake cables would be inspected, tyres would be looked at for faults and, as ever, the entire chassis and interior would be scrutinised for anything even vaguely resembling an explosive device. That was Hendry's job. The cars and everything to do with them were his province.

He had brought William Duncan home safely some two hours ago and listened while Helen Duncan related the news about the mutilated horse. Duncan himself had nodded as his wife had spoken then hugged her tightly.

Doyle had looked on impassively then decided on one more tour of the grounds before darkness threw its impenetrable blanket over the land.

As he had done earlier in the day, he had wandered as far as the maze. Except this time he had not ventured inside the privet-lined walkways. The hedges were fully eight feet high, immaculately trimmed and decorated with topiary animals that seemed to look down mockingly upon those who were foolish enough to enter their domain. The paths that turned left and right were gravel and Doyle had managed to find his way into the centre of the puzzle earlier that day, dropping pieces of cigarette packet to guide him out.

At its heart the maze boasted a delightful ornate centre-piece comprising two stone benches and sculptures of lions and swans. Like their topiary counterparts, these sentinels seemed to gaze upon newcomers with disdainful eyes. Doyle had sat and smoked a cigarette before making his way out again.

Hendry closed and locked the garage and wandered over to join Doyle. 'Maybe whoever's doing this will leave it at the horses,' the driver offered.

'Yeah, right,' Doyle said dismissively. 'No, they're not going to be happy until Duncan's six foot under. And his missis too.'

The two men made their way inside.

Doyle secured the front door.

Mel emerged from the sitting room and smiled at her colleagues.

'Are they okay?' Hendry wanted to know.

'They're just talking,' Mel explained. 'I left them to it.'

'The grounds are clear, as far as I can tell,' Doyle told her.

Mel looked at her watch. 'One of us ought to keep an eye on the monitors,' she said. 'Just in case.'

'I'll do it,' Hendry offered.

'No, you get something to eat, Joe. I'll watch,' said Doyle.

'Want some company?' Mel asked.

Doyle nodded.

65

The bank of monitors flickered and Doyle rubbed his eyes, his gaze moving slowly from one screen to the next. Every now and then he would press a button and alter the angle of a specific camera.

Mel reached over and turned on some of the security lights around the house. Others were triggered by motion sensors and would be activated if anything passed before them.

Doyle yawned and sipped his coffee, wincing when he realised it was cold.

'Boring, isn't it?' Mel said. 'All this sitting around.'

'It beats the shit out of sitting in a car,' he replied, patting the chair he sat on.

'Did you do a lot of that when you were in the CTU?'

'My share.'

'Do you still miss it?'

He nodded. 'It was all I knew,' he told her. 'It was what I was best at.'

'You seem to have taken to this kind of work very well.'

'Needs must and all that crap.'

There was a long silence between them, finally broken by Mel. 'What do you think of Mrs Duncan?' she asked smiling.

'I think *you've* got more chance with her than I have.'

Mel raised her eyebrows quizzically.

'She likes sleeping with women,' Doyle continued. 'She told me. Fuck knows why. Perhaps she was trying to shock me.'

'And did she?'

'I couldn't give a shit if she sleeps with donkeys, Mel. That's the first rule of this game, isn't it? The only thing that matters is the safety of the clients. What they get up to in their own time is *their* fucking business. Right?'

Mel regarded him silently. 'It's ironic, isn't it?' she finally murmured. 'We're expected to protect people we probably won't like. Expected to risk our lives for someone we might despise.'

'Does that bother you?'

'It's the job, isn't it?'

'And the job's all that matters?' It was Doyle's turn to look at her. 'Is this how you see yourself in ten years' time, Mel? Carrying a gun. Waiting for some mad bastard to try and kill the person you're guarding. Wondering if you're going to have to put your own life on the line to save them?'

'I haven't thought about it. What are the options? Get married? Settle down?'

'It probably wouldn't be so bad.'

'Then why haven't *you* done it?'

'I told you, this kind of thing's all I know.'

'Even if the right woman comes along?'

Doyle swallowed hard and returned his attention to the bank of monitors. 'I think she did, once,' he said softly.

'Georgie?'

Doyle nodded.

'How did she die?' Mel wanted to know.

'We were working together,' he said slowly. 'I can't remember all the details. It seems like a fucking eternity since it happened. She got shot. Simple as that. Occupational hazard.'

'Did you love her?'

Doyle smiled humourlessly. 'What difference does it make?' he said scornfully. 'We were . . . alike. There was *something* between us. I don't know what the fuck you'd call it. But it doesn't matter any more, does it?' He looked at Mel. 'You remind me of her in some ways.'

'Is that a compliment?'

He nodded.

She reached out and gently touched his hand.

He looked down and she slowly withdrew it.

'I'm sorry,' Mel told him. 'I didn't mean to pry. I just—'

'Forget it,' he said, cutting her short. 'No harm done.' He adjusted two of the cameras scanning the grounds then looked back at Mel. 'What about you? How come the right bloke hasn't turned up yet?'

'Married to the job, I suppose.'

'And if he did? Would you give it all up to play the little woman?'

'Maybe. I'm not even sure what I want out of life any more.'

'Looks like we're *both* fucked.'

Mel grinned. 'Kindred spirits,' she chuckled.

Doyle focused on one of the monitors. His eyes narrowed.

'Perhaps you and I should—'

Doyle interrupted. 'Look at that,' he said, pointing a finger at the screen that held his attention. 'Is it a shadow?'

'Which camera is it?' she wanted to know.

'The one near the swimming pool.'

A dark shape was clearly visible now, scuttling quickly along the side of the pool then back into the welcoming darkness.

'Zoom in,' Mel said. 'That's no shadow.'

Doyle hit the necessary button. The image became larger rather than sharper.

'The sensor lights around there are motion activated,' Mel said. 'How come they haven't been tripped?'

Doyle squinted at the shape. 'It's definitely a man,' he said. He reached forward and drew his index finger around the outline of the shape. 'And he's carrying something.'

They both recognised it immediately. The outline of the AK47 assault rifle was unmistakable.

The shape moved, its motion fluid.

'Stay with him,' Mel murmured.

There was movement on another monitor. Two more shapes.

'By the stables,' Doyle said.

'And on the drive,' Mel added. 'Four of them, at least.'

Doyle pulled the Beretta from its holster and worked the slide, chambering a round. 'You'd better get Hendry,' he said. 'It looks like we've got some work to do.'

On the bank of monitors Doyle counted six figures moving

quickly and furtively around the grounds, all heading towards the house.

'I'll call the police, get some help,' Mel said, snatching up the phone.

The line was dead. 'No calls tonight,' she said. 'They've cut the wires.'

'Try your mobile.'

She dialled but a shriek of static forced her to move the Nokia away from her ear. 'They've jammed the frequency,' she told him.

'Party time,' Doyle murmured under his breath.

The dark figures continued towards the house.

66

'Get upstairs now,' Mel said, gesturing towards the Duncans who looked on helplessly.

'We could help you,' William Duncan offered.

Mel shook her head. 'Please do as I say,' she insisted. 'Lock yourselves in your room and stay down. Don't go near the windows.'

Duncan slid an arm around his wife's shoulder and the two of them made their way hurriedly through the hall and up the broad staircase to the first storey of the house.

Mel was holding the small automatic that she'd taken from her shoulder holster. Doyle glanced at it and saw how comfortably it fitted into her slender hand. It was a Heckler and Koch VP70. He knew it held eighteen 9mm rounds in its magazine.

'Still coming,' shouted Hendry who was posted before the screens. 'I can see eight of them now. All armed as far as I can tell.'

'How do you want to play this?' Doyle said. 'Go out to meet them or let them come to us?'

'Let them come,' Mel said. 'It'll be more difficult for them to get inside. We can cover the entrances.'

'Not all of them,' Doyle said warily.

Mel looked at him for a moment then headed off towards the sitting room.

The first burst of automatic fire raked the building.

Doyle spun round in the direction of the shots.

Two windows shattered and part of one frame was blasted to matchwood by the impact of the heavy-grain bullets.

'Put the interior lights out and all the exterior ones on,' he called to Hendry, moving towards one of the broken windows. 'We'll be able to see them but they won't be able to see us.'

Hendry nodded and hit a number of switches. Immediately the area within a hundred yards of the house was illuminated by the cold, white glare of more than a dozen security flood-lights.

Doyle saw several of the oncoming figures freeze, caught like moths in a torch beam. He took his chance.

The former counter terrorist swung the Beretta into position and pumped the trigger. The sound was deafening as the 9mm spewed its deadly load towards the attackers.

Two went down. There were shouts of anger and surprise from the others. Doyle fired again. Another of the men was hit, his body spinning round violently as the slug caught him in the shoulder, pulverised his collar bone and dropped him like a stone. He tried to crawl away, leaving a trail of blood behind him.

Another burst of automatic fire tore into the house. Doyle ducked as several bullets ripped over his head and drilled into the wall of the room, blasting chunks of plaster free and sending more broken glass showering on to the expensive carpet.

He could smell cordite and gunpowder.

Just like old times.

There was more firing from another part of the house. He recognised the sound of the VP70. Mel chose her targets as carefully as she could and shot down another of the furious attackers.

More automatic fire. Doyle heard fresh glass shattering.

This was fucking crazy. There was no way three of them could cover every part of a house this size.

He glanced out of the window and fired again, the muzzle flash from the 9mm momentarily searing his retina. Spent shell cases spun into the air and landed on the carpet beside him.

'There's more of them over by the stables,' Hendry shouted, gazing at a monitor. 'Another two at least.'

Doyle himself had shot three. Mel another two.

'How many of these bastards are there?' Doyle hissed under his breath.

Doyle was about to snatch another look at the garden when a concentrated burst of fire sent him diving for the floor. Bullets blasted holes in the walls and obliterated ornaments. Several hit a sofa and stuffing exploded from it like innards from a gut-shot body.

More firing. Part of the garden was plunged into darkness. 'They're shooting out the lights,' Hendry yelled.

'This is bullshit,' snarled Doyle. Then, into his microphone, 'Mel, they're going to pin us down in here.'

No answer.

'Mel,' he shouted.

He heard a thunderous blast in his earpiece and winced.

'I can hear you, Doyle,' she said breathlessly.

'I'm going outside,' he said.

'No, stay in here.'

'You want to die like a rat in a fucking trap?' he snarled.

Silence.

Doyle scrambled to his feet and, ducking low, he scuttled through the house towards the front door.

He could see nothing moving in the darkness outside.

Just because you can't see it doesn't mean it's not there.

More gunfire, from the rear of the house.

Doyle could feel his heart thudding that little bit faster against his ribs.

'What are you doing?'

The voice made him look round. William Duncan was standing at the top of the stairs.

'You were told to stay up there and keep your fucking head down,' Doyle called back.

'I can help you,' Duncan insisted. He was already advancing down the stairs.

'Doyle.' He heard his name in his earpiece.

'I'm going out there, Mel,' he told her, his hand already on the lock of the front door. 'They'll box us in and blow the fucking place to pieces. It's only a matter of time before they get in.'

'You watch yourself,' Mel told him.

Duncan was at the bottom of the stairs by now. He saw Doyle lift his trouser leg and check the .38 tucked in the ankle holster there.

There was another thunderous roar in Doyle's earpiece. More gunfire.

'Let me help you,' said Duncan forcefully.

'All right,' Doyle snapped. 'Lock this behind me.'

67

The night air felt cool against Doyle's skin. He glanced quickly left and right to check it was clear. As he stepped away from the door he heard the bolts being slid into place behind him.

At least Duncan was doing as he was told.

There was little cover between the house and the trees that lined the driveway but Doyle sprinted towards them with a speed he'd forgotten he had.

He reached the first and pressed himself up against the damp bark, looking back at the house.

Apart from the odd bursts of fire from the attackers (who he guessed now numbered about six) and the occasional return shots from Mel or Hendry, the night seemed relatively still.

Doyle pressed the magazine-release button on the 9mm and saw that he was down to three slugs. He slammed a fresh, fifteen-shot clip into the butt and worked the slide, chambering a round.

Now. Think this through. Don't fuck it up.

He peered through the gloom towards the house and beyond it in the direction of the swimming pool. Nothing moving.

There were trees planted thickly around the path that led to the pool.

A hundred, two hundred yards away?

He could make it if he ran fast enough. And what bigger incentive was there than getting caught in the sweep of an AK47?

Doyle drew a deep breath and sped off across the grass. He heard voices shouting in a language he didn't recognise. At first he couldn't work out which direction they were coming from.

Straight ahead. Behind the trees and the low wall that ran along-side the path.

Doyle reached the trees and dropped down, the Beretta gripped firmly in his fist. From his vantage point he could see four of the attackers gathered around the rear of the house. Three were attempting to clamber through a broken window into the building itself. There was another close to the swimming pool, apparently reloading.

Where the hell were the other two?

Doyle could feel his heart hammering against his ribs.

Come on. Come on.

He looked towards the house. One of the men was now inside. His two companions were attempting to follow him.

Doyle held the pin microphone between his thumb and forefinger and pulled it close to his mouth. 'Mel,' he whispered, looking round.

Silence.

'Mel, can you hear me?'

Still nothing.

He watched as the second attacker slipped inside.

'Mel, they're inside the house,' he said, raising his voice a little more. 'Check the fucking monitors.'

Close to him he heard words barked in a guttural voice. When he turned he saw one of the remaining men.

Two were inside. Another was about to join them. One more moving up from the direction of the swimming pool. A fifth just beyond the wall behind which he now crouched.

Where the fuck is the other one?

He wondered if the other attacker might be at the front of the building. Perhaps he was trying to break in there. Force the defenders to split up.

The metallic rattle of a cocking lever cut through the night.

Doyle turned to see the sixth man leering at him.

The AK47 he held was levelled and ready to fire.

68

D oyle knew he was going to die.
From six feet away, even if he was a complete fucking idiot, there was no way his opponent could miss. Not with a submachine gun on auto. The weapon fired over seven hundred rounds a minute and the slightest pressure on the trigger could empty the thirty-round magazine in seconds.

The barrel yawned before him, ready to spew out its deadly load.

As if he were moving in slow motion, Doyle swung the Beretta up, preparing to fire.

You'll go with me, you fucker.

There was a high-pitched whoosh just above Doyle's head. It reminded him of the sound a bullet makes when it parts air. But there was no accompanying bang.

He heard a dull thud and the man facing him dropped the Kalashnikov. For interminable seconds he remained on his feet, his bulging eyes still locked on Doyle.

Blood ran in thin ribbons from both his nostrils. Only then did the former counter terrorist realise why.

The arrow had pierced the man's throat just below the chin and erupted another foot from the back of his neck. Its 30-inch, fibre-glass shaft had penetrated to the flight. The pointed end dripped blood.

There was another similar sound and Doyle saw a second arrow thud into the man's chest. He fell backwards and lay still.

'What the fuck . . . ?' Doyle gazed at the corpse then heard the sound of movement close to him. He turned, the automatic pointed at the noise.

William Duncan scrambled across the damp grass towards him, the longbow gripped in his fist, another arrow already held in position. 'I thought you needed some help,' the industrialist said, glancing at the dead man.

'I told you to stay in the house,' said Doyle.

'If I had you'd be dead now.'

Doyle looked at Duncan but said nothing.

There was an eruption of fire close to them. Bullets drilled into the wall behind which they sheltered and Doyle instinctively put out a hand to push Duncan closer to the earth.

The smell of cordite filled the night air.

Doyle motioned for Duncan to remain still as another burst of fire raked the wall. Splinters of stone flew up and showered the two men.

Doyle heard a shout, then a metallic click as the hammer of the AK47 slammed down on an empty chamber. He swiftly rose to his feet and caught the fifth man in his sights.

Doyle pumped the trigger five times. Bullets hit the man in the face, chest and shoulder, drilled through and erupted in several places leaving exit wounds the size of a man's fist. Blood sprayed into the air and the man toppled backwards, arms flailing.

Doyle swung himself over the wall, scuttled across to the body and put one more shot squarely between the eyes of his opponent. The blast took off most of the back of his head.

The former counter terrorist snatched up the Kalashnikov and motioned to Duncan to join him. 'Hey, Robin Hood,' he murmured, beckoning to the industrialist. 'Follow me. And keep your fucking head down.'

They scurried back towards the house.

69

'They're inside.' Joe Hendry spoke quietly and without panic.

'How many?' Mel wanted to know.

'Three of them.'

'Where's Duncan?'

'I don't know.'

'Jesus Christ, Joe. He could be dead by now. Contact Doyle. Find out if he's got him.'

'Doyle went outside, remember? If Duncan's out there with him chances are we're all out of work by now.'

Mel didn't answer. She hurried along the gallery landing that overlooked the main hallway of the house, glancing over the balustrade occasionally, the 9mm gripped tightly in her fist.

Two of the intruders walked into the hall and Mel caught sight of the AK47s they were carrying. She swung the VP70 up and sighted it, pumping the trigger.

The first two shots caught the leading man in the shoulder and cheek. He dropped like a stone, his companion spinning round, finger tightening on the trigger.

A blast from the Kalashnikov deafened Mel and she dropped to her knees as bullets tore into the wall, pieces of plaster flying into the air all around her.

She fired again. Three shots. All well placed. One in the stomach doubled the attacker up. The second slammed into the top of his skull and the third clipped his elbow, shattering bone and causing him to drop the assault rifle. He toppled backwards on to the polished wood of the hall floor, already awash with the blood of his companion. Both men lay still.

Mel advanced slowly down the stairs.

Where was the other one? Hendry had said three were inside.

Her earpiece crackled and she put a hand to it as if to silence it. The door to her left was open. The third attacker could be there. Waiting.

Mel moved a little further down the stairs, her heart thudding against her ribs.

There were two thunderous blasts from her left. A muffled groan.

She swung her automatic up and sighted it.

The body of the third intruder fell face down at her feet, two bullets in the back of his head.

Doyle stepped over the body, glanced at the other dead men then up the stairs in Mel's direction.

She had him in her sights. He nodded and she lowered the weapon.

'Is that all of them?' Doyle said, indicating the bodies in the hall.

'Joe said three got inside,' she told him. 'I don't know about the rest.'

'Two more dead outside,' Doyle informed her. He tapped his microphone. 'Joe. Anything moving?'

There was a hiss of static.

'Nothing that I can see,' said Hendry finally.

'There were six,' Doyle murmured. 'The other one's either fucked off or he's waiting in the grounds.'

'There's nothing showing on any of the monitors,' Hendry offered.

'We'll give it an hour,' Doyle said quietly. 'Then we'll check the grounds again. Every inch of them.'

70

Morning had dawned grey and with the threat of rain but, Doyle was relieved to see, without the presence of any more men intent on killing William Duncan and his wife.

For the time being anyway.

The drive into central London had taken the former counter terrorist just over an hour.

The phone call that had made the journey necessary in the first place had been both unexpected and puzzling.

As Doyle brought the car to a halt outside the building in Hill Street he sat behind the wheel for a moment, looking up at the former town house of John Paul Getty, wondering why he was here. Wondering why he was back at the headquarters of the Counter Terrorist Unit.

He shut off the engine and walked to the door, pressing the buzzer.

'Doyle, 239 . . .' He corrected himself.

Old habits died hard, didn't they? Forget your code number. You don't work here any more. Remember? They binned you off.

'Sean Doyle,' he said into the grille. 'I've got an appointment with Jonathan Parker.' There was a loud buzz and the door opened. Doyle stepped inside and the door closed behind him.

There was a new receptionist on duty. Mid-thirties. Shoulder-length blond hair. Pretty. Easy smile.

Old habits.

'I've got an appointment with Parker,' Doyle said.

The receptionist smiled again. 'I'll take you through,' she said, getting to her feet.

'I know the way,' Doyle told her, heading for the all-too-familiar door. He knocked. Thought about walking straight in but hesitated.

'Come in,' called Parker.

Doyle walked in and looked blankly at his old superior.

On the sofa to his right sat another familiar figure. Sir Anthony Pressman ran appraising eyes over the former counter terrorist then returned to the file he had balanced on his lap.

Doyle looked at the Home Secretary then back at Parker.

'Take a seat, Doyle,' Parker said.

Doyle hesitated a moment then accepted. 'Why the welcoming committee?' he wanted to know, glancing at Pressman.

'There have been certain developments,' the Home Secretary said without looking up. 'We felt they should be discussed.'

'Declan Leary's been arrested,' Parker interjected. 'He's in police custody in Belfast right now. They got him two days ago.'

'He wants to deal,' Pressman added. 'Presently he's looking at life for his part in recent Real IRA activities. He says he has information that would be valuable to the security forces. He's willing to trade that information for a lighter sentence. The Prime Minister is prepared to listen to a plea for clemency in view of the way the peace talks in Northern Ireland are progressing.'

Doyle considered each man carefully and silently.

'As you know there are many IRA victims hidden in secret graves in both the Six Counties and the Republic,' Parker continued. 'Some dating back over fifteen years. Leary's prepared to reveal the whereabouts of ten of these graves in exchange for leniency. That's the deal he's proposing.'

'Naturally the Provisionals are anxious to prevent him revealing information of this kind,' Pressman said. 'Our latest intelligence reports indicate that they have sanctioned one, possibly two, of their own men to eliminate Leary before any of this information can be disclosed.'

Doyle looked at each of the men then snorted. 'So fucking what?' he said. 'What's any of that got to do with me? I don't work for this organisation any more, remember? You threw me out.' He began to get to his feet.

'Doyle, wait,' Parker said, raising a hand.

'We have a proposition to put to you,' Pressman added.

Doyle reached for a cigarette and lit it. 'I'm all fucking ears,' he spat.

'Full reinstatement in the Counter Terrorist Unit,' Parker told him.

Doyle shook his head. 'Fuck you,' he said. 'Both of you.'

'*Full* reinstatement,' Parker pressed. 'You'd be back on active service within twenty-four hours.'

'Leary needs protection,' Pressman told him. 'We're not sure that the RUC are equipped to offer it to the degree necessary. *You* are. Besides, I'm not prepared to risk the number of officers that could be involved in this operation.'

Doyle drew slowly on the cigarette then blew out a stream of smoke. 'So what are you saying?' he said finally. 'I go back to work for the CTU just so I can hold the hand of some cunt who tried to kill me?'

'You're the best equipped operative for this job, Doyle,' Pressman told him.

'Bollocks. I'm expendable. That's *my* best qualification.'

'So, what's your answer?' Parker asked. As he spoke he slipped his hand into one of the drawers of his desk and pulled something out. He dropped it on to the polished wood in front of Doyle.

It was a slim leather wallet.

Doyle recognised it. He picked it up and flipped it open. His ID.

'In or out?' Parker persisted.

Doyle slipped the wallet into his jacket pocket. 'There's one condition. I pick my own back-up team.'

'There are many capable agents in the organisation that you can work with and—' Pressman began.

'Fuck that,' snapped Doyle, cutting him short. '*My* people or forget it. You can start digging the hole for Leary now.'

Pressman nodded. 'Very well,' he said stiffly. 'But they'd better be reliable, Doyle.'

Doyle got to his feet. 'Trust me,' he smiled.

IMAGES AND IMAGININGS

Ward sat watching the tape, his hands clasped together as if in prayer.

Forty minutes of his empty desk then the picture began to break up. He guessed that was when the battery had begun to lose power.

He exhaled deeply, eyes still on the screen. There was something dark in one corner of the picture.

He moved nearer the television set, trying to get a better view. He still couldn't see.

He hit the pause button and tried to study the still frame more closely.

What was the dark shape? He tried to run his index finger around it. To trace the outline.

He re-wound the tape slightly. Moved it on frame by frame. One second an empty office, the next, the dark shape looming over his chair. Unformed. Somehow intangible.

He saw an oval shape at the top of it. Then it broadened. There was another thinner strand to one side.

Ward re-wound again. Watched again. And again.

The shape . . . Jesus Christ. It was a shadow. The oval shape was a head. The broader part the torso. The thinner strand an arm.

A shadow. His own?

The tape had run out after forty-odd minutes. He had blacked out around 1.55. And . . . and what?

He'd blacked out. On the sofa. Inside the house. If that was the case then the shadow could not be his.

So what did he have before him? A benevolent and very

creative burglar? A figure who crept into his office every night and wrote thirty pages for him?

He turned over the possibilities in his mind.

If the blackout, and others like it that he'd been experiencing, were manifesting themselves as some form of short-term memory loss then that might be an explanation. He passed out. Lost consciousness, or at least his grip on the consciousness that he knew and then he worked. Simple.

Ward shook his head. The writing had taken place between 2.00 and 5.00. It was physically impossible to complete thirty pages in less time than that. Wasn't it?

He studied the shadow once more. It was that of a man. Wasn't it? If not a man then what?

Ward ran a hand through his hair. Perhaps he was closer to insanity than he thought.

It was his own shadow. There was no other logical explanation for it.

He would try the camcorder again that night. The answer was there somewhere.

And he had to find it.

71

It had taken Doyle less time than he'd thought to persuade Mel and Hendry to join him. He had also encountered less opposition from Brian Cartwright than he'd expected. The head of Cartwright Security had agreed to release two of his most valued employees with a minimum of fuss.

As for William Duncan and his wife, they were no longer Doyle's concern. As he sat in the back of the car watching the all-too-familiar Belfast landmarks passing him, his mind was focused on just one thing. Declan Leary.

Almost unconsciously the counter terrorist touched his thigh, remembering where Leary's knife had penetrated. He massaged it through his faded jeans. The leather of his jacket creaked as he moved.

Beside him Mel was also dressed in jeans. They were tucked into black suede boots that reached to her knees. Her short, black jacket was undone to reveal a tight, white T-shirt, and the strap of her shoulder holster was visible as she moved.

Hendry brought the car to a halt and prepared to get out but Doyle put a hand on his shoulder. 'Stay here, Joe,' he said. 'This won't take long.'

'What about me?' Mel wanted to know.

'Come in with me.'

Mel nodded and clambered out of the car behind him.

The two of them walked unchallenged through the police station, Doyle merely flipping his ID at whoever moved to stop them.

As he drew nearer the room he sought, a large figure emerged from an office nearby.

Chief Inspector Peter Robinson looked quizzically at Doyle for a moment then at Mel.

'You got my call,' Doyle said. 'I want to see Leary.'

'There's no one with him,' Robinson answered. 'Help yourself. Just hit the four-digit code on the key pad beside the door.'

Doyle nodded.

'Do you need me in there with you?' Mel asked.

'If you want to come in that's fine. Otherwise you can watch through there.' He nodded in the direction of the open doorway to the office next to the interview room. There was a two-way mirror stretching the length of the wall. Through it he could see Declan Leary.

'Time to renew old acquaintances,' said Doyle and jabbed the four digits into the key pad.

The interview-room door opened with a hydraulic hiss and Doyle stepped inside.

The room smelled of stale cigarettes and coffee, and contained a wooden table and two chairs.

Leary looked up as Doyle entered, his eyes narrowing.

Yeah, recognise me, do you, you bastard? I'm the one who killed your fucking mate and almost got you too.

'Declan Leary,' Doyle said, a faint smile on his lips.

'Do I know you?' the Irishman said, uninterestedly.

'We've met. Briefly. How's your sister?'

Leary looked puzzled.

'Good-looking girl as I remember,' Doyle persisted.

'Who the fuck are you?'

'I'm your babysitter. I work for the Counter Terrorist Unit.'

Leary grunted dismissively. 'Am I supposed to be impressed?' he muttered.

'No. Just grateful. I'm supposed to keep you alive, you piece of shit. Save you from your own people.'

'Which people would they be?'

'The Provos. You know what I'm talking about. What's the matter, lose your fucking bottle when they caught you? Couldn't face the thought of doing a twenty stretch? Is that why you're prepared to grass up your mates?'

'I don't know what you're talking about.'

'The graves, Leary. You're going to tell us where they are and who's in them. What'll you get in return? New identity? A five stretch maybe? At least your brother had the balls to do his time. Before someone blew his fucking head off.'

'Who are you?' Leary snarled, getting to his feet.

'Sit down,' Doyle sneered.

Leary did as he was told.

'Understand one thing,' Doyle said slowly. 'I couldn't give a flying fuck if the IRA kill you, if you end up getting arse-fucked in prison for the rest of your life or if you walk under a bus. But, for the time being, it's my job to keep you alive and I intend to do that. When I say I'm going to do something I do it.'

'You're going to protect me, are you? How touching.'

'Only until you're not needed any more. Until you become irrelevant again.' Doyle drew the Beretta 9mm from his shoulder holster and aimed it at Leary's head. 'And when that happens, we'll talk. Just you and me.'

'I remember you,' Leary breathed, his gaze moving from the barrel of the automatic to Doyle and back again.

'You should.'

'How's the leg?' sneered the Irishman.

Doyle lashed out with the pistol and caught Leary across the face with it. The impact sent him toppling from his chair. He hit the ground hard, blood running from his split bottom lip.

'You bastard,' he spat, wiping the crimson fluid away with the back of his hand.

Doyle nodded. 'Spot on. But *you* can call me Doyle.'

72

Mel guessed that the dirt track leading to the house was close to a hundred yards long. On either side of it towered high hedges. Beyond those lay fields. The road at the bottom of the muddy thoroughfare was barely wide enough to allow the passage of two vehicles moving in opposite directions.

Positioned more than twenty-five miles from Belfast, the safe house was perfect. It was a white painted building with a slate roof, although many of the slates were missing. There was a small garden to the rear, again protected from the fields by tall hedges. To the front of the building was a rutted, mud-slicked area.

It was here that Joe Hendry had parked the car. He'd thought about leaving it in the garage but hadn't been 100 per cent sure that the rickety construction wouldn't come crashing down on the car. In the end he'd decided to leave the vehicle out in the open.

Mel could see it now, the rain bouncing on its chassis. She was standing in the sitting room of the sparsely furnished house looking out at the countryside.

Doyle was in the kitchen finishing his breakfast. Hendry was upstairs sleeping.

'You never told me your name.'

The words came from behind her and she turned slowly to look at Declan Leary. He was tied to a chair in one corner of the room.

'Is it important?' she wanted to know.

'It might be. You never know how long we might be together here. I know *his* name.' Leary jerked his head in the direction of the kitchen. 'But not yours.'

'My name's Blake.'

'You got a first name or couldn't your parents afford one?'

'Mel.'

'What's that short for?'

'Melissa.'

'Very nice. What is it between you and Doyle? Is he fucking you?' Leary grinned.

Mel took a step towards the Irishman. 'What do you think?' she said quietly.

'I think if he is then he's a lucky man. You're a grand-looking woman.'

'I'll take that as a compliment.'

'That's how it was meant.' Again he smiled.

'Why don't you shut the fuck up.'

Mel turned as she heard Doyle's voice from the kitchen. The counter terrorist wandered into the room and glanced contemptuously at Leary.

'He has a way about him, doesn't he?' said the Irishman, looking at Mel. 'You're a real charmer, Doyle.'

'And *you* talk too much.'

'I was just making conversation with the lady. Sorry if you object to me talking to your girlfriend.'

Doyle smiled humourlessly. 'You make the most of it,' he murmured. 'It might not be so easy to talk with a gun barrel stuck down your throat.'

'Is that what you've got planned for me?'

'I didn't mean me. I meant whoever the Provos send after you. Your little revelations aren't going to go down too well with them.'

'It must be a pain for you, Doyle. Having to protect a man who nearly killed you.'

Mel looked quizzically at Doyle.

'It's part of the job,' the counter terrorist told his captive. 'That's all you are, Leary. A job. Nothing more.'

He hooked a thumb in the direction of the kitchen. 'There's

some breakfast if you want it, Mel,' Doyle said. 'I'll watch this
prick for a while.'

Mel nodded and wandered into the other room.

Doyle crossed to the window and looked out at the muddy
yard and the track that stretched away from the house. In
the sky, rain clouds were gathering menacingly. Doyle lit up
a cigarette and sucked hard on it.

'Have you got one of those to spare?' Leary asked.

Doyle looked at him for a moment. 'No,' he said. 'I wouldn't
give *you* the steam off my shit.' He took another drag on the
cigarette and blew the smoke in Leary's direction. 'So, what
made you bottle it, Leary? Why the deal? Was it just for a
lighter sentence?'

'What the fuck do you care?'

'I don't, I'm just curious.'

'I haven't got anything to be ashamed of.'

'You're selling out your own people.'

'And they're selling out their own *country*. Sinn Fein couldn't
give a fuck about what's happening here. This is my country.
I don't want it run by Proddies and Brits.'

'Things change.'

'Not if I can help it. At least I can say I tried. I didn't
surrender *my* principles.'

'Very philosophical. Is that what you're going to say to the
Provo hitmen who bag you?'

'It's your job to make sure they don't.'

Doyle nodded and blew out more smoke. 'Then you'd
better hope I'm good at my job,' he said. 'Or you're going to
end up in the same kind of grave as you're supposed to show
us.'

DEADLOCK

Ward couldn't work. He had sat at his desk for over three hours staring at the screen, the keyboard and the plastic carriage clock.

Nothing came. No words flowed.

At 1.16 p.m. he gave up and retreated inside the house. There were two messages on the answerphone but he didn't bother to listen to them. Instead he made his way into the sitting room and poured himself a large measure of Glenfiddich. Then another.

He wanted to get drunk. Wanted to fall asleep but it seemed no matter how hard he tried, he could not drink himself into the oblivion he sought so badly.

His mind was spinning. Events of the past few weeks. What was going on in his life?

He smiled wanly. 'Your life,' he told himself, 'is collapsing around your fucking ears. And so is your sanity.' He laughed humourlessly.

He didn't want to be in the house surrounded by his thoughts. He knew he needed to escape, albeit fleetingly.

He wandered out into the hall and scooped his car keys out of the small dish beside the front door. It took him fifteen minutes to drive to the cinema. All the way over, the cassette-player blasted loudly and Ward sang along occasionally, joining in the words that ripped from the speakers.

He parked and sat motionless behind the wheel for a moment.

'When you get home, your novel might be finished,' he said to himself. He laughed loudly. A little *too* loudly. There was desperation in the sound, not joy.

A WELCOME DARKNESS

Ward stood looking at the electronic board that carried the titles and times of the films showing at the multiplex. The newest comedy from the Farrelly Brothers, an adaptation of a bestselling novel (there was always one of those), some mindless Steven Seagal action picture.

Not much choice and he'd seen most of them already.

Then he noticed with delight that there was a special one-day presentation of *La Reine Margot*. He'd seen it before, he owned it on video, but it was a welcome alternative to the other dross on display.

The girl behind the cash-desk window eyed him warily as she gave him his ticket.

'You know where to go by now, don't you?' she said, attempting a joke.

Ward smiled and nodded.

There were few people at the cinema. One of the advantages of being able to attend in the afternoons.

He found the screen he wanted and selected his seat. Two other people came in before the picture began but, thankfully, they sat at the back of the auditorium.

The darkness closed around Ward as the film began. And he welcomed it.

PRODUCTIVITY

I t had happened again.

Ward didn't count the pages. He didn't know whether to feel gratitude or bewilderment at what had happened. He merely glanced at the desk and its contents.

It was almost 5.30 p.m.

73

M el was the first to hear the noise. She assumed it was just the beams of the house settling. Expanding with the constant downpour of rain. Nevertheless she stood motionless on the landing of the safe house and looked up.

The white ceiling was discoloured in places, the paintwork peeling. Especially around the entrance to the attic. There was a single rusty ring in the hatch. A small pole with a metal hook could be used to pull it open. Doyle had clambered up there when they'd first arrived, and according to him all that was up there was some battered furniture, cardboard boxes full of old magazines and Betamax video tapes and a water tank. All covered by a layer of dust.

Mel wondered if the water tank was responsible for the noise. She stood still a moment longer then walked slowly towards the window at the end of the narrow landing.

Cupping her eyes to her face she peered out into the night. She could barely see ten yards in the gloom. The rain that had been hammering down for most of the day and night did little to help visibility. She knew that Joe Hendry was somewhere out there. Doubtless complaining about the weather and wondering how long it would take him to dry off in front of the two-bar electric fire that provided most of the heat inside the house.

Doyle too was wandering around in the gloom. He'd already made two treks around the building, on one occasion walking as far as the end of the dirt track that connected to the road beyond. Mel had accompanied him, watching as he scrutinised every single inch of hedgerow, checking for anywhere that might provide cover.

The house possessed three security lights on its battered walls but none of them were switched on.

Mel heard the sound again. This time she was certain that it came from above her.

She slid a hand to the butt of her pistol and pulled it gently from the polished leather. Again she stood motionless, ears alert.

The noise was definitely coming from the attic.

Mice?

'Mel.'

The sound of her name startled her but she didn't move, merely held up a hand to silence the source of the voice.

She beckoned Doyle up the stairs then raised one index finger as a sign for him to remain quiet.

The counter terrorist moved swiftly to join her.

Mel tapped her ear then pointed at the peeling paintwork above them.

Doyle looked at her quizzically.

She mouthed the words, 'Something moving.'

Doyle pulled the 9mm automatic from its shoulder holster and nodded, his own gaze now fixed on the ceiling.

'Everything all right,' he called, raising his voice slightly.

'Fine,' she answered, also increasing the volume of her response.

From above there was another creak. Louder this time. It was a foot or so in front of him.

He raised the Beretta, following the sound with the barrel.

Another creak.

Mel also raised her pistol and trained it at the noise.

A louder creak.

Doyle opened fire. Six shots drilled into the ceiling blasting pieces of plaster and timber in all directions. Empty shell cases spun from the Beretta and landed with a metallic clink on the wooden floor next to the counter terrorist.

He waited a moment, the thunderous retorts still ringing in his ears, the smell of cordite stinging his nose.

Blood began dripping slowly through two of the holes. It puddled on the landing.

Doyle reached for the hooked pole and tugged at the rusty ring in the attic hatch. The body fell with a loud thump and lay before him.

The counter terrorist lowered his pistol and trained it on the corpse. There was a Browning Hi-power gripped in one fist.

One of Doyle's bullets had hit the man in the thigh. Another in the stomach. A third in the neck just below the left earlobe.

'How the hell did he get in?' Mel wanted to know.

Doyle didn't answer.

'How did he know we were here?' Mel persisted. 'The only people who knew our location were the RUC.'

Doyle knelt beside the body and rifled through the dead man's pockets, finally pulling out a wallet which he flipped open.

'Call CI Robinson,' he said, his face set in hard lines. 'I want that bastard here now.'

74

D oyle stood beside the body, watching as Chief Inspector Peter Robinson took in the scene. 'Daniel Kane,' he said, tossing the wallet at the RUC man. 'Name ring a bell?'

'I don't know what you're talking about, Doyle,' Robinson protested. 'What you should be asking yourself is how he managed to get inside this bloody house. You were meant to protect Leary. How the hell did Kane get in here?'

'Perhaps he had a helping hand.'

'Meaning what?'

'Oh come on, Robinson, don't bullshit me.' Doyle took a menacing step towards the CI. 'The only people who knew where Leary was going to be held were me and my team and two or three of your boys. Now I know that no one connected with me opened their gob so that narrows it down, doesn't it?'

'What the hell are you trying to say?'

'That someone grassed us up. Somebody in *your* organisation gave Kane the whereabouts of this fucking safe house so that he could get inside and kill Leary. You've got a rat in your cellar, Robinson. You'd better find them and quick.'

'That's absurd.'

'Is it? Then how did Kane know where Leary was?'

'There's nothing to link Kane and Leary.'

'Leary's brother was killed by Kane. Leary himself had murdered a number of Daniel Kane's men. I'd call that a link, wouldn't you, *Chief Inspector*?' He emphasised the last two words with disdain. 'I read the files.'

Robinson exhaled deeply. 'There's no proof he was tipped off as to Leary's whereabouts.'

'Give me a break,' Doyle snapped. 'How big's the Six Counties? And out of all that space, all those places, on the first night Leary's in a safe house a member of a rival terrorist organisation just *happens* to stumble on this place. Fuck off. Someone pointed him in this direction. They might as well have put the fucking gun in his hand. For all I know, they did. And if it's happened once, it'll happen again.'

'What do you intend to do?'

'That's my business.'

'He's still my prisoner, Doyle.'

'Not any more. Not as long as you've got an informer working with you. From now on, *I'll* decide where Leary's kept. I was hired to make sure the bastard stayed alive long enough to supply the relevant info and that's exactly what I'm going to do.'

'It's not up to you. You have to report to me and—'

'Bullshit. We're moving out of here tonight. I'll make sure Leary shows me the sites of the ten graves. When he has, I'll phone through their locations. When all ten are revealed I'll give you a time and place where you can pick him up.'

'You can't do that,' protested Robinson.

Doyle took a step towards the policeman. 'Don't tell me what I can or can't do,' he hissed. 'This is my fucking job and from now on I do it *my* way.' The counter terrorist walked to the top of the stairs then paused and looked back at Robinson. 'If it's any consolation I want Leary dead as much as you.'

'Why should *I* want him dead?' Robinson asked, swallowing hard.

'Four years ago your daughter was killed in a bomb blast. Responsibility for that bomb was claimed by the Real IRA. A cell known to contain Declan Leary. You tipped off Kane, didn't you?'

There was a long silence.

'How did you know about my daughter?' Robinson said finally, his voice cracking.

'I did some checking. It's part of the job. Did you really think that Kane was going to get past *me*?'

Robinson didn't answer.

'Don't try to find us until this is over,' Doyle said. He hurried off down the stairs.

Robinson continued to gaze down at the bullet-riddled body of Daniel Kane. He was still staring at it when he heard the car engine roar into life outside the house.

It was another fifteen minutes before he walked slowly downstairs, crossed to the phone and dialled.

75

J oe Hendry eased his foot off the accelerator of the Astra and flicked the headlights on to full beam. The twin rays of white light cut through the darkness and the fine mist of drizzle but illuminated only hedges, trees and fields.

'Are you sure we're in the right place, Doyle?' he asked.

'There's a left coming up,' the counter terrorist told him. 'About fifty yards ahead. Take it.'

'Maybe you're lost,' Declan Leary offered from his position in the back seat next to Doyle.

'Shut it, Leary,' Doyle snapped without looking at him.

Hendry slowed down, found the turn and guided the car on to a bumpy road that was pitted and holed. The Astra lurched alarmingly as the driver struggled to keep control.

'It's like driving over the bloody Somme,' he remarked, using the back of his hand to wipe some condensation from the windscreen.

'There, just up ahead,' Doyle said, pointing in the direction they were travelling.

There was a high wire fence stretching away on both sides of a heavily reinforced gate. Razor wire had been laid in rolls across the top of the fence, some of the wickedly sharp blades now rusted. Beyond the gate there were a dozen or more buildings. Grey, monolithic structures with gently sloping roofs.

'What is it?' Mel wanted to know.

'An old army base,' Doyle informed her. 'It overlooks Lough Egish. It's perfect for us.'

Leary looked ahead then back at Doyle.

The counter terrorist patted Hendry on the shoulder and

the driver brought the car to a halt. Doyle clambered out
and walked up to the gate. He pulled and, to his delight, found
it unlocked. He waved Hendry through, the strong wind whip-
ping his long, brown hair around his face. Doyle pulled up the
collar of his leather jacket and strode in behind the car. The
vehicle had stopped in front of the nearest Nissen hut.

Doyle pulled open the rear door and dragged Leary out.

'I was expecting more luxurious surroundings,' the Irishman
smirked.

Doyle shoved him hard in the back, pushing him towards
the hut, watching as he struggled to stay on his feet. He was
finding it hard to keep his balance with the handcuffs pinning
his arms behind his back.

The hut was also unlocked.

'There's a generator in that building, Joe,' Doyle told
Hendry. 'See if you can get it started. We'll at least have some
light.'

Hendry nodded and moved off in the direction indicated.

'Won't that attract attention?' Mel wondered.

'You can't see this place from the road,' Doyle assured her.
'You could have a firework display on the drill square and no
one would notice.'

Mel led the way into the hut, recoiling immediately from
the cloud of dust that enveloped her. 'How long has it been
empty?' she coughed.

'Eighteen months,' Doyle said.

As he spoke one of the bare bulbs in the ceiling flickered
orange then died. It flared again, more brightly this time then
gradually swelled into a purer white luminescence.

'Well done, Joe,' Doyle murmured. He crossed to the bank
of switches on one wall and flicked them all on. Then he
looked around the room.

Apart from a couple of broken plastic chairs it was empty.
A carpet of dust covered everything.

'Looks like we're sleeping on the floor,' the counter
terrorist said.

'I don't know how long that generator's going to run,' said
Hendry, walking into the hut. 'There's not much fuel left. The

army must have taken everything with them when they left.'

'We can always get extra,' Mel interjected. 'And food as well.'

'Hopefully we won't have to worry about that for too long,' Doyle said, turning his gaze towards Leary. 'We're only here until shithead gives us the locations of those ten graves. After that he's not our responsibility any more.'

'I said I'd tell you where they were and I will,' Leary protested. 'That was the deal.'

'You didn't make any fucking deals with me.'

'I'll tell you where the graves are. I said I would.'

'No, fuck that,' Doyle hissed. 'We're not running around like headless chickens on your fucking say so. You're not going to *tell* us where they are, you're going to *show* us. Every one of them. And when we get to the locations, *you're* going to dig up the bodies. Got it? You show me ten corpses and your part of the deal is fulfilled. You try to piss me about and I'll put *you* in the fucking ground myself.'

Leary eyed the counter terrorist angrily.

'There's a shovel in the boot of the car,' Doyle said. 'You start digging tomorrow. And you'd better hope you can remember where all those poor bastards are planted.'

76

The stench was appalling.

Mel put a hand to her nose and stepped back from the edge of the shallow grave.

Doyle merely stood impassively, hands dug deep into the pockets of his leather jacket. There was a cigarette screwed into one corner of his mouth.

The grave was less than three feet deep and the counter terrorist could only guess at how long its contents had been there.

The skeleton still wore its clothes. A sweatshirt. A thick anorak. Jeans. All rotting, just as their owner had done.

There were bullet holes in the coat. In the skull. Pieces of jawbone had come loose.

Leary looked up from the grave and tossed the shovel to one side.

'Right?' he said, sucking in lungfuls of the rancid air.

'One down, nine to go,' said the counter terrorist. He reached for his mobile phone and jabbed a number. He wandered back and forth waiting for it to be answered. When it finally was he spoke immediately. 'Robinson? It's Doyle.'

The RUC man wanted to know where they were.

'Just listen to me,' Doyle said. 'You wanted bodies? You've got them. First one's in a field off the A31, about two miles south of Milford. There's woods on either side of the road. Send your forensics boys about fifty yards in. They'll find it. I'll call the others in as we find them.'

Robinson wanted to know if Leary was co-operating.

'All the way to a nice cosy five stretch,' Doyle said. He

drew on his cigarette one final time then tossed the butt at Leary. 'We're moving on.'

He switched the phone off.

They found two more bodies that first day.

77

Doyle lit a cigarette, drew on it then passed it to Mel. She accepted it gratefully and sank lower in the passenger seat of the Astra.

'So this was your world, Doyle,' she said, staring out of the windscreen.

About fifty feet from where the car was parked, Declan Leary, his clothes spattered with mud, was digging again. Ten or twelve yards away, leaning against an old barn, Joe Hendry stood with his arms crossed. He gazed at the grey sky, at Leary working away with his shovel and at the hills that rose steeply all around. Most of them were heavily wooded and the trees seemed to be clinging to the precipitous slopes with difficulty.

The farm that Leary had brought them to had been abandoned over a year earlier. The farmhouse and most of the outbuildings lay over five hundred yards away at the perimeter of the field in which they now found themselves.

'My world,' Doyle muttered. 'What do you mean?'

'People like Leary. Jobs like this.'

'It was all I knew. All I wanted. I was good at it. I still am.'

'I'd noticed.'

'We're not *that* different, Mel. It's just the surroundings.'

'I'd take a hotel in Mayfair over a field in Ulster.'

Doyle chuckled. 'I might have to agree with you on *that* one,' he smiled.

'Why did you want to get back to it so badly?'

'I told you. It's all I know. What made *you* want to come with me?'

She shrugged. 'I'm beginning to wonder,' she confessed.
Again Doyle smiled.

'And when it's over?' Mel asked. 'What then? Leary's only
got to show us two more graves and that's it. Job done. What
do you do then? What do any of us do?'

'It's up to you, what *you* do. I'm sure Cartwright would be
more than happy to have you and Joe back working for him.'

'What about you?'

'I belong here, Mel. You asked me what I'll do when it's
over. That's simple. It's never over.'

'You sound happy about that.'

'What am I supposed to do? Retire? Sit around in a cardigan
and slippers for the rest of my fucking life waiting for the day
when I can't take it any more and I decide to chew the barrel
of a 9mm?' He drew on his cigarette. 'Maybe somebody like
Leary'll catch me out. Perhaps *I'll* be the one in a shallow
grave in the middle of nowhere. But I can't give up. I don't
want to give up.'

'Do you love it so much?'

'Perhaps I'm just scared of what I'll be without it. I've had
a taste of that and I didn't like it.'

'You were great in the security business, Doyle. Why not
come back to it?'

He shook his head. 'Like you said, Mel,' he told her. '*This* is
my world.'

'And you're happy here?'

'I never said that. I just said it was where I belonged.'

'*Are* you happy?' She glanced at him.

All he could do was shrug. 'To be happy, you have to want
something, don't you?' Doyle murmured.

'And what do you want?'

'I have absolutely no fucking idea. What about you?'

'I've never really thought about it.'

'So think now. You've got the time. Husband? Kids? What
would make you happy?'

'I wanted a career in the police. That was taken from me.
I found something else I could do and I enjoy it. But ask me
where I want to be in ten years' time and I couldn't tell you.'

'If I *last* another ten years it'll be a fucking achievement,' Doyle grunted.

'Does that bother you?'

'Why should it? If I don't know what I'm living for then I'm hardly likely to be scared about the prospect of dying, am I? Besides, so many doctors have told me how lucky I am to be alive now. How I should thank God I can still walk. All that other bullshit. I've got scars on every part of my fucking body and I'm supposed to thank God that I'm lucky. I should have been dead long before now. Sometimes I think it might have saved some pain if I had been.'

So much pain.

'Pain for who?'

'Me. Others too. The only thing I've ever learned from this job is that you should never get close to anyone. They might not be around for too long.'

They locked stares for a moment then Mel returned to gazing out of the windscreen. 'Do you know what frightens me about dying? That no one will come to my funeral. That the only one at the graveside would be the priest. I've got no family. No close friends. I don't think anyone would miss me if I died tomorrow.'

The counter terrorist sucked hard on his cigarette and tossed the butt out of the open window. 'Join the fucking club,' said Doyle, with an air of finality. 'I told you we weren't that different, Mel.'

'Doyle.' The shout came from Hendry.

Both the counter terrorist and Mel clambered out of the car and began walking towards their companion.

'It's another body,' the driver called, gesturing into the grave.

'Two more to go,' Mel said.

Doyle nodded.

'Then what?' she persisted.

Doyle didn't answer.

A LIGHT IN THE BLACK

W ard finished numbering the pages then sat back and
scanned what had been printed. Again he felt that schizo-
phrenic feeling of joy and bewilderment.

Where had the pages come from? Who had written them?

He took a deep breath and decided to return to the house.
Perhaps he might be able to eat something. Perhaps.

He promised himself he would return an hour later.

When he did, he found more.

78

'We're just about finished with you,' said Doyle, staring at Leary.

The Irishman was covered in mud. It was smeared on his cheeks. Even in his hair.

'Last two locations,' Doyle demanded.

'I thought you wanted to see them,' Leary protested.

'We're *going* to see them,' Doyle assured him. 'You and I will go to one.' He turned to look at his companions. 'Mel, you and Joe take the other one.'

'Why split up now, Doyle?' Mel wanted to know.

'I've got business to discuss with this piece of shit. There's no need for you two to be there when that happens.'

Mel held Doyle's gaze for a moment then shook her head.

The counter terrorist turned back to face Leary. 'Locations of the last two graves,' he snapped.

'One's buried in some woods near Mountnorris,' Leary said wearily. 'The other one's in a church at Whitecross.'

'Which church?' Mel asked.

'St Angela's. It's in a crypt under the nave.'

'No bullshit?' snapped Doyle, leaning closer to the Irishman.

'Listen, I'm as anxious to get away from you as you are from me. Why would I lie now?'

'Those locations aren't more than ten miles apart,' Doyle mused. 'Joe. Drop us at the one in Mountnorris. The woods will be nice and quiet for me and this prick to have a chat.' He looked at Leary. 'You and Mel check out the one in Whitecross. If it's kosher, let me know then come back and pick me up. I'll ring both locations through then we'll drop this fucker off some-where the RUC can pick him up.'

Hendry nodded.

The Astra sped on through the gathering dusk.

Doyle checked his watch. 6.04 p.m.

Mel and Hendry should be at the church in Whitecross soon. They'd left Doyle and his captive more than twenty minutes earlier. The counter terrorist had been following Leary through increasingly dense woods ever since. He walked five or six feet behind him, carrying the shovel like an over-sized club. He prodded Leary in the back with it and the Irishman continued leading the way. He was still handcuffed.

Birds returning to their nests were black arrowheads against the sky. Clouds were forming into menacing banks and Doyle thought he felt the first drops of rain in the air.

'Who was he?' Doyle wanted to know.

'Who was who?'

'This one? The poor bastard buried in here.'

'Brit. Proddie. Tout. How the fuck do I know?'

They continued on through the trees, the gloom made more palpable by the canopy of branches above them.

'What about the one in Whitecross?' Doyle persisted.

Leary didn't answer.

'I'm talking to you, you cunt,' Doyle snarled, pushing the Irishman hard in the back.

He fell forward, catching his head on a fallen branch hard enough to break the skin. He rolled over, looking up at Doyle. 'There's no body in the church,' he hissed.

'I told you not to fuck me around,' Doyle said angrily.

'There's something there but it's not a body.'

'What the fuck are you talking about?'

'It's an arms dump. The organisation hid weapons and explo-sives there. It's booby-trapped.'

Doyle's grey eyes blazed. He dropped the shovel and pulled the Beretta from its shoulder holster, pointing it at Leary.

'As soon as they open it, it'll explode,' the Irishman continued. 'You'll be able to bury them both in the same matchbox. I knew you'd prefer to get me alone in the woods in case we were interrupted in the church. Looks like you lose again, Doyle.'

Doyle lowered the Beretta slightly. He shot Leary once in the right kneecap.

Moving at a speed in excess of twelve hundred feet a second, the heavy-grain slug shattered the patella as if it were porcelain. It tore through the leg, ripping away cruciate ligaments and muscle.

Leary screamed in agony.

'How do they disarm it?' Doyle said, kneeling beside the wounded Irishman. He pressed the barrel of the automatic against the younger man's chin. 'How?'

'They can't,' Leary said through gritted teeth.

Doyle fired again. The second shot pulverised Leary's left kneecap.

His screams echoed through the woods, mingling with the thunderous retort of the pistol.

The counter terrorist thrust a hand in his jacket, reaching for his mobile. He stabbed in Mel's number and waited.

Leary was still screaming. Doyle spun round and kicked him hard in the face. It shut him up for long enough.

'Hello.'

'Mel, listen to me,' Doyle said breathlessly. 'Don't go inside that fucking church.'

'Doyle . . . can't hear . . . breaking up,' Mel said, her voice fading.

'Don't go inside the fucking church,' Doyle bellowed into the mouthpiece.

'Still . . . hear . . . saying . . .'

The counter terrorist looked around him.

The trees. There are too many trees. That's what was fucking up the signal. Get back to the road.

He looked down at Leary who lay motionless on the mossy floor of the forest.

The road was two hundred yards away.

You'll never make it.

Doyle turned and ran as he'd never run in his life.

79

As he ran, Doyle ducked to avoid low branches, crashed through bushes, ignored twigs that scratched at his face. And, all the time, the road seemed to be miles away from him.

The breath seared in his lungs.

You're not going to make it.

He was fifty yards from the road now.

'Stay out of the church,' he shouted into the phone as he ran. There was still a deafening hiss of static.

'Mel,' he roared.

Thirty yards. 'Mel, can you hear me?'

'Breaking up . . . to go in now . . .'

Twenty yards. 'Don't go inside the church,' Doyle bellowed frantically.

'Off now . . . call you back . . . Leary was talking about . . .'

Ten yards. He crashed through the hedge, almost sprawled on to the road.

'Mel, keep away from the church,' he shouted.

There was no sound at the other end.

Doyle switched off. Dialled again. Waited.

'Come on. Come on.'

No answer. He tried Hendry's phone. It rang twice.

'Answer it,' Doyle snarled, his eyes bulging madly.

'Yeah.'

'Joe, get out of there now. It's a set-up.'

'What?' Hendry said, his voice echoing.

They must be inside the church.

'Leary's fucked us over. The crypt is booby-trapped. Don't open it,' Doyle gasped.

He heard Mel's voice in the background. Something unintelligible.

There was a creak. A sound that almost split his eardrum. Then silence.

80

D oyle dropped the mobile back into his pocket and turned back towards the woods. He moved slowly, retracing his steps, his face set in hard lines. The knot of muscles at the side of his jaw was pulsing angrily.

It took him fifteen minutes to reach the place where he'd left Leary. The Irishman was still lying face down, both his legs shattered. It looked as if he'd been dipped in red paint from the knees down.

He walked up to Leary and kicked him hard in the ribs. Hard enough to roll him over on to his back.

Doyle took out his mobile again and dialled a number.

He recognised the voice on the other end. 'Robinson. It's Doyle,' he said quietly.

'Doyle . . . can hardly hear you . . . breaking up,' the CI told him.

'Listen carefully.'

'What . . . hell is going on?' the RUC man wanted to know. 'Been an explosion . . . church in Whitecross. All hell's . . . loose.'

'I know about the explosion. You'll find two bodies in the church. My back-up team. Leary double-crossed us.'

'Where is he?'

'Here, with me.'

'Thank God for that.'

'I need to ask you something. What was your daughter's name?'

'What?'

'Your daughter? The one who was killed in that bomb blast. What was her name?'

'Angela. Why?'

'Next time you go to visit her grave tell her everything's all right.'

'Doyle, what . . . talking about? You're not making any sense and I can hardly hear you . . .'

'I shouldn't have killed Kane.'

'Doyle . . . say again . . .'

'I'll call you back in twenty minutes.'

The counter terrorist switched off the phone. He looked down at Leary impassively.

The Irishman tried to hold his gaze but was forced to close his eyes due to the unbearable pain.

Doyle shot him five times.

He stood there for a moment longer then turned and trudged back towards the road.

81

LONDON; TWO DAYS LATER:

S ean Doyle held the crystal tumbler in his hand and studied
the amber liquid in it before taking a mouthful. The brandy
burned its way to his stomach.

'Perhaps we should have had a toast first,' said Sir Anthony
Pressman, raising his own glass. 'I'll be the first to admit that
your methods are somewhat irregular, Doyle, but they seem
to get results.'

Jonathan Parker glanced at Pressman then at Doyle as he
sipped his drink.

Sunshine was streaming through the windows of Parker's
office at the CTU's Hill Street headquarters. Motes of dust
turned lazily in the air.

'Sinn Fein seemed fairly happy with the way you handled
Leary,' said Pressman.

'I'm glad they approve,' Doyle said disdainfully. 'I saved them
the job of killing him. What did they have to say about the
graves he showed us?'

'That's a matter that will have to be discussed in the future,'
Pressman said.

'Yeah, I bet it fucking will,' grunted Doyle getting to his feet.

'Most of those responsible for the murders are no longer
associated with that organisation or the Provisional IRA,'
Pressman continued. 'The recovery of the bodies was a
cosmetic exercise anyway. Designed to help the families of
the victims as much as anything else. It's just rather unfortu-
nate about your colleagues.'

'Shit happens,' Doyle said flatly, moving towards the door. Pressman rose too.

'There's a message you can give to Sinn Fein when you see them,' the counter terrorist said. 'The same one I want to give to you.'

Pressman smiled efficiently.

Doyle caught him with a perfect right hook. The powerful blow knocked the politician off his feet and sent him crashing backwards into the sofa, his nose broken, blood spilling down his perfectly laundered shirt and tie.

'Get out,' Parker said quietly.

'I was on my way,' Doyle told him.

And he was gone.

THE END

PARTING OF THE WAYS

The end.

Ward looked at the two words. To him they may as well have been glowing in neon.

The end.

Who had decided this was the end? When had he completed this novel? This novel he could remember barely a third of.

He swallowed hard and laid the last of the pages on the pile.

It was over.

The book was finished.

As he sat at his desk, he found that his hands were shaking.

AN ALL-SEEING EYE

As before, Ward peered through the viewfinder of the camcorder and trained it on his desk.

The night was humid and more than once he had to wipe the lens with the corner of his handkerchief. Perspiration was running down his back. He could feel it like a clammy sheath on the nape of his neck.

He glanced at his watch. 11.36 p.m.

He took one more look, then satisfied he had done everything he could, he pressed the red record button.

The small cassette began to turn its spools. Ward watched it for a moment then made his way down the stairs. He locked the office door and wandered slowly back towards the house.

The sudden breeze that sprang up was a welcome cooling touch on his hot skin and he stood for a moment, enjoying the temporary respite from the cloying humidity.

It was a second or two before he noticed the smell. A rank, pungent odour that made him cough.

Ward put a hand to his nose and stared in the direction from which the odour was coming.

Carried on the breeze, it seemed to be wafting up from one of the darker parts of the garden.

At opposite corners there were two large and very old oak trees. He had guessed, when he bought the place, around three hundred years old. One was close to his office, the other about a hundred yards away towards the wooden fence that formed one boundary of his property.

It was from there that the stench was coming.

Ward took a step towards it, trying to hold his breath.

There were only two lights on inside the house so very little illumination spilled into the garden. It was almost impossible to see more than a few yards ahead.

Ward stood still once more, trying not to gag.

He heard sounds of movement in the high blackberry-and-laurel hedges at the bottom of the garden. Cats sometimes prowled there and he'd seen hedgehogs and even squirrels in the past. But none of them smelled like this.

He knew the stench. Knew it but . . .

Rotten meat. The realisation hit him as palpably as the vile odour itself. This was what was filling his nostrils with so noxious a scent.

During his days as a student he'd had a summer job on a farm in Normandy and two of the cows had been attacked and killed by gypsies' dogs. Their carcasses hadn't been discovered for two days. Left to putrefy in the blistering sun, they had swelled and bloated like corpulent balloons.

Ward could remember finding them in one of the fields. Smelling their rankness. The foul stench had never left him and he knew that was what he was sampling now.

The smell seemed to grow stronger. He expected to hear the sound of buzzing flies.

There was more rustling from the hedge. Ward wasn't sure whether to move towards it or head back into the house. There was a torch in one of the drawers near the back door and he wondered about fetching it. Shining it in the direction of the smell and noises.

For brief moments he wondered if it could be a fox. If it was, best not to get too close. They spread rabies.

A badger? He shook his head. His house wasn't *that* close to the countryside.

And, even if the nocturnal visitor proved to be any of these creatures, that didn't account for the rancid stench.

He stroked his chin thoughtfully then wandered towards the back door. The smell was making his head spin.

He'd just put his hand on the door handle when he heard more movement. Louder. Closer.

Ward pulled open the door and fumbled quickly for the

torch. He stepped back into the garden and flicked it on, allowing the cold, white light to cut through the blackness.

'Jesus Christ,' murmured Ward, the torch quivering in his grasp.

For fleeting seconds the beam caught and held the source of the sounds.

Ward took a step back. He blinked hard. The shape in the cold light was still there.

Squat, low to the ground. Carrying all its weight on its front legs. Legs that were bowed but extremely powerful. Like an ape.

It seemed to have hair on most of the upper part of its body. Glistening black in the torchlight.

Then it moved. Moved like lightning.

Ward swung the beam back and forth. There were others. He counted three.

All, it seemed, anxious to escape the probing glare of the torch.

They scattered in all directions. And when they ran they made a sound that raised the hairs on the back of his neck. A sound that resembled a deep retching noise. As if they were vomiting something up from their seething bellies.

Ward hurried back inside and slammed the door, his breath coming in gasps. His head was spinning.

He crossed to the light switch and hit it hard. Security lights illuminated the garden. He scanned the area for any signs of movement. Nothing.

Ward stood there for what seemed like an eternity then he switched off the lights and ensured the back door was firmly locked and bolted. Once those tasks had been completed, he padded into the sitting room.

He poured himself a drink and sat down, breathing heavily.

It was barely five minutes before he heard a knock on the front door.

IN DARKNESS

For a moment Ward wondered if this was another product of his disintegrating mind.

Smells that didn't exist. Sights that could only be the product of a furtive, drink-fuelled and troubled imagination. Visions that could not be explained. His senses seemed to be conspiring against him. Could his hearing have joined the alliance?

He waited. The knock came again. Louder and more insistent.

He put down his glass and wandered out into the hall, peering through the spy-hole in the door. The motion-triggered security light in the porch illuminated a figure standing before him.

He swallowed hard then slid the chain back and unlocked the door.

'Hi, Chris,' said Jenny. Five-foot-two Jenny wearing the long black coat. Jenny with the streaked brown hair. Jenny the prostitute.

He stepped back and ushered her inside.

'I wasn't expecting an appointment so late,' she told him, slipping off her coat. She was wearing a pair of knee-length boots, denim shorts and a yellow T-shirt.

'Is it a problem?' he wanted to know.

'No. Some customers . . .' she coughed and corrected herself, 'I mean, clients, call at any time of the day or night.'

He stood looking at her.

'Do you want me to go upstairs?' she said, almost apologetically.

In that moment she reminded Ward of a naughty child waiting to be sent to her room.

He shook his head and nodded in the direction of the sitting room. 'Go through,' he told her.

She hesitated a moment then did as he instructed. 'It's a beautiful room,' she said, looking round.

'Drink?' he said, ignoring her observation. He handed her a brandy and coke.

'You remembered my favourite.'

'Listen, I need to ask you a few things.'

'You just want to talk this time?' She sat down next to him and put one hand on his thigh. 'If you just want me to talk then that's fine,' Jenny continued. 'Whatever you want, Chris.' She slid her hand higher, towards his groin.

'Listen to me, will you?' he snapped. He got to his feet and refilled his glass.

'You said I rang you the other day. A couple of days ago. I can't remember exactly when. Something to do with you and another girl. What the fuck was that all about?'

'Me and Claire. You rang and asked if I could bring another girl with me when I came.'

'Why?'

'Why do you think?' she chuckled.

'What did I say?' he snapped.

Her smile faded. 'You asked me if I could arrange to bring another girl to your house. You wanted to watch us while we did each other. You said you might join in. You might just watch.'

'And that was *all* I said?'

She looked puzzled.

'How did I sound?'

'Chris, I don't understand what you mean.'

'Did I sound the same? The way I always sound. My voice.' He sucked in a deep breath. 'This is fucking useless.'

'I don't know what you mean,' she protested. 'I'm trying to help but—'

'Could it have been someone pretending to be me? Someone imitating my voice?'

She shook her head. 'Why would they want to do that?' Jenny enquired.

'That's what I want to know.'

'You rang me. You said you wanted me to come here and you said you wanted me to arrange to bring another girl too. You said you'd pay whatever it cost. *That's* what you said.'

Ward poured himself another drink and began pacing the sitting room slowly.

'What about tonight?' said Jenny finally. Her voice was hesitant, as if she was reluctant to break the oppressive silence.

'What do you mean?'

'Do you want me tonight?'

He stopped pacing and looked at her with something approaching contempt.

'Well, you're *here*, aren't you?' he muttered.

She finished her drink then made her way upstairs.

Ward followed a moment later.

UNEXPECTED VISIONS

There was blood everywhere. Ward woke up in it. He smelt it in his nostrils. That acrid, coppery stench.

When he opened his eyes he saw it all over the walls. It had soaked into the duvet like ink into blotting paper. It was splashed on the carpet. There was even some on the ceiling.

He sat up on the bed and realised he was naked. His body was covered with the sticky, crimson fluid. Some had congealed. Some had the tacky texture of drying paint. His hair was matted with it. Barely an inch of his flesh was untouched by the red splatters.

Ward felt his stomach contract. He gritted his teeth to prevent himself from vomiting.

He ran his hands over his body, his eyes scanning the flesh. There were no cuts. This was not *his* blood.

He dragged himself off the bed, gazing at his reflection in the mirrored doors of the wardrobe. He ran a hand over his face and smeared more of the crimson fluid over his cheeks.

Ward turned towards the bathroom, blundered in and turned the shower on to full power. He didn't even wait for the jets to become warm but dived straight beneath them, anxious to wash away this foul coating that covered him like a second skin. The cold water hit his skin like pinpricks and he looked down to see the blood swirling away down the plughole.

All the time he stood beneath the spray he forced himself to think what might have happened. He could remember nothing. Nothing from the previous night. Nothing that might have caused this carnage.

He washed the last of the blood from his body then reached for a towel and wrapped it around himself.

Again he tried to think. As he stepped back into the bedroom he saw something lying beside the bed. It was a piece of material. Like everything else in the room, it was soaked in blood.

Ward turned it between his shaking hands and realised that it was lace. Once it had been white. Now it bore the indelible colour of life fluid. But whose?

He rubbed the material between thumb and forefinger. The realisation hit him like a sledgehammer. He was holding a pair of knickers.

He touched the smooth gusset. Pulled gently on the elastic around the waist area. The clothing looked like a bandage that had been pressed to an arterial wound. A cloth plug attempting to staunch an unstoppable flow of blood.

He shook his head. 'Oh, God,' he murmured.

He sat on the floor beside the bed, still holding the knickers.

Beneath the stained counterpane he spotted something else. It was a knee-length boot.

Ward reached under the bed and pulled it out. The leather was new. He smelled it. Held it close to him as a child might grip a comforter.

There was a sock inside it. That too was also covered in blood.

There was something familiar about this boot. Something . . .

A vision drifted into his mind. Of a girl with streaked brown hair. A girl in knee-length leather boots, denim shorts and a yellow T-shirt.

Jenny.

The boot was hers. So were the knickers. By implication, so was the blood.

Ward swallowed hard. What the fuck had happened in here last night? Where was Jenny?

Questions raced through his mind. He knew he had no answer to any of them. He sat naked beside the bed, surrounded by the blood and he tried to think. He remembered answering the door to her. Remembered giving her a drink. Then, after that, nothing. Just empty blackness where his memory should be.

Ward got to his feet and hurried out of the room, heading for his bedroom. He snatched up the phone and dialled Jenny's number. It rang three times.

He knew she shared a flat with another girl. If *she* was there she might know where Jenny was.

The phone still rang.

'Come on,' Ward gasped.

Finally it was answered.

'Hello,' said Ward quickly.

'Hello,' said the voice at the other end.

'I want to speak to Jenny.'

'Who is this?'

'Just let me speak to her, will you? I want to arrange an appointment to see her.'

'She's not here at the moment.'

'Where is she?'

'I don't know. She was out all last night and—'

'When will she be back?'

'Well, she said she'd be back this morning but—'

'What's her mobile number?'

'I can make the appointment for you if you like.'

'No, just give me the number.'

'Hang on a minute.'

He heard rustling, papers being shifted.

'I've got the number. Have you got a pen?'

'Just give it to me,' he snapped.

The girl had barely finished speaking when Ward slammed the phone down. He lifted the receiver again then dialled Jenny's mobile number. And waited. And . . .

There was a high-pitched ringing inside the room. Ward dropped the phone and ducked down on to the blood-spattered carpet. The ringing was coming from beneath the bed. He reached under and pulled out Jenny's mobile.

She had been here. No doubt. But where the hell was she now?

Ward dropped the phone and sat motionless on the floor.

SEARCH

It took him over five hours to clean the bedroom. Wearing just a pair of shorts, he slaved inside what had become a charnel house, washing and scraping away the crimson fluid. He carried the duvet downstairs and shoved it into the washing machine.

The initial clean-up was followed by more detailed ablutions and Ward removed the worst of the bloodstains from the carpet, curtains and furniture.

The scraps of clothing and the boot he saved.

It was approaching five in the afternoon when he finally collapsed, exhausted, on to his bed. His body was sheathed in sweat and he had a raging headache.

He needed to go downstairs and take a couple of Nurofen but he just lay staring at the ceiling, his mind spinning.

It was another hour before he finally hauled himself upright.

Thirty minutes more before he remembered the camcorder inside the office.

NO WORDS OF WISDOM

Ward unlocked the office door and trudged slowly up the stairs.

Four pieces of paper had spewed from the printer.

He approached them and picked each up in turn.

THE

CUNT

DESERVED

TO die

there was no other way

A REVELATION

Ward stared at the four pages for what seemed like an eternity then he laid them carefully with the rest of the manuscript on his desk.

He crossed to the camcorder and took it from its tripod.

The cassette had been used up. All ninety minutes of it. He had to see what the machine had caught on film.

Before he left the office, he switched off both the monitor and the printer.

FILM SHOW

Ward poured himself another glass of Jack Daniel's while he waited for the tape to rewind. Once it was ready, he changed the necessary cables and leads that connected the camcorder to the television then pressed the play button. He sat back in his seat and exhaled deeply.

There was a second or two of blank leader, then a startling flash of black and white across the screen.

Ward swallowed what was left in his glass.

The picture on his television screen came into focus.

He sat forward in his seat.

What he saw before him wasn't his office. It was the spare bedroom of his house.

He swallowed hard and studied the images before him.

Jenny was tied to a wooden chair. She was naked. The bonds that held her securely in place were strips of sheet. One around each ankle and one around each wrist. She was wearing a blindfold. Also made of sheeting.

The camera panned slowly from her perfectly pedicured feet, up the smooth curve of her calves to her slim thighs. It paused at the neatly trimmed triangle of her pubic hair then continued to rise until it came to her breasts. The nipples were already hard and prominent.

Further it moved. Up the hollow of her neck then to her face. She was smiling.

Ward moved closer to the screen, his hands shaking.

He could see her lips moving but he couldn't hear what she was saying. He reached for the TV remote and increased the sound. She had stopped speaking now.

He saw her clothes scattered around the bedroom. Some on the bed. Others on the floor.

'Are you ready?' The voice he heard on the tape was his own.

It came from off-camera.

The gaze of the camcorder was still riveted on Jenny.

His own image stepped into shot. Naked.

He knelt between her spread thighs and rubbed his hands over the smooth flesh before pushing two fingers into her vagina.

Jenny moaned expertly.

Then he withdrew the digits and concentrated on her breasts, massaging them, turning the nipples between his thumb and forefinger.

Again she moaned with practised accomplishment.

Ward watched himself stand up. Saw his throbbing erection as he paused before her. Then he stepped out of shot again.

'Don't tease,' Jenny said, still smiling.

When he stepped back into shot he was holding a knife. It was at least a foot long. Serrated and wickedly pointed.

Ward shook his head as he watched the video, transfixed by what he saw.

The image on the screen moved towards Jenny and again stood between her open legs.

'Take this blindfold off, Chris,' Jenny said. 'I like to see what you're doing.'

On screen he moved the blade to within inches of her throat.

'Chris,' she persisted, her voice soft and coaxing. 'Let me see you.'

Ward tried to swallow but his throat was chalk dry.

On screen, the knife was practically touching the flesh of her neck now.

'Open your mouth,' the on-screen Ward told her.

Jenny did as he instructed. She licked her lips exaggeratedly.

He touched the blade to her tongue.

Her smile faded. 'What's that?' she said.

They were the last two words she uttered.

SNUFF MOVIE

Ward watched as the images on the screen suddenly became more animated.

The knife was driven forward with incredible power. He saw it slice through Jenny's tongue. Saw most of that appendage severed. Saw the blood erupt into the air.

She tried to scream but the blood gushing back into her throat made the noise little more than a liquid gurgle.

The knife sped back and forth with incredible speed and ferocity.

Through her cheek. It was torn free, ripping the flesh.

Into her neck. More blood bursting from the wound.

Then into her chest. Once, twice. One breast was practically severed.

Four, five times. Every cut was deep.

Blood spurted madly into the air but the hacking and slashing continued.

The blade was driven into her belly and pulled upwards. A slippery, seething mass of intestines spilled from the eviscerated body. He saw the green of bile as the gall bladder was hacked in half by another frenzied cut.

A nipple was severed and fell to the floor.

The blade was drawn across the throat from side to side. Ear to ear. The throat opened and yawned like a blood-filled mouth.

And still the stabbing went on.

Several deep wounds were inflicted on the thighs. One severed a femoral artery and blood sprayed several feet into the air.

Another buried the blade, handle deep, into Jenny's vagina like some lethal, metallic penis.

She made no sound after the first five or six cuts. The only noises audible on the tape were the liquid sounds of blood spurting or flesh being hacked and then the soft hiss as her sphincter muscle collapsed. Faeces and urine mingled with the blood that was already soaking into the carpet.

Ward watched with his eyes bulging.

Ten. Twenty. Thirty more devastating incisions. Unnecessary. Life had long since left her body along with most of the blood it had contained.

Finally he removed the blindfold and, almost carefully, plunged the knife into first one eye then the other.

Left it stuck in the right socket.

Glistening.

Christopher Ward turned away from the screen, his stomach contracting. For long moments he was sure he was going to vomit but the feeling gradually passed.

It was another five minutes before he could bring himself to look at the screen again.

AFTERMATH

W ard reached for the bottle of Jack Daniel's. He poured himself a full glass and drank it in two massive gulps. He drank until he passed out.

OBLIVION

W ard didn't wake until after one that morning.
He stared at the now-blank television screen, rolled
on to his back and blacked out once again.

Life sometimes seems so pointless. What is the reason for it? What is the reason for our being? Scholars throughout the ages have laboured over the question and none have come to a satisfactory conclusion. I myself have often wondered what the true nature of life and being is but they are fleeing thoughts in a world too preoccupied with relevances more tangible than anything so ethereal. Why would any man want to devote his life to discovery of the object of being? Of being on this planet and in this life. How incredibly supercilious of man to imagine, for one moment, that he is the only inhabitant of this world. There are many worlds about which mankind has no understanding. The world inside a man's mind is the most uncharted territory ever. No one fully understands, nor will they ever, the workings of the human mind. What some desire others find abhorrent. What some find beauteous, others may barely countenance. So many contradictions within the mind of man and none will ever be truly and irrevocably solved.

Take the question of morality. Who is to say what is moral? By whose criteria are we to judge this question? That of God? The morality embodied within those commandments that the Bible speaks so proudly of? Those ten rules designed for destruction. Rules that man is incapable of keeping. God issued those rules knowing that those he had created were unable to uphold them. God is a trickster. God wishes his children to fall by the wayside because if they do then they call on him with even greater volume. Their prayers grow more desperate and they rely upon their deities to an even greater extent. A vengeful God. A caring God. The God of cancer and war. The Lord of child abuse and illness. The Holy Spirit of madness and destruction. The Trinity of suffering.

In every man there is the capacity for evil and yet has anyone ever truly defined the meaning of that word. Is it evil to kill? Is it evil to steal? No. I feel it is not. If a man has the strength to commit any act, no matter how depraved then he should be applauded for his honesty. There is a purity in the act of anyone who knows he is answerable to no one but himself. The law is unimportant. Man must live by the law he creates for himself. He must live by a code of honour that he himself invents, not that handed down to him by the church, society or the masses. Man's biggest crime is to lose his identity. Without it he is nothing and that identity is defined by a man's actions. Not as they are perceived by the world at large but by himself. Once that code of behaviour has been established, one that is peculiar to each individual, then its rules and parameters must not be broken for the retribution that accompanies such a transgression is limitless.

STRANGE WORDS

Christopher Ward read the words but they made no sense to him. He sat at his desk and scanned the two sheets endlessly.

The only thing he knew was that the handwriting was not his.

DILEMMA

Christopher Ward sat staring at the blank monitor before him then, as if a switch had been thrown somewhere deep in the recesses of his mind, he typed:

1. Where is the girl?
2. Did I kill her?
3. Who wrote the words I found today?
4. Hallucinations?

He underlined the last one three times.

5. If I killed the girl, where did I hide the body?
6. What would have made me kill her in the first place?

Ward sighed almost painfully and looked at what he'd typed. He picked up the two handwritten pages he'd found in the office that morning and re-read them. When he'd finished, he placed them gently on the desk to his right, next to the box of printer paper he kept there.

He got to his feet and crossed to one of his bookshelves. He selected a *Dictionary of Psychology* and flicked through the pages.

'Amnesia,' he murmured to himself as he found the entry. He read it quickly then replaced the book on the shelf. There was nothing worthwhile there. Nothing that helped him.

He switched the monitor off and made his way down the stairs, locking the office door behind him.

Inside the house it was cool, almost chilly, and he shivered as he wandered through into the study. He switched on the computer there and waited. No point in checking e-mails. No one ever sent them any more. He went straight to the Internet and tapped in: Short-Term Memory Loss.

The computer buzzed and whirred. Ward got to his feet and padded back into the sitting room where he retrieved a bottle of Glenfiddich and a clean glass. He carried these back into the study and sat down at the computer once again.

A series of different coloured images appeared before him. He placed his hand on the mouse and waited.

Search Results: 11 matches found
2 in symptoms and conditions
1 in special topics
3 in medical abstracts
5 in drugs

1. Memory loss
2. Stress in childhood
3. Post-cardiac defibrillation
4. Zopiclone (systemic)
5. Temozolomide (systemic)
6. Zaleplon (systemic)
7. Zolpidem (systemic)
8. Dronabinol (systemic)
9. The nature of early memory
10. Memories lost and found – part II
11. Acute traumatic brain injury in amateur boxing

Ward scanned what was before him then clicked on 'The nature of early memory'. He read quickly then took a gulp of his whisky and shook his head.

He clicked on 'Memories lost and found'. He read that more slowly, occasionally reading aloud.

'There are different kinds of memory,' he read. 'Declarative or explicit memory includes learning of facts . . . culture of victimisation . . . may cause patients to deny responsibility for their problems . . . memories can contain varying elements of truth and distortion.'

He sat back in his seat and drank more whisky. In less than an hour, he'd finished the whole bottle.

It eventually becomes impossible to separate what constitutes reality and fantasy. One passes over into another with such ease that to discern their individuality is almost futile. The fine line which is trodden between the world of the imagination and the everyday world becomes indistinct. Sometimes this is a desirable state of affairs but, more often than not, it signals the refusal of the mind to accept reality. It chooses instead to retreat into fantasy. It is a world more comfortably inhabited. In such a state, what was recognised previously as catharsis becomes prophetic. The mingling of worlds is amplified to such a degree that it may be possible to influence the outcome of that which had previously been subject to the whims of fate. And with that comes responsibility. One that does not always sit easily with those who possess it.

I seek a knowledge that others have sought but failed to find. I seek with a ferocity some find disturbing. With a single-mindedness which produces confrontation, but then, what is life but a series of conflicts? Without conflict, life is worthless. Without confrontation, man is nothing. Only from confrontation can true knowledge come. The battle is fought inside the mind to begin with but then it evolves into a more tangible fight. With the passing of time, one learns to thrive on conflict, to seek it. To welcome it. How tedious to pass the days in silent subservience. How much better to confront. To challenge. To triumph. For without the pleasure of triumph there is no sense in entering into a conflict. One should only do so with the express purpose of leaving it as the victor. Defeat is something to be despised. To be ridiculed. Those who accept it are to be similarly loathed and treated with the contempt one would reserve for lesser beings.

But victory can be viewed in many different ways and from many different aspects. The true nature of triumph is again a personal matter. Man measures his victories against others. Only a man who values victory above all things is worthy to retain his place in the natural order. There are no aspects of defeat that are tolerable or worthwhile. The single overriding factor in the mind of any man should be to stand unchallenged atop the mountain of ambition he has seen fit to climb. To fall short of that summit is to fail. To fail is to show weakness and weakness is the most vile and contemptuous attribute that any man can be cursed with.

There

are

others

SALVATION

Ward placed the five pages to one side and slumped forward on his desk. He was drifting off to sleep when he heard a loud noise away to his left. It took him a few seconds to realise that the noise was a car horn. A little more time to work out that the sound was coming from the driveway of his own house.

He got to his feet and crossed to one of the velux windows of his office. By standing on a chair he could just make out the bonnet of a car pointing towards the house. Another moment and he saw a figure walk around the vehicle, lean through the open driver's door and hit the hooter three more times.

Ward blinked hard. He was sure he recognised the figure.

Martin Connelly walked towards the front door of the house, disappearing from Ward's view.

Ward moved away from the window and stumbled towards the stairs. He gripped the banister to prevent himself falling then finally blundered out into the garden and headed for the tall, wooden gate that led out into the drive.

'Martin,' he called.

Connelly heard him and hurried over, slowing his pace as he drew nearer.

'Jesus Christ,' murmured the agent, his eyes widening. 'What the hell's happened here?'

'What are you talking about?' Ward wanted to know. 'Why are you here?'

'I've left God knows how many messages on your answering machine. You haven't returned any of the calls.'

'So what else is new?'

'The last time we spoke was over ten days ago, Chris. What have you been doing? Why didn't you answer the calls?'

'I've been busy,' Ward said and he laughed.

The sound raised the hairs on the back of Connelly's neck.

'You look terrible,' he said.

'Thanks. You drove from London to tell me *that*?'

'Can I come in?' Connelly asked. 'I need to speak to you, Chris.'

'Actually, there's something I need to show *you,*' Ward confessed. 'Come into the office.'

Connelly followed the author up the stairs, recoiling from the smell of body odour that hung in the air.

There were several flies buzzing around inside the office, one of them occasionally landing on a pile of rotting tea bags by the sink.

'The book,' said Ward, indicating the manuscript. 'The book no fucker wants.' He laughed again. A humourless, empty sound. 'And this.' He passed the handwritten pages to Connelly.

The agent took them and sat down on the chair near the window. He read them quickly, a frown creasing his forehead. 'I don't get it,' he said finally, offering the pages back to Ward.

'Neither do I,' Ward told him.

Again Connelly shook his head.

'I didn't write it,' Ward said flatly.

EMPTY WORDS

Inside the house Martin Connelly watched as Ward poured two large measures of whisky into tumblers. The agent was holding the handwritten pages in one hand, his gaze drifting between them and Ward. He accepted the drink and sipped at it.

'None of this makes any sense, Chris,' he said quietly.

'I know,' Ward agreed. 'I've read it over and over again and—'

'Not just that. What's happening with *you* makes no sense.'

'What the fuck are you talking about?'

'Look, I know things aren't going too well at the moment but—'

Ward cut him short. 'Not going too well,' he snarled. 'A masterpiece of understatement, Martin. My career's in ruins, my life's falling to bits around my fucking ears. Jesus, not going too well. That's a bit like saying the Jews had a rough time in Dachau. No shit.'

'You're not helping yourself.'

'What do you mean? It's the *publishers* who aren't helping. Publishers who won't publish what I write. What am I supposed to do? What do you think I can do to help myself, Martin? *Beg* them to publish me?'

'This stuff doesn't help,' said Connelly, raising the glass. 'How much are you drinking these days?'

'If you drove all the way from London to lecture me about my drinking then get in your flash car and fuck off now.' Ward downed a sizeable gulp of the fiery liquid.

'You've always had a problem with it, Chris, you know that.'

'Drink is the least of my problems at the moment. Now tell me, why are you here?'

'I was worried.'

'Ah, the agent caring about one of his clients, how touching. I'm hardly the meal ticket I used to be, am I, Martin? I'd have thought you could have found more deserving causes. What was the name of that publicity girl at Headline you were shagging? She seemed like a more worthwhile object for your attentions.'

'Do you want me here or not?'

'I don't know what I want. Because I don't know what the fuck is happening to me.'

Ward slumped into the chair opposite his agent. 'Things . . . have been happening,' he said, realising that what he was about to say was going to sound ridiculous.

'What kind of things?'

'Things I can't explain. Stupid things. Weird things.'

'Like what?'

Ward sucked in a breath, held it a moment then exhaled slowly. 'I've been having . . . blackouts. I don't know what else to call them,' he said evenly. 'I'll fall asleep and when I wake up, there's part of the book completed. Stuff that I know I must have written but that I can't remember. More than a hundred pages of that novel out in the office, I can't remember writing.'

Connelly listend intently. 'Some kind of short-term memory loss?' he offered.

'I thought that but there've been other things too. I've seen things. At night.'

'What kind of things?'

'Apparitions,' he smiled humourlessly. 'There, I've said it now. I don't know what else to call them.'

'But you can remember *them*?'

'Because I'm awake when I see them.'

'How can you be sure? Couldn't it be a dream? I mean, if there's something wrong with your mind then—'

'You mean if I'm going fucking insane?'

'Do you think you are?'

'Sometimes.'

'Then get help. Let *me* help you.'

'Take me to a doctor? Get me pumped full of happy pills? Job done. No. Besides, it's gone too far for that.'

'Chris, if you get help now—'

Ward got to his feet. 'Come through to the other room,' he said, refilling his glass. 'There's something I want you to see.'

A TROUBLE SHARED

The camcorder was already set up in the study. The television in the smaller room was on.

Ward indicated the small sofa and Connelly sat down, still holding the five handwritten pages.

'You think you can help me?' said Ward, looking at his agent. 'Tell me again after you've watched this.'

As Connelly sat forward on the seat, Ward pressed the play button.

Images began to fill the screen.

SHOCK TACTICS

For long moments Connelly looked as if he was going to be sick. Even after the images on the screen had vanished. He clutched his belly and blew out his cheeks.

'I told you it had gone too far,' said Ward, gazing at his agent.

'You killed that girl,' Connelly murmured.

'I did warn you,' he said. 'So, what do you want to do, Martin? Ring the police now?'

Connelly put a hand to his mouth. 'God,' he whispered, still clutching his stomach. 'Who was she?'

'Her name was Jenny. That's all I know.'

'What was she doing here?'

'We'd done business before. I called her.'

Connelly nodded. Understood. 'Where's the body?' he wanted to know.

'I don't know. I don't know *anything* any more. Martin.'

The two men regarded each other silently for what seemed like an eternity.

'Chris, you've got to go to the police,' Connelly said finally. 'Tell them what's happening to you.'

'I don't *know* what's happening to me. And what if I do go? What are they going to say? "All right then, Mr Ward, as you've been having trouble remembering things we'll just let this matter of the murder go. Don't worry about it. People who are losing their minds always cut up prostitutes and film it. Off you go." Give me a fucking break, Martin.'

Connelly regarded him warily.

'You're afraid of me, aren't you?' Ward said quietly.

Connelly didn't answer.

'Well, perhaps that's understandable after what you've seen,' Ward murmured. 'I appreciate that you may want to go.'

'I didn't say that. But try and see it from my point of view, Chris. I just watched you murder someone. How the hell am I supposed to feel?'

'Do you think there's a book in it?'

Ward laughed and, once more, Connelly felt the hairs on the back of his neck rise.

'And this?' Connelly said, holding up the handwritten pages.

'I told you, I didn't write it.'

'Then who did?'

Ward could only shake his head.

'You must have done it,' Connelly insisted. 'You said you thought you'd written other parts of your book without remembering. While you were blacked out.'

'That's different,' Ward said, pointing at the pages. 'The words are different. The structure's different. The cadence. Everything about it. I did *not* write that, Martin.'

Again the two men looked silently at each other.

'Now, are you going to help me or not?' Ward said.

'Help you do what? Murder someone else?'

'Very funny. Give me twenty-four hours. Stay here. In the house. Watch what happens. Watch *me*.' Ward swallowed hard. 'Things happen at night mainly. Stay here and see.'

'Twenty-four hours,' Connelly murmured.

'That's all I'm asking.'

Connelly nodded slowly.

WATCHFUL EYES

1.06 p.m. Connelly found some tins of spaghetti in one of Ward's kitchen cupboards and heated them. Ward made some toast then the two men sat at the kitchen table and ate.

'When was the last time you went out?' Connelly wanted to know.

Ward could only shrug. 'I can't remember,' he said. 'That's the problem, Martin. There isn't much I *can* remember these days.'

'You said things happened at night. You mean these blackouts?'

'Not just that. *They* seem to happen at any time of the day or night,' he murmured. 'No. I've been seeing things too. Hallucinating. At least I think I'm hallucinating. If I'm not then things are weirder than even I thought.'

'What have you seen?'

'Things,' Ward said vaguely. 'I don't know what the fuck you'd call them. Apparitions.'

'Ghosts?'

'No.'

'Then what?'

Ward swallowed hard. 'Figures,' he said quietly. 'It's hard to describe them. It sounds even more fucking stupid sitting here in the middle of the day. In the light.' He ran a hand over his unshaven cheeks. 'They look like apes. I know it sounds ridiculous.'

'Where have you seen them?'

'In the garden. Around the office. But always at night.'

'Have you ever found any physical evidence?'

'Like what? Footprints? That kind of thing?'

Connelly nodded.

'No,' said Ward. 'Never.' He sat back in his chair and laughed. 'And you wonder why I drink?' he said bitterly.

Connelly regarded him indifferently. 'How much do you know about this house?' he asked.

Ward looked vague.

'Its history,' Connelly continued. 'Who lived here before you?'

'Oh, come on. The fucking house is new. It had been standing empty for two years before I bought it. It's not built on some fucking Indian burial ground or a cemetery or any of that kind of Hollywood bullshit. It's a new house. I was the first tenant. Nothing happened here before I moved in, Martin. The house is *not* haunted.'

There was another long silence finally broken by Connelly. 'And these . . . apparitions?' he said. 'You think they'll come again tonight?'

'I don't know.'

'Could they be linked with what's happening though?'

'I don't know,' Ward said a little more loudly.

The two men locked stares.

'This is like something you used to write,' said Connelly.

Ward didn't answer. He merely got to his feet and dropped the dirty plates into the sink.

'Want a drink while we wait?' he said.

'Wait for what?' Connelly asked.

'For the night to come,' Ward said.

TIME TO SPARE

4.29 p.m.

'What do you think this means?' Connelly held up the sheets of handwritten paper.

'I told you, I don't know,' Ward rasped, sipping his drink.

'Perhaps the answer is in here somewhere. The answer to all of this. It can't hurt to go through it.'

Ward shrugged. He watched as Connelly spread the sheets of paper out on the coffee table, gazing at each one in turn.

'"Reality and fantasy become inseparable",' Connelly read.

'It's a pity they don't. I'd write a novel about an author who wins the fucking lottery,' sneered Ward.

'Is that what you think this means? That what is written eventually becomes fact?'

'Who knows? The point is not what it means but how it got in my office in the first place. We need to know who wrote it, not what they're trying to say.'

Connelly read more. 'It talks about confrontation,' he said thoughtfully. 'How conflict is good. How power is good and weakness is bad.'

'Perhaps my office is haunted by Nietzsche,' chuckled Ward.

'I'm glad you find it funny, Chris. I wonder if the police will be laughing when they see that video.'

'Are you threatening me, Martin?'

'Why? What if I was? Are you going to do to me the same as you did to her?'

'Fuck you.'

'I'm trying to help. You asked me to help. That's what I'm trying to do.'

Ward regarded him balefully for a second then refilled his glass. 'All right, go on,' he murmured.

'It's this last bit. "There are others." I wonder if it means others like you.'

'Murderers, you mean?'

'What do *you* think it means?'

'I told you. I don't know and I don't fucking care. All that bothers me is how it got into my office.'

'Are you *sure* you didn't write it?' Connelly was growing agitated.

'How many more times? I told you—'

'Are you *sure*?' shouted Connelly.

'It's not my writing. It's not the *way* I write. I'm *sure*.'

Connelly got to his feet and wandered over to the French windows that looked out on to Ward's back garden. In the sky, clouds were building steadily like gathering formations of troops preparing for a final onslaught.

'It looks like there's another storm coming,' murmured Connelly.

Ward didn't answer.

THE COMING STORM

6.42 p.m. Rain hammered down unrelentingly, falling from the seething banks of black clouds in torrents.

Ward gazed out of the French windows and watched the droplets pounding against the concrete outside. Part of the garden near one of the oak trees was already under half an inch of water. Elsewhere on the grass, other puddles were growing larger as the downpour showed no sign of abating.

The first distant rumble of thunder rolled across the sky like artillery fire.

When Ward turned his head, he saw that Connelly was also looking out of the window. The agent looked a little apprehensive.

'If this keeps up it'll be dark in an hour,' said Ward.

'And then?'

Ward shrugged. He sat still a moment longer then got to his feet.

'I'm going out to the office,' he said. 'Just to shut the computer down. Turn off the monitor. I'll lock it up for the night.'

'Do you want some company?' Connelly asked, also rising.

'No. I'll only be a couple of minutes. Pour us some more drinks.'

The agent nodded.

Ward stepped out of the room.

Outside, a brilliant white shaft of lightning tore through the clouds and illuminated the sky.

Think hard and consider the situation in which you now find yourself. Contemplate the possibilities and mull them over in your mind for there is but one outcome. When first our union was sublimated there was no questioning. There were no doubts or remonstrations. The terms were accepted. The price was set. A valuation put upon that which is ordinarily thought to be above remuneration. Consider this and also contemplate what has been given and accepted without question. For all deeds and acts there is a manifest set of circumstances. An outcome. Irrevocable and irretrievable in its finality. Terms were set. Accepted. Acted upon. Now is the time for payment.

Many others have walked the same path. Many more will do so. There *are* others. Others who seek what you have sought. Who will attain what you have attained and who will pay as you must pay. With the passing of the years has come no remembrance. No recollection of what was desired and what was offered in return. Something offered more priceless than the treasures of the ages.

Consider the following and prepare to settle that which must be accounted for: 12 12 84 the choice was made. Now must come the reckoning.

COMMUNICATION

Martin Connelly heard a sound from inside the study. He approached the door slowly.

'Chris,' he called.

No answer. Just that insistent noise he'd heard a moment earlier. Like . . .

Like what?

Like the mechanical and electronic sound made by a printer as it transfers the images from a computer screen on to paper.

He pushed the door wider and stepped inside the room.

The computer was indeed on. The monitor was active. Connelly could see words spreading across it. He crossed to the machine and stood staring at the screen.

Names. Hundreds of them.

And the printer dutifully transferring them on to paper.

Connelly read them:

Dante Alighieri
Ludwig Van Beethoven
Adolf Hitler
Napoleon Bonaparte
Bram Stoker
Hieronymus Bosch
Christopher Marlowe

And still they continued.

He was still gazing at the screen when Ward walked in, his hair and clothes dripping. A single sheet of paper gripped in his fist.

'What the fuck is going on?' Ward said, looking at the names dancing across the screen.

Connelly could only shake his head. 'It just started,' he said, indicating the computer.

Ward stared at the names.

Edgar Allan Poe
Caravaggio
Frank Sinatra
John Dillinger
Stalin

He was still staring half an hour later.

The rapidity and profusion with which the names continued to appear showed no signs of stopping.

'What do we do?' Connelly asked.

Ward could only shake his head. He held out the piece of handwritten paper he'd found in his office.

Connelly took it and read it.

'It was there when I got to the computer,' Ward told him.

'Any idea what it means?' said Connelly.

Ward shook his head.

The computer continued to rattle off an increasingly long list of names. And it showed no signs of stopping.

AN INVENTORY

9.34 p.m.

'Seventy-six pages,' said Ward.

The names on the sheaf of paper he held were in non-alphabetical, random order. Many he recognised, many more he didn't.

Connelly was also flicking through some of the printed sheets.

'These names don't have anything in common,' Ward said. 'Not as a whole. There are groups of them that you can match up. Musicians. Writers. Artists. Even some sportsmen. Some are old, some are new.'

'What do you make of it?'

'Christ knows. What the fuck do Edgar Allan Poe and Madonna have in common? Or Christopher Marlowe and Lenny Bruce for that matter? Joseph Goebbels and Bill Gates?' He shook his head. 'There are hundreds of names on here that I don't recognise either. They're not well-known people.'

'Perhaps if we looked them up,' Connelly offered.

'Where, Martin?'

Connelly merely shrugged.

Ward continued looking at the names. 'Jesus,' he whispered.

'What is it?'

'These names sound familiar,' said the writer. 'Declan Leary. Melissa Blake. Joe Hendry.'

'I don't get it.'

'They were all characters in that book I've just finished. They all died.'

Connelly stared at the list. 'What was that about imagination becoming reality?' he said quietly. 'In one of those hand-written sheets.'

Ward nodded. 'But I created those characters. Why are they on this list?' he asked. 'They weren't real.'

'Somewhere they might be. Somewhere in this world there are probably people with the names Declan Leary, Melissa Blake and Joe Hendry. The names aren't that uncommon, Chris.'

'We'll see,' Ward snapped and hurried out to the hall. He returned with a copy of the phone book and flipped it open, running his index finger down the list of names. 'There's an M Blake,' he said. 'A J Hendry and a D Leary.'

'I said they weren't uncommon.'

Ward scribbled down the numbers.

'What are you doing?' Connelly wanted to know.

'I want to speak to them.'

'Chris, what for?'

Ward was already heading for the hallway. He snatched up the phone and dialled the first number. And waited.

No answer.

He tried the number for J Hendry. It rang.

And rang.

Then was finally answered. 'Hello.' The voice at the other end was that of a woman. Subdued, barely audible.

'I'd like to speak to Mr J Hendry, please,' said Ward.

Silence.

'Hello, I said I'd like to speak to—'

'Yes, I heard you,' the woman said softly. 'I'm sorry. Joe died two days ago.'

Ward put down the phone. He tried the number for Leary.

A young man told him that Declan Leary had been killed in an accident two weeks earlier.

Ward exhaled and wandered back into the sitting room. 'Two of them are dead,' he said.

'It must be a coincidence,' Connelly told him.

'What if these other names are names of characters I've created in the past? Characters I've killed off.'

Connelly shook his head. 'Art mirrors life?' he said. 'Not

that literally. Anyway, you didn't create all the names on this list. Also a lot of them are still alive.'

Ward ran a hand through his hair. 'Perhaps there's an answer in this,' he said, holding up the piece of handwritten paper. 'Like this date. Twelve, twelve, eighty-four. Twelfth of December, 1984.'

'Does that date have any significance for you?' asked Connelly.

'Not that I can remember.'

'What about some of the other things mentioned.'

'"The terms were accepted,"' Ward murmured. 'Terms of what? "Now is the time for payment".' He took a sip of his drink. '"Many others have walked the same path." Which path?'

'You work it out.'

'Twelve, twelve, eighty-four,' Ward whispered. 'Jesus Christ. If those numbers *are* a date, then I recognise them and so should you. It was the date I signed to your agency. The day you became my agent.'

'Can you remember what you said when you signed? You said you wanted to be so rich it was obscene. You said you wanted everything. The world.'

'I *was* rich. But not any more.'

'Terms were set,' Connelly said quietly. 'Nothing lasts for ever, Chris.'

'That still doesn't explain the names on this list.'

'Run through them again. Just the first three or four.'

'Napoleon Bonaparte. Beethoven. Christopher Marlowe.'

'A general who became an emperor. A composer who wanted immortality,' Connelly began.

'And a writer who wrote about a man who made a pact with the Devil,' Ward added.

'I had to let *you* work it out, Chris.'

'I still don't understand.'

'What was Marlowe's most famous work?'

'*Doctor Faustus.*'

'Remember the story?'

'A man who wanted wealth and fame sold his soul to the Devil in return for it. He had to face a reckoning. So did

Marlowe himself. He was murdered in a pub in London.'

'He was paying his debt.'

'What the fuck are you talking about?'

'Marlowe *wrote* about a man who sold his soul to the Devil.
A man like himself. Like all the others on that list. How do
you think they got what they wanted? Everything's got a price,
Chris. Anything can be attained if you've got the right goods
to barter. All those people had. Some wanted fame. Some
wanted power or money. Some wanted entire nations, the
world. They all signed. And when the time came, they all paid.
But it doesn't have to be as grand as fame and power. Some
of those on that list just wanted little things. "Can you let my
sick child live?" "Can the results of the biopsy I had be benign?"
Just *little* things, Chris. Because not everyone prays to God.
And even those who do get fed up with him never answering
them. So they look for alternatives. And I don't ask a lot in
return for what I give.'

'Who the fuck *are* you?'

'I would have thought that was obvious by now.'

Ward was suddenly aware of a smell in the room. A cloying
acrid stench that made him cough. It was the noxious odour
of hydrogen sulphide. Bad eggs.

Sulphur.

Connelly got slowly to his feet and walked towards the rear
of the room, to the French windows which looked on to the
garden. Slowly he pulled the curtains open so that Ward could
see out into the rain-drenched darkness.

'What are you doing?' the writer asked. 'What's going on?'

'A reckoning, Chris.'

There was movement close to the windows and Ward saw
several familiar shapes there. One was scratching at the glass
with its ape-like hand.

For the first time he saw them up close. Three of them.
Bent low to the ground. Their weight resting on their front
legs. They looked like the bastard offspring of a dog and a
baboon.

'Not apparitions, Chris. Messengers,' said Connelly. 'And all
those names on that list, the hundreds you recognise and the

thousands you don't, they all saw them or will see them when
their time comes.'

Ward's heart was hammering against his ribs. Was this another
hallucination?

The three creatures threw themselves at the glass.

'The line does blur between fantasy and reality,' said
Connelly. 'Every name you've ever used in one of your books
has been a real name and the possessor of that name has died
within weeks of you using it. That's been part of the agreement. You just never knew it. But it was all part of the bargain.
It was just necessary that *you* were the one to discover that,
Chris. I don't like loose ends.'

Connelly unlocked the French windows, allowing them to
open slightly.

'You've known from the beginning what's been going on,'
Ward stammered. 'Everything.'

'I'm just glad you finished the book. It'll be a monument.
And sales always get a boost when the author dies.'

Ward took a step towards the sitting-room door.

'Don't try to run, Chris,' Connelly admonished. 'At least face
it with a little dignity. After all, it is only the repayment of a
debt. Nothing much. Just think what you've had. I don't ask
for *much* in return.'

Connelly fully opened the windows.

The creatures bounded in. Screams, howls and maniacal
growls rose in one deafening cacophony.

Outside the rain continued to fall.

SOUTH BUCKS EXAMINER

August 18th

Police are still investigating the disappearance of writer Christopher Ward who vanished from his Buckinghamshire home almost two weeks ago.

Ward was the author of a number of bestselling novels in the horror/thriller genre.

Film rights to three of his newest books had recently been purchased and Ward was expected to write the scripts for at least two of them.

His disappearance was discovered after his agent, Mr Martin Connelly, visited the writer's home and found it in what was described as a 'derelict' state.

Ward was single and lived alone.

The police do not suspect foul play and the search continues.

Nothing's all right, nothing is fine. I'm running and I'm crying . . .

Papa Roach

Here I stand at the crossroads' edge,
afraid to reach out for eternity.

Queensryche